ROMANCE
& FINANCE

ONCE READ, ALWAYS REMEMBERED

G G Gench

A CIP catalogue record for this book
is available from the British Library.

ISBN 978-1-9996093-0-6

Publisher: G G Gench LLP
3 Jarvis Close, Barking, Essex, IG11 7PZ

Website: www.poetgench.com

All drawings by Bruna X
All photos of drawings by Martin Zvara
Cover design by Lynne Triplett
Typeset by Elaine Sharples

A NEW BEGINNING

A NEW BEGINNING

When a lady is mature and mellow,
She needs the company of a jolly good fellow.
She does it with her magic touch,
And is the pretty pick of the bunch.
She takes care of me like my beloved mother.
She treats me like my true friend,
And loves to live like a perfect lover.
Now I have a new beginning.
I am ready to be
Fresh and free in spring,
Calm and comfortable in summer,
Fabulous and fruitful in autumn,
Hot and happy in winter.

Ms Mili Tokkan earned her second doctor of philosophy degree at the age of twenty-seven and was very lucky to be one of those bright and beautiful people in the world. She could proudly use *Doctor* as her title, but for some reason she didn't like to do so. She preferred to be called Mili and was also known as Leyla Lovebird. All those years she had focused on her studies and playing her Storioni violin for a few orchestras as a guest musician. She hadn't had time to have a proper relationship with anybody and had been working for her father's investment company since finishing her studies.

It was the twenty-eighth of November 2000. She woke up and was eager to start her daily routine of having a shower before her morning meditation, as she had been doing for the last twelve years. She'd had a dream about a golden glider on her fifteenth birthday and had been creating an image of it in her head since then. Her morning meditation usually lasted about half an hour, or sometimes a bit longer. She enjoyed her morning meditation more than her afternoon and evening meditations, which usually lasted about ten minutes each.

Meditation for Mili was a mental journey which took her to the astral world of the past and the present. During her meditation, she had a golden glider and a golden guide. Her virtual golden glider took her wherever she wanted to go, in any direction, and to whomever she wanted to meet. Her golden guide was an invisible person in the astral world who helped her whenever she needed direction during her meditation. She called her golden guide by his initials, GG. She met various people while she was in her golden glider, whom she called golden guests. She loved these interactions and knew the knowledge gained in the astral world could easily be used in surprising ways in the real world.

While she was having her shower, she remembered the poem *A New Beginning*. She had read the poem a long time ago and heard about the poet many times. Perhaps it would be the right time for her to have a new beginning. There were so many thoughts on her mind. She remembered one of her golden guests, who had said:

"Remember, my dear, when you have a vision, you are on a mission. If you wish to fulfil your mission, you need concentration and dedication. Perhaps that is all you need."

After having her shower, she sat on her chair and started meditating. She took three deep breaths, counted from one to eleven, and was in her golden glider.

"Good morning, GG! Where can we go this morning? It's the twenty-eighth of November, and it has been snowing gently. My chrysanthemum is covered in snow. It's like a bride wearing her wedding dress and waiting for her groom. Let's fly over London and look for the poet of peace and pleasure. I'm in a good mood this morning. We have been to East, West and South London a few times. He must be somewhere in North London these days."

After flying over North London for about fifteen minutes, her golden glider gave her a green signal, and she descended onto a street. She was excited to meet the poet. Without hesitation, she entered a studio flat on the ground floor. A man was lying on his bed. The flat was in a great mess. Neither doors nor windows had been opened for a few days. It smelled awful. He definitely needed help. She found out the door number, the street name and the phone number of the flat and returned home immediately.

After her meditation, she was excited and anxious. She wasn't sure what to do next. She looked in the mirror and talked to herself.

"It's the right time to take action now, but before anything else, let me find out about the poet."

She decided to meditate again that morning. During the meditation she found out more of the poet's past life in detail. He had met a doctor on the twenty-eighth of November twelve years ago, and on that day, it had been raining.

"This can't just be a coincidence, after all. It must be destiny. Today I must meet this poet and help him. He needs me," she thought.

She went to the kitchen and met her mother.

"Good morning, Mother."

"Good morning, Mili. Your father left early. He's going to have a breakfast meeting with one of his business associates."

"I'm not interested in his business associates. I know all

about their business affairs and adventures. Sometimes it's so boring. What they do seems very primitive to me."

"Mili, darling, what's the matter with you?"

"I'm fine, Mother. I want to meet the poet Goldash today. He isn't well and needs my help. You told me about his poems, but you haven't told me much about the poet."

"No, my dear. I didn't want to tell you about him. Sometimes I cry when I remember Oya and Goldash. She and her mother were my good friends. I didn't know anything about the poet. A few years ago, the psychic Mrs Gulizar Gulbar told me about Oya and Goldash. Their love affair was short. They joined the Golden Guide Group and travelled the world for nine months. Oya died in a traffic accident together with her mother and father in August about ten years ago, and Goldash learned about it in September. That year, in October, a bicycle knocked him over from behind, and he lost his memory. He couldn't even remember his own name for a while, but he remembered her name."

"Would you stop it please, Mother?" she cried.

"Finish your breakfast and go to Goldash, my dear. I'll tell your father you're not going to the office today."

"Thank you, Mother."

After having breakfast, Mili went to her room and checked she had everything that would be needed for the visit. She looked in the mirror. There was both nervousness and excitement on her face. While she was thinking about how to impress the poet, she caught sight of her violin in the mirror.

"Yes, playing *Romance* for him would be very exciting and entertaining," she thought.

She went to her car and sat in it for a few minutes without moving. How exciting to see him in the snowy weather. She watched children in the street; some were playing with snowballs, and some were trying to make a snowman. They were all happy and having fun. She was as happy and excited as the children in the street. She needed to go to Edmonton from Hampstead. She hoped there wouldn't be heavy traffic on the North Circular. After a journey of about half an hour, she came to the door of the poet's studio flat.

She knocked on the door many times. The door wasn't opened. She phoned his landline.

He lifted the receiver and said, "Hello!"

"Hello, Goldash, I want to see you. Can you open the door please?"

"All right!" He hung up.

He was able to get up from his bed and went to the door. He managed to unlock it before he fell down. She pushed the door open and entered the flat. She helped him onto his bed. He was very weak and drowsy. She opened the rear door of the flat to let some fresh air in. On either side of the door stood a chrysanthemum and a peace rose.

She checked the refrigerator. It was empty. There was no food anywhere in the kitchenette. She took the key to the front door, went to the shop, bought water, milk, brown bread, ready-made vegetable soup, some fruit and nuts. When she got back to the flat, she felt oddly excited by the prospect of preparing soup for him. She had never cooked anything before in her life. Her mother always cooked for her.

"I wish my mother were here to help me now," she thought.

She read the instructions on the box of soup and prepared some for him. She carefully poured it into a bowl and put it on a tray.

"Goldash, come on, have some soup."

He was half asleep and half awake. He looked at her and said, "Thank you, angel. You are so kind to me. I would never have thought an angel would prepare soup for me."

While he was having the soup and bread, she looked at him strangely and wasn't able to say anything to him. When he had finished the soup, she asked him, "Would you like to have some fruit?"

"Yes please."

She peeled a banana and cut it into a few pieces. She offered it to him on a plate with a fork.

"I haven't had a banana with a fork before. You don't need to be so kind to me. I'm not afraid of dying and have been waiting for this moment. I'm ready to go to the world of angels. Take my breath away please."

"I'm not an angel of death. I do have news for you from the world of angels, though."

"Why don't you take my breath away? I've told you, I'm not afraid of dying."

"Yes, Goldash. I know you are a brave man. Remember, you have some unfinished business in this world."

"Come on, angel. I've had lots of fun and fulfilled all my fantasies in this world."

"Do you remember what you promised your beloved mother?"

"Yes, I remember very well. I promised her not to return to our village without a qualification. I did my very best to get a qualification and failed. I am not ashamed of my failure. She would understand and be so proud of me. She is a wise woman."

"I promised Oya to support you."

"What?"

"You heard what I said. She is one of my friends in the spirit world. I promised her to look after you as long as I live. You must have a qualification before you go to the world of angels."

"How is Oya these days?"

"She is very well and has been enjoying the world of angels."

"I'm unable to join my beloved Oya in the world of angels today. I miss her so much! Do you understand me?"

"Yes, I understand you very well. Once again, you have to start from scratch. It's another new beginning for you."

"Thank you for visiting me and bringing me news from the world of angels. Would you be kind enough to leave me alone please?"

"Yes, I would. No man has kissed me before. I would love to have a kiss from you. Would you be kind enough to kiss me please?"

"I would never have imagined I would kiss an angel. I haven't had a shave or shower for a few weeks, and haven't brushed my teeth for a few days. My mouth smells awful. I'm very sorry, but I won't kiss you."

"That's fine. I'll help you have a bath. I'm going to prepare it for you. You're a true gentleman."

"I'm very impressed. You're determined to have a kiss from me before you go, aren't you?"

She went to the bathroom and cleaned the bath.

"He needs a nice bubble bath," she thought.

While she was preparing the bath for him, he managed to get up from his bed. He took his pyjamas off and put on his bathrobe. Then he went to the bathroom slowly, took his bathrobe off and lay down in the bath.

"Dear angel, I would like to stay in the bath about half an hour. Would you make linden tea for me? I usually have it with lemon."

"Yes, with pleasure. I'll go to the shop again."

"Thank you, angel."

After buying linden tea, honey, lemon and mouthwash, she changed his bed sheets.

She knocked on the bathroom door and entered.

"How are you feeling, Goldash?"

"I always feel better when I have a nice nurse around me."

"Remember, I'm here to comfort you."

"It's difficult to believe that an angel is doing all this for the sake of a kiss. Angels must be interesting creatures."

"You're right. Now I'm going to shave you."

She shaved him and helped him to clean his teeth and body. He put on his bathrobe and went to his bed.

"Dear angel, can I introduce my friends to you?"

"Your friends?"

"This is Teddy Tulin, and this is Bunny Benny. They've been my friends since the fourteenth of February 1989. Oya gave them to me. They know all my secrets."

He kissed Teddy Tulin and Bunny Benny.

"Would you like to kiss my fabulous friends? They love you."

"Yes, I would."

She kissed them and held his hands.

"You are supposed to kiss me, aren't you?" she said.

"I am sorry, angel. I have forgotten all about it."

He kissed her.

"You've had what you wanted. Now you can go," he said.

"I have a question for you."

"You can ask me whatever you like. What is it?"

"I like the drawing on the wall. It is unusual and original. I would like to have a drawing like that. Where did you buy it?"

He sighed. "I didn't buy it. Somebody sent it to me as a birthday present last August. I don't know who sent it. I'm not supposed to sell it to anybody, for any price. If I sell it, that money will bring me bad luck. It was written in the letter that came with the drawing. The title of the drawing is *Now You See Me*."

"You surprise me, Goldash. You are a fascinating fellow. I would love to play the violin for you."

"Play the violin for me? What are you talking about? You are supposed to leave me alone after kissing me."

"Oya asked me to play *Romance* for you. I'm a professional violinist. I couldn't say no to Oya. Do you understand me?"

"All right, angel, I can't say no to you either. Where is your violin?"

"It's in my car."

"I would never have thought an angel would drive a car and play the violin. You surprise me, angel."

"We surprise each other, don't we? You keep saying the same thing: 'I would never have thought an angel would do this and that.' You treat your toys as human beings. Why don't you treat me as a human being and your soulmate?"

"Yes, now you are my dearest soulmate. Would you promise to leave after playing the violin for me? I told you I wanted to be alone, didn't I?"

"Yes, I promise."

She brought her violin from her car into the flat.

"Can I introduce my violin friend Storioni to you? She was born in 1770. She is a two hundred and thirty-year-old lady."

"Bless her! She is older than the USA, and looks younger than you and me. So, you treat your violin as a human being. I'm delighted to meet your friend."

"Would you close your eyes and try to relax for a few minutes?" she asked.

He closed his eyes. There was silence in the flat.

"Now you can look at me, Goldash."

He opened his eyes and saw a naked violinist.

"Good grief! What are you trying to do, angel? I'm physically and psychologically run down and wouldn't be any good for you. Would you be kind enough to get dressed please?"

"Relax, Goldash, relax. Tell me what you think."

He looked at her beautiful hourglass body for a minute.

"This is unbelievable. Your body is almost identical to Oya's."

"Are you sure about that?"

"Yes, I am one hundred per cent sure about it. My hands and tongue will always remember every inch of her body."

"Wow! I haven't heard anything like that before. It's a very strong statement. No man has touched my body yet. Would you like to touch my body?"

"I would never have thought I would have an affair with an angel."

"Would you stop saying the same thing again and again? When would you like to touch my body?"

"You and your violin represent two sexy and sensual ladies, but I feel very weak, and neither of you are able to turn me on. I need a few weeks to regain my strength and sensuality."

"I'll be away for a few months."

"That's even better. I'll wait for you. You should be calm and comfortable. I feel sleepy. Would you play *Romance* for me and leave me alone after playing it?"

While he was listening to the seductive sound of Storioni, he fell asleep peacefully.

He slept for a few hours and woke up late in the afternoon.

"What a delightful dream that was."

He touched his face and realised that he had no beard.

"It can't have been a dream. She shaved me. She must be an angel," he thought.

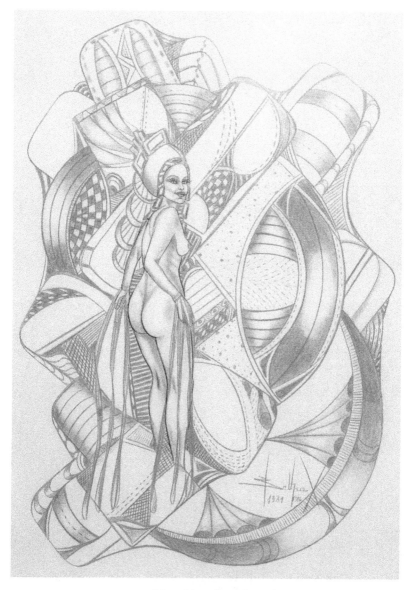

Now You See Me

He was confused and wondered about what had happened that morning. He got up from his bed and had a shower. After making a cup of fresh coffee, he saw a note on the table.

My dearest soulmate Goldash,

I am so thrilled to meet you in person. I wish I had met you a long time ago.

I found the ring that Oya bought for you in the drawer. I think you should wear it all the time. I am going to talk to your landlord about your rent arrears and your finances. You must start to study as soon as possible.

Hugs and kisses!
Your loving angel
LL

After reading the note, he looked at his right hand. He had a ring on the ring finger of his right hand, because the middle and ring fingers of his left hand had been joined since birth.

"Now I am engaged to an angel. I'm so excited," he thought.

He read her note again and wrote a poem.

SOULMATE
My dearest soulmate,
It really doesn't matter
How far away you are.
Tonight,
I can hear
The seductive sound of your magic violin.
It is all around here.
I am so relaxed and released.
Tonight,
It really doesn't matter.
I can even sleep forever.

He wanted to see his landlord, Mr Bernie Barnaby, and knew he needed to be smart and sensible. He wore his suit and his piano tie and went to see his landlord, who lived next door.

"Good evening, Mr Barnaby."

"Good evening, Goldash. Come on in. I want to talk to you."

They went through to the sitting room.

"Can I offer you something to drink?"

"A fresh coffee please. I feel like I'm still dreaming. Did you see any women coming to my flat this morning?"

"Yes, I saw a beautiful woman. I must say I haven't seen any woman as stunning as her before. You must be a very lucky boy. Her long hair, green eyes and smile mesmerised me instantly. I saw her as she was coming out of your flat. She told me you weren't well. She knew my name. I guess you told her."

"No, I didn't tell her anything about you."

"Later, I saw her as she was taking her violin from her baby blue Bentley. She made me very envious of you."

"You don't need to envy me. I haven't paid my rent for a few months."

Bernie nodded. "You don't need to pay me rent any more. She visited me and talked to me about you. I am not going to take any further rent from you."

"You said you were behind with your mortgage payments. You even wanted to increase the rent more than you were supposed to."

"I'm so sorry. I lied to you. Please forgive me, Goldash."

He smiled. "I forgive you, and may God forgive you too! You are a greedy landlord."

"You see, I'm an investment consultant. I have a few properties and no mortgage. She asked me to do a few things for you. She is so sweet, but scary, and knows all about me."

"I guess she knows all your secrets. Now I know why you are scared of her."

"You're right. We shouldn't play games with her."

"Interestingly enough, she wanted me to play with her. Unfortunately, I wasn't feeling well. Did she tell you her name?"

"Yes, she said it was LL. She said it: L for love, and L for love. It's an unusual name."

"What were her requests?"

"She asked me to write off your rent arrears, take no rent from you in the future, pay all your course fees and exam fees, give you five hundred pounds on the first day of each month during your studies, give you one hundred pounds for passing each exam, and adopt you as a son."

"I don't like the last one. I'm a grown man and don't need an adopted father."

"Remember, her request is an order! I'm going to see my lawyer next week and arrange those formalities for you. Would you be happy with that?"

"Yes, I would. You must do whatever is necessary to make her happy. Otherwise, you will have all sorts of problems."

"I'm so happy for you. I am a changed man now. Let's go to a restaurant and celebrate this evening."

He smiled. "I want to be on my own this evening and would like to go to a restaurant in Highgate. I don't have any money, though. Could you give me one hundred pounds please?"

"Yes, son. I'll go to the cash machine and get the money for you."

"I haven't met that woman before. She knows what I promised my mother, and about Oya. I am puzzled, Mr Barnaby."

"Who is Oya? What did you promise your mother?"

"Oya was my fiancée, and she passed away a long time ago.

I promised my mother I wouldn't return to our village without a qualification. It must be a university degree, or equivalent to a university degree."

"I'm sorry about your fiancée. I'm confident you will get the qualification you want, now you don't have money problems. What are you going to study?"

"I want to be a member of the Association of International Accountants. First, I will check to see if I can get any exemptions. I will let you know all about it, now you are my sponsor. I never thought my greedy landlord Mr Barnaby would become a generous landlord. I feel as if I am living in a dreamworld."

"Now excuse me. I'll go to the cash machine and get one hundred pounds for you."

He came back with the money and gave it to Goldash.

"Here is a cheque for two thousand pounds. I dated it the first of December. Five hundred is your monthly allowance, and the rest is for your course fees. When you need more money for your course and exam fees, you can let me know."

"Congratulations, Mr Barnaby. You are now a fully fledged philanthropist. You must be enjoying it."

"Yes, I'm very happy and enjoying it very much. She told me you were a sensational ambidextrous snooker player. People used to call you Mr One-Four-Seven. They still talk about your hat-trick of maximum breaks on the evening of the twenty-eighth of July 1989."

"Yes, that's something to remember for a long time."

"I love playing snooker. Perhaps we can play together at the weekends. I would love to see your snooker skills and get my first century break."

"How long have you been playing snooker?"

"I've been playing for more than twenty-five years."

"My dear sir, you've been playing snooker more than twenty-five years and you haven't broken your century break duck yet. You must be an excellent snooker player!"

"You don't need to be sarcastic. When can we play snooker together?"

"It would be very nice to play snooker with my sponsor. Unfortunately, on the twenty-eighth of August 1989, I promised Oya I would never play again."

"I'm sorry to hear it. I assume there must be a good reason why you promised her not to play again."

"There was a good reason, but I don't want to talk about it."

"I understand, son."

"Would you like to learn how to be a sensational snooker player?"

"Yes please. Tell me all about it."

"If you want to be a sensational snooker player, you need three Cs and three Ps. The three Cs are confidence, concentration and consistency. The three Ps are potting, position and passion. When you master the three Cs and three Ps, you will be a sensational snooker player. I mastered them within three months. If you master them within three months, I would love to see your century break on the twenty-eighth of February. Today is the twenty-eighth of November. I will be the first person to congratulate you. That's the beauty of snooker: when you get your maximum break, your opponent congratulates you before anyone else does. When I had my first maximum break, on the twenty-eighth of January 1989, my snooker partner, lovely Lorna, congratulated me and kissed me. I was very shy at that time."

"I wish I had been there to congratulate you. I would love to get my century break on the twenty-eighth of February."

"You can do that. I wish you all the best, Mr Barnaby."

"Thank you, Goldash. Now you go and enjoy yourself. You deserve it this evening."

"I'm very grateful for your kindness and generosity."

Goldash went to his flat and got his overcoat. It was a cold and icy day, and the drive to Highgate wouldn't be a comfortable one. He drove slowly and parked in the car park of La Lune, the French restaurant, and pondered. He had mixed feelings when he thought back to his first night out with Oya, and entered the restaurant. It was more or less the same as before, with the same decor and the same staff.

"Good evening, sir. I am so delighted to see you. You were here on the twenty-first of March 1989. Would you like to have your dinner at the same table? It is the best table in this restaurant."

"Yes please. You must have a good memory and remembered me very well."

"You were here with Dr Oya Oydash. How could I forget such a fascinating face? I remember everything she said to me. When I brought menus to you, she spoke to me in French and said, 'My precious poet has expensive tastes, and his wine must be at least forty years old.' Unfortunately, we didn't have that kind of special wine for you that evening. You and Oya had our special dinner. When she paid the bill with her credit card, I read her name and have never forgotten it. I had a dream about you and Oya that night. In my dream, both of you were in a beautiful garden, and I was serving you. After I had served dinner and forty-four-year-old wine to both of you, Oya said, 'My gorgeous Goldash has healing hands. If he gives you reflexology, you will feel ten years younger, Rodrigue.' You gave me relaxing reflexology. I fell asleep on the chair. When I woke up, Oya and you weren't there. The following week, I went to

France and bought a few bottles of special wine. I hoped you would come back here one day. Days, weeks, months, seasons and years went by, but you didn't come back here, although I didn't lose hope. I had the same dream a few times. That was the reason I stayed at this restaurant. I married the daughter of my employer on the twenty-first of March 1997. Now I am a partner in this restaurant. We have a delightful daughter. When my wife comes here, we always have dinner at this table. I haven't opened any of those bottles yet. I have been keeping them for you. I knew you would come back here one day."

"Thank you, Rodrigue. That's very kind of you. Congratulations! You've been doing very well, and I'm very happy for you. After all these years, I'm lonely and penniless. My landlord gave me some money to come here this evening."

"What happened?"

"Oya was my fiancée. She passed away on the twenty-seventh of August 1990."

When Rodrigue heard this, tears quietly fell down his face.

"Dear Rodrigue, I know the feeling."

Rodrigue couldn't say anything to Goldash and nodded his head. Goldash wrote his address and phone number on a piece of paper and gave it to Rodrigue.

"If you come to my place tomorrow morning at eleven o'clock, I'll give you relaxing reflexology. Would you open one of your special wine bottles for me? I'm going outside to have a cigarette. I'll order dinner in half an hour."

"As you wish, sir."

When Goldash came back, his wine was ready for him. There were so many thoughts on his mind. He felt so lonely and wrote a poem.

LONELY HERO

Breaking every rule
And being a lonely hero is
Not an honour.
After all,
My desire still silently burns.
The journey of my life
Never sets me free from my loneliness.

He was deep in thought, drinking a glass of wine, when he heard the voice of a woman.

"Excuse me, sir."

A tall, attractive woman caught his attention instantly.

"I'm sorry to bother you. Are you Goldash?

"Yes, I am."

"My name is Barbara Bigsby. When I was parking my car, I received this text message. I was curious, so I came over. I usually have dinner at this table."

He smiled. "I like curious and creative ladies."

She laughed and showed him the message.

Hi Barbara, there is something in common between you and Goldash, the gentleman wearing a piano tie in the restaurant. He is ambidextrous and a qualified accounting technician. You may need him to prepare your accounts in January. He knows how to play acey-deucey. LL

He stood up, kissed her hand and pulled a chair out for her.

"Please take a seat. I'm not expecting anybody. If you would like to, we can have dinner together."

She gave him her business card.

"Thank you, Barbara. I'm sorry, I don't have a business card. So, you are a barrister. Are you ambidextrous?"

"No, I'm not."

"My fiancée passed away. Did your husband pass away?"

"Yes, he did. Why are you asking me these questions?"

"I'm trying to find out what we have in common. You're not ambidextrous. You lost your loved one, and I lost my loved one. Not many people know how to play acey-deucey. Where did you learn to play it?"

"My grandmother was Greek. I used to play acey-deucey with her and enjoyed it very much. My mother is also Greek, and my father is English."

"I have a few good Greek friends. How is your Greek?"

"It's very good. Do you speak Greek?" asked Barbara.

"No, I speak Turkish. How many languages do you know?"

"I am fluent in French and Italian too."

"You must be very talented in languages," he nodded.

"I was born in London, but we lived in Paris for a few years when I was young. We have a villa in Italy, so it all came to me naturally. Many of my friends are bilingual."

"Yes, you're right. Many people are bilingual in London these days."

Rodrigue brought a glass of wine and a menu for Barbara.

"I'm going to have a special dinner this evening. Would you like to have the same?" asked Goldash.

"Yes please. That would be very nice."

"Rodrigue knows just what we would like to have for dinner."

"Yes, he knows very well. I'm a regular customer here. Rodrigue doesn't look happy this evening. He is usually a cheerful person. I wonder what has happened to him."

"I told Rodrigue my fiancée, Oya, had passed away. She and I were here about eleven years ago. It's the first time I've been here since then."

She held his hands and said, "I'm so sorry about your fiancée."

"It's fine. It took me a while to cope with it, but now I know that triumphs and tragedies are part of my daily life, I must take them as they come. Oya was a medical doctor and medical psychic. She was a double delight. Would you tell me about your husband? What happened to him?"

"My husband, Brandon, was a barrister and my business partner. We worked together for many years. He was diagnosed with idiopathic pulmonary fibrosis about four years ago. It's a type of lung disease. We were told he had about two years to live. Sadly, he passed away two years ago. I miss him so much."

"I'm so sorry about your husband. Do you have any children?"

"Yes, I have two sons. My parents-in-law took them to the theatre this evening. They have been very supportive for the last four years."

"Bless your sons and your parents-in-law."

"I like your tie. It suits you. Do you play the piano?"

"Yes, I do. I have joined fingers, so I only play the piano to please myself."

He showed her his joined fingers, then took his notebook from his jacket pocket and wrote a poem while Barbara looked on.

REALLY?

I play the piano
But I am not a pianist.
I write poems
Because I am a poet.

He gave her the poem and she read it.

"So you are a poet."

"Yes, I am. A few years ago, I met a lawyer. I wrote a poem for her. Can I write it down for you?"

"Of course. Can you write it with your left hand please? I want to see how an ambidextrous person writes."

AS LONG AS MY FEE IS PAID

Right or wrong,
It doesn't matter.
I act!
It is my job,
I am a lawyer.

"I like this poem very much. So, you wrote it from a lawyer's point of view. Can you sign this with your left hand please?"

He signed the poem *As Long As My Fee Is Paid* with his left hand, and the poem *Really?* with his right hand.

"I wrote a poem that my Greek friends like. Let me recite it to you," said Goldash.

THE GREEK ARTS

I admire the Greek arts.
They are fantastic and futuristic.
Their beauty and bounty are incredible.
After thousands of years,
They still stand against
Many destroyers and invaders.

"It's excellent. Have you been to Greece?"

"Yes, I've been there. I wrote this poem when Oya and I were in Athens."

There was a long pause.

"I wonder how LL knows we are here. I didn't tell anybody about coming to this restaurant," said Goldash.

"I don't know who sent that text message to me and don't want to know. I am just happy to have met you."

"It's been a pleasure to meet you too. I've just remembered my poem about the game of acey-deucey. I wrote it a long time ago. Shall I recite it for you?"

"Yes please."

ACEY-DEUCEY

My dear lady,
Let's play acey-deucey.
It is my favourite game.
Let's throw our dice and move our pieces.
You try your luck and strategy.
I try my luck and strategy.
You play whatever you like.
I like to play all doubles.
Double six and double one;
Double five and double two;
Double four and double three;
They all represent my initials.
Perhaps you can have a nice crossing.
Perhaps I can have a nice crossing.
You will hold me and push me back.
I will hold you and push you back.
And later we will try to catch each other.
Perhaps I will be a casualty of crossing
More than you will be.
Perhaps you will be a casualty of crossing
More than I will be.
You win and I lose.

I win and you lose.
In the end it makes no difference.
Let's play another acey-deucey.
It won't be the same game.
After all
A company of two is bored.
A company of three is bold.

"Thank you, that's so lovely."

"It's my pleasure. I'm glad you like poetry."

After dinner, she felt a little bit tired and wanted to go home early.

"Can I have another one of your business cards please?" he asked.

She gave him a card. He wrote his mobile and landline numbers on the back of the card and gave it back to her.

"When can we meet again, Goldash?"

"I'm going to be busy for a few weeks. Perhaps we can meet in January. I know solicitors' accounts must be audited. I have experience and can assist you in preparing them."

"That would be great. I have received another text message. Would you like to read it?"

Hi Barbara, would you be kind enough to pay the bill? Goldash is a poor poet and student. LL

"What do you study?"

"I'm trying to be a qualified accountant."

Rodrigue brought the bill.

"The wine is on the house. It's so lovely to see you after eleven years, Goldash."

"Thank you, Rodrigue. I want to come here as often as possible."

Goldash and Barbara went to the car park together.

"That Vauxhall must be your car. I like the number plate, Y4 TAX."

"Thank you, Barbara. You must be a brilliant barrister. You worked it out so quickly. All the other cars in this car park are expensive, and a poor poet couldn't afford any of them. Where is your car?"

"My car is the Bentley over there."

"How splendid, Barbara the beautiful barrister with a Bentley."

She laughed. "Well, Goldash, it's been an enjoyable evening. I hope to see you soon."

"Yes, see you soon, Barbara."

He got in his car and thought for a few minutes.

"What an astonishing day! This morning I thought it was all over and I would soon be in another world or another life. Then an angel came into my life and changed everything. My greedy landlord became generous. I dined with a beautiful barrister, and had two glasses of fifty-two-year-old wine and didn't pay a penny for them. I almost forgot; I wrote two poems too. My life has become more unpredictable than the British weather. When I met Oya, it was the first turning point in my life. Today, I met an angel; this is now the second turning point in my life. I'm sailing solo against the storm again."

He chose a different route and drove home slowly. Before going to bed that night, he did the Alexander technique, an exercise to promote well-being by retraining body posture. He cuddled Teddy Tulin and Bunny Benny.

"My dearest friends, it looks like we are going to have long lives together. You've been my good friends for more than eleven years. I love you so much."

While he was kissing his toys, he received a text message.

Next time you should talk with your angel, not with your toys. She can hear you all the time. Hugs and kisses. LL

He replied:

Yes, indeed. Next time I will talk with my loving angel.

He didn't feel sleepy and was still thinking about his angel. Suddenly, he looked at his digital clock on the wall. It was midnight.

"Yes, it's zero again. This is a new beginning for me," he thought.

He looked at his bookcase. There were textbooks on business administration, taxation, financial accounting, management accounting, economics, business law, auditing, and his favourite book on the unwritten laws of finance and investment.

"Every society and community must have some unwritten laws," he thought.

He had read them while he was studying to become a qualified accounting technician. He looked at the contents section of each textbook. He remembered what his economics teacher had told him: "In economics, everything is based on supply and demand. If you teach supply and demand to a parrot, you will have an economist."

He tried to remember the name of his economics teacher but couldn't. He was still suffering from a weak memory, and he shook his head.

"I used to be able to memorise whole books. Now I'm not able to remember the name of my teacher. May God help me!"

After going through all the contents sections of the textbooks, he felt sleepy.

As arranged, Rodrigue came to his door at eleven o'clock.

"Good morning, Rodrigue. Come on in, my good friend."

"Good morning, Goldash. I'm so excited. Finally, my dream has come true."

"I'm sure you'll feel much better after having reflexology."

He offered Rodrigue a cup of herbal tea. While they were drinking the tea, Goldash explained to him about reflexology and how it works. He set up the chair and started the treatment. When he had finished, Rodrigue was sleeping like a baby on the chair. He covered him with a blanket and let him sleep for a while.

Goldash looked at his bookcase again and saw a prospectus from the Association of International Accountants. He had been a student member of the Association twelve years before, but he hadn't paid his membership subscription for many years, so he would need to re-enrol. He remembered how he had failed his last exams, and how embarrassed he had been when Oya saw his exam results. However sad or bad, they were always sweet memories of Oya.

While he was reading the prospectus and syllabus of the Association, he forgot Rodrigue was there. He was awake and waiting for Goldash.

"How are you feeling now, Rodrigue?"

"I feel relaxed. Thank you so much."

"You have slept more than an hour. You must be relaxed, rebalanced and reconnected."

"Oya was right. I feel ten years younger. I had an interesting dream about Oya while I was sleeping. In my dream she said, 'You are having reflexology now. You are not dreaming, Rodrigue.' Do you think her spirit is here and watching us?"

"She is always in my heart," said Goldash.

He helped Rodrigue get up, and offered him a glass of water.

"I feel lighter. It's so relaxing. I wish I'd had reflexology a long time ago. How often can I have it?"

"You can have it once every two or three months, or whenever you feel you need it."

"I hope to see you soon. You can visit our restaurant whenever you like."

"Yes, see you next week."

Once Rodrigue was gone, Goldash phoned the Association and requested all the necessary information to re-enrol with them. He had to take ten professional level exams and hoped to pass them all on his first attempt.

"Perhaps I can pass all my exams in two years. Yes, I can do it," he resolved.

He received a text message:

Yes, you can do it. Perhaps you should visit Doctors Nigel and Narine Nesbitt tomorrow. Hugs and kisses. LL

He replied:

Yes, I will call them now.

He hadn't visited the Nesbitts for a while.

"Yes, it would be nice to visit them, cook for them and give them reflexology. I'm sure they will be delighted to see me again," he thought.

He received another text message:

They are dying to see you. Their niece Araks is visiting them tomorrow. She is a delightful doctor and was a friend of Oya. LL

He replied:

Thank you for the information.

The next day, he bought three dozen red roses for the Nesbitts and drove from Edmonton to Buckhurst Hill. The couple lived in a big house with a swimming pool and a tennis court. He parked his car in the visitor's parking space and rang the doorbell. A young lady opened the door.

"Good afternoon, sir. You must be Goldash."

"Yes, I am, and you must be Araks."

She led him in with a shy smile. The Nesbitts were in the sitting room, lounging on a plush sofa. They stood up and welcomed him.

"We are not happy with you, Goldash. You should visit us once a month, not once a year. We miss you so much. You know it very well," said Narine.

"You're right. I should visit you once a month. I'm not happy with you either. Why didn't you tell me about your niece? She is so beautiful. Her beauty flows into my heart as the River Aras flows into the Caspian Sea."

"Goldash certainly knows how to flatter a lady," said Araks.

"What would our golden boy like to drink?" asked Nigel.

"Tea with lemon please."

While they were having their tea, Goldash told them what he had been doing for the last year. He wasn't shy about telling them anything and everything.

"That's fine, but you haven't told us you are engaged. You are wearing an engagement ring," said Narine.

"I was going to tell you about it. I'm engaged to an angel."

"You mean her name is Angel?" said Narine.

"No, her name isn't Angel. Honestly, I don't know her name. Sometimes she sends me text messages. She uses her initials, LL."

"My dear Goldash, are you all right?" asked Nigel.

"Yes, I am perfectly all right and very happy."

"If you're perfectly all right, why on earth do you talk nonsense?" asked Narine.

"Surely you don't expect us to believe you," said Nigel.

"I knew you wouldn't believe me. What I'm telling you is true. Yes, I'm engaged to an angel."

"My dear boy, you definitely need professional help," said Narine.

"We have a psychotherapist friend. She is one of the top psychotherapists in London. She has many famous clients," said Nigel.

"I don't need any psychotherapy at the moment. I'll visit your friend when I am rich and famous. I'm sure she will be delighted to see me and take my money."

"We all love you, Goldash. We are trying to help you," said Narine.

"Thank you so much for your kind support. You've been supporting me for many years. I love you as I love my parents. I want to start studying accountancy next month and need your help."

"We can help you with that. How much money do you need?" asked Nigel.

"I don't need money. My angel talked to my landlord. He is happy to sponsor me. He is going to pay all my course and exam fees and will give me five hundred pounds per month. Yesterday, I remembered what my economics teacher had said to us but couldn't remember his name. I read a few pages of my auditing book and didn't remember anything that I had read. I need your help to improve my memory."

"That isn't a problem at all. If you visit us once a week, we will help you. I knew you were joking about being engaged to an angel," said Narine.

"I'll visit you once a week, and I wasn't joking about my angel. It was her suggestion to visit you today."

Goldash showed them the text message.

"She knows all about my past and present."

"How did you meet her?" asked Nigel.

"I wasn't well for a few weeks and had let myself go. She came to my flat, cooked for me, helped me bathe and played the violin naked for me. It's so amazing that her body is almost identical to Oya's. Here is the note she left for me."

"I don't understand. How could it happen just like that?" wondered Nigel.

"I don't understand either. Perhaps we don't need to understand it. I'm still thinking about the name of my economics teacher. He said something about assumptions in economics. I don't remember exactly what he told us."

"Is it important?" asked Narine.

"No, I don't think so. Today, I'm going to pretend that I've caught a few trout in the River Aras and will bake them for you. We'll have a delicious dinner all together. Before dinner, I want to give the three of you reflexology. After dinner, we can play bridge, if you like. I haven't played bridge for a long time."

"Now what you say makes sense," said Nigel.

"This is unbelievable. I've just received this text message," said Araks.

"You look shocked. What's the matter with you, Araks?" asked Narine.

Araks read the text message:

Hi Araks, you shouldn't have reflexology today. You are having your period. Next week it is your mother's birthday. After next week, Goldash won't be available for you. By the way, I like the tattoo on your right hip. It is a red rose. LL

"I didn't know you had a tattoo on your hip. Is it true, Araks?" asked Narine.

"Yes, it's true."

"If it's true, would you show it to us? I would love to see it," said Goldash.

Araks had no choice and reluctantly showed them her tattoo. She was embarrassed that she hadn't told her auntie about it. There was the letter L on the left side of her tattoo, and the letter A on the right side of it. Goldash didn't ask her about these letters.

"Perhaps she wants to live in Los Angeles," he thought.

"Do you have a tattoo, Goldash?" asked Narine.

"No, I don't. Now you all believe me, don't you? Yes, I'm engaged to an angel."

"It's unbelievable," said Nigel.

"When Oya was having her period, she would always want to have hugs. Can I give you a hug, Araks?" asked Goldash.

"Yes please. That's all I need at the moment."

He gave Araks a hug and held her hands for a while.

"First, I'll go to the supermarket to buy trout and some other things for dinner. They will be better if I marinate them for a few hours."

"Can I come with you please, Goldash?" asked Araks.

"Yes, certainly. I always enjoy the company of a beautiful and intellectual lady."

He enjoyed shopping with Araks, and asked her some questions about her friendship with Oya. He gave Narine and Nigel reflexology. While he was preparing dinner, Araks helped him. They enjoyed dinner and afterwards played bridge.

"You know, playing bridge will improve your memory. You can visit us whenever you like. All our neighbours like to play bridge too, so we never have a shortage of bridge players," said Nigel.

"I thought that doing a role play with a delightful doctor would improve my memory," replied Goldash.

"Yes, that would improve your memory too," said Narine.

By the time Goldash left, it was almost midnight. He thought of many things. Was he lucky or unlucky? Had his life been a comedy or a tragedy? What he'd had in the past was like a dream. Perhaps many people would like to have had what he'd had. He thought it didn't seem real, although he had enjoyed every minute of it.

A text message took his attention.

Dear Goldash, there is no use thinking about the past. You must concentrate on what you want to achieve. Be positive, pleasant and practical please. LL

He replied:

Yes, my loving angel. I will try to be strong and sensible again.

The following afternoon he decided to take the auditing, company law and management information exams in June and wanted to read his books on these subjects before the courses began in January. As he was reading the auditing book, he received another text message.

Hi Goldash, Rodrigue gave me your mobile phone number. I need your help to prepare a business plan. Talk to you later. Nicole

He couldn't remember who she was, and he phoned her.

"Hello, Nicole, this is Goldash. I'm sorry, I can't remember who you are."

"Remember, we attended a cooking course together a long time ago."

"Oh yes, I remember you now. How have you been doing?"

"I've been doing fine. I worked with Rodrigue for a few years. When I visited him yesterday, he spoke about reflexology. I asked him the name of his reflexologist. When he said Goldash, I knew it had to be you. He told me all about you. When Rodrigue was telling me about Oya, both of us cried. I'm so sorry, Goldash."

"It's all right, Nicole. Why do you need a business plan?"

"I want to buy a café in Greenwich. My mother gave me thirty thousand pounds, and I need to borrow another thirty thousand. The bank wants a business plan for the loan."

"I can do that, as I've prepared a few business plans including cash flow forecasts, forecast profit and loss accounts and balance sheets, and I can prepare one for you as well. I just need some information about you and the café."

"That's perfect. If we meet at Greenwich Market tomorrow afternoon at one o'clock, I will show you the café that I want to buy. After that, we can go to my place. Would you give me reflexology and a massage as well please?"

"Yes, that would be very nice indeed. See you tomorrow, Nicole."

"See you, Goldash."

The next morning, he turned his laptop on, looked at a few business plans and prepared a business plan template for Nicole. He prepared his briefcase and took his reflexology chair and massage couch out to his car. After a journey of about forty minutes, he arrived at Greenwich Market. He was expecting a phone call from Nicole. Instead, he received a text message.

Nicole came to the car park and parked her car next to yours. She didn't notice you, and you didn't notice her either. She had forgotten to take her mobile phone with her and went back home. She can't make it again today. If you wander around the market, you might meet a lovely lady. It is your lucky day. LL

He replied:

Thank you, my loving angel.

He took his time and looked at the people and goods carefully. Shops were selling items for Christmas, and people were busy buying things for presents.

"That's the beauty of the festive season, everybody is trying to be a winner," he thought.

He enjoyed being an observer at the market. He forgot why he had gone there and continued looking around. After a while he grew bored and decided to go home. He was going to the car park when he heard the voice of a woman.

"Hello, Goldash!"

"Susanna, hello!"

They hugged and kissed each other.

"What a sweet surprise to see you here. How are you, my darling?" asked Susanna.

"I'm fine. I'm surprised to see you here, too. I was supposed to meet a friend here, but somehow we missed each other."

"What a coincidence! I was supposed to meet an estate agent. He didn't turn up. I miss you so much, my darling. Finally, after thirteen years I've met you again."

"I have missed my sexy and sweet English teacher Susanna Smith."

"If you don't have any other plans today, we could take a walk in the park and have dinner together."

"Yes, that would be very nice."

"Have you had lunch, Goldash?"

"No, I haven't."

"All right, let's go to a café and have lunch."

She held his hand and took him to a nearby café. They ordered two mixed salads and two cups of coffee.

"After all these years, you haven't changed. You have the same young face and body. You are as desirable and delightful as ever. Do you still teach English?"

"Thank you for the compliment. No, I stopped teaching English a long time ago. You were such a shy boy. I'm glad you've got rid of your shyness. You made me sexy, sweet, desirable and delightful. I was so flattered."

"Yes, it's true. Your smiling face, long blonde hair and hourglass body make you very sexy and desirable. Are you married? Do you have children?"

"I'm not married. I don't have my own children. I adopted a boy and a girl. My sister looks after them. Half of my income goes to my sister, her children and my children. I help my sister whenever she isn't available for the children. I remember you were looking for a special lady. Have you found her?"

"Yes, I found my dream lady and enjoyed every second of my time with her. Unfortunately, she is no longer in this world."

"I'm so sorry to hear that."

He looked into her eyes and said softly, "I'm still single and straight."

She stood up and gave him a hug. When she sat down, she noticed the ring on his finger.

"If you're single, why are you wearing an engagement ring?"

"I'm engaged to myself. This ring protects me from lustful lionesses."

She laughed. "That's very interesting. I married myself a long time ago. My dearest Goldash, I love you so much. You changed my life."

"I don't understand. How could a poor and shy boy change your life?"

"Do you remember the last day of our class? It was a Friday. We went to a pub after class. Everybody was happy and enjoying themselves. You were quiet and thinking about something. You and I went to the park and walked there for a while."

"Yes, I remember it very well. You were supposed to prepare dinner for us, but you changed your mind. I bought takeaway shish kebabs instead. You said you owned the house, but I saw a rent reminder from your landlord on the table. You also said you lived there alone, but there were shoes of different sizes at your house. I thought you were tipsy and acting strangely."

"I'm still sorry for my strange behaviour that evening, which I won't forget for the rest of my life. That night was the turning point of my life."

"I didn't say or do anything wrong to you."

"The truth is, I wanted to seduce you that night. I offered you a glass of red wine. You said you drank wine, but it had to be at least forty years old. After playing acey-deucey for the best of three, you took a black cab home and left me alone. I didn't have a car at that time and couldn't give you a lift. I couldn't sleep that night. It was the only sleepless night I've had. I wanted to buy a car, a house and old wines. That Monday, I went to Sweden and stayed with my grandmother for a few months. Then I came back to London and started dating men with money."

"I remember what your grandmother told you. When you were telling me about the KISS principle, you told me some variants of it, and your grandmother's favourite was Keep It Strictly Swedish."

"What is your favourite variant of KISS?" she asked.

"Keep It Sweet and Seductive."

"That's very good. That's exactly what I expect from you."

"Can you tell me what exactly you do for a living?" he asked.

"I'm in the property business. I have a few properties. I buy and sell them and have made lots of money."

"Well done, Susanna. You must be proud of yourself. Many people want to be healthy, happy and wealthy like you."

"Thank you, Goldash."

"My reflexology chair and massage couch are in my car. If you like, I can give you reflexology and a massage and cook something special for you this evening. By the way, I am a qualified reflexologist, massage therapist and accounting technician."

"That would be splendid. It must be my lucky day. Interestingly enough, I was thinking about you last week and remembered your short story *The Boy With A Broken Briefcase*. I enjoyed reading it very much. I wish I had a copy of it."

"I kept the original in my briefcase. When my flat was burgled, my briefcase was stolen. I had an accident, lost my memory and confidence for a while. I remember the title of it but not its content."

"I'm so sorry to hear that. How are you doing these days?"

"My memory has never been the same since the accident. It's getting better, though. I feel more confident these days. I know a place in Blackheath where I can buy ostrich meat and some organic foods. If you give me your address, I'll come to your place after doing my shopping."

"I live in Blackheath and had no idea about that shop."

"Perhaps you don't need to know about it. Goldash will do the shopping for you," he laughed.

"Where do you live these days?"

"I live in Edmonton."

"That's on the other side of the river. How do you know that shop in Blackheath?"

"Once I was the housekeeper of a heart surgeon, and we lived in Blackheath. I used to cook for him and his lovely ladies."

"Oh my God! I was looking for you everywhere but in Blackheath."

"I didn't know my beloved English teacher was looking for me everywhere."

She held his hand.

"When I bought the house you visited, I thought of you and wanted to invite you there and offer you a glass of your favourite wine. I knew you wouldn't have said no. I got your address from the college. I hoped you were still at the same address. It was somewhere in Woolwich. Your landlady told you you had moved to Hackney. First, I advertised about you in the *Hackney Gazette* and *Evening Standard* but heard nothing. Then I tried the national newspapers including the *Financial Times*, *The Guardian*, *Daily Mail*, *Daily Mirror*, *The Sun* and *The Times*, but still heard nothing from you. No news isn't always good news, is it? I hoped you would visit me one day and hadn't moved away. How long did you live in Blackheath?"

"I think it was for about two years. There are so many open secrets that people don't see. What a shame we didn't see them either."

"Can I join you for the shopping please?" she asked.

"No, I don't think that's a good idea. Once I had an affair with the daughter of the shop owner. You are a mature woman and don't need to make a young lady jealous. Do you understand, Susanna?"

"Yes, I understand. No problem at all."

"Thank you, your ladyship. Don't worry, I won't run away with her. You can have my mobile phone number, and let me have yours. If she kidnaps me, you can come and save me," he laughed.

"You used to be a quiet and shy boy. How long have you been a naughty boy?"

"I've been a naughty boy since this afternoon."

She smiled. "I wish I could believe you."

"No, you don't need to believe me this time. My memory has failed me again. I don't remember her name. I know you are the best beauty of Blackheath. Is it all right if I also call her the same thing?"

"Yes, Goldash. You have my permission. You can make her happy."

"I'm sure my young lady will be very happy. See you soon."

"See you soon, my darling."

He went to the shop under the assumption that Susanna had no food in her house. He bought ostrich meat, pink oyster mushrooms, sweet potatoes, duck eggs, spices, vegetables, some exotic fruit and everything else necessary for cooking.

"What a surprise. What a weekend I'm having," he thought.

Once back in the car, he checked his *London A-Z* street map and got the directions to her house. There was a big parking space for visitors. He parked his car next to her maroon Mercedes-Benz. She saw him arriving and went to the door to meet him.

"That was quick. Didn't you see your young lady?"

"No, she wasn't there. She and her parents had gone to the funeral of a relative. Otherwise, I wouldn't have come here until this evening."

They went inside the house. She opened a bottle of red wine and offered him a drink.

"I bought this wine twelve years ago and have kept it for you. It is well matured. Welcome home, Goldash. Cheers!" said Susanna.

"Cheers to our health and happiness. It's thirteen years since I was here last. You've made some changes. It looks so beautiful."

"I have indeed. I had a nice Victorian conservatory and a garage built."

He looked around the sitting room and said, "I remember you used to ride a bicycle. You have been doing very well."

"I still have that bicycle. Would you like to see my Rolls-Royce?"

"Yes, I would."

She showed him around the house and took him to the garage.

"Here she is. This is our beautiful baby."

"This royal red Rolls-Royce is your baby, not ours."

"Come on, my darling. I would love to share my wealth with you. Would you like to drive it?"

"Yes, I would, but not today. Perhaps another time I'll drive it and take you to Epping Forest."

"I haven't heard of that place. Where is it?"

"Bless you, Susanna. You are a Londoner and don't know much about the beauties of London. May the Mayor of London forgive you! Perhaps you can study the beauties of London and write a book about them. You have a degree in English literature. You have the time and money. It wouldn't be difficult for you, would it? You may include some of my poems in your book."

"Did you write a poem about Epping Forest?"

"Yes, I did."

He recited it to her.

MYSTERIOUS EPPING FOREST
On a Thursday evening,
My lady and I were at a Chinese restaurant
Somewhere on Stratford Broadway.
I had stir-fried duck breast
And she had sizzling prawns.
When we have something delicious,
We usually feel adventurous.
So we decided to go to Epping Forest.
During the day, Epping Forest is marvellous,
And at night, it is mysterious.
After fifteen minutes driving in Epping Forest,
We saw a judge
Judging a pair of bubbly breasts.
We saw a GP
Examining a shapely body.
And we saw an MP
Rewarding a street beauty.
Without hesitation,
We started to play our game.
When I was in a position to score,

I saw a shadow at the back of my car.
I said,
"Hey baby!
There is an intruder in our field."
She said,
"Come on, don't be silly!
He is not an intruder.
He is a spectator without a ticket."
While she was still playing with my toy,
The policeman approached
The right front door of the car
And said,
"Hey boy!
You are in Epping Forest.
Don't stand here like a tree.
Do whatever you want to do.
Feel absolutely free."

"It's very good. I like this poem very much. Would you tell me about the lady in your poem?"

"She was Rachel, a recruitment consultant."

"How did you meet her?"

"Last year, I was looking for a temporary job…"

I saw an advert about a temporary accounts assistant job in a newspaper. It paid twenty pounds an hour. I thought it would be good to have that job. I made an appointment with the recruitment agency on a Thursday and went to the interview. Rachel, the recruitment consultant, interviewed me. After looking at my curriculum vitae and asking me the usual questions about my accountancy experience, she said it would be twelve pounds an hour. I realised it was another case of legalised lying.

I asked, "Is that before tax or after tax?"

"Of course it's before tax."

"It isn't good enough to take you out, unfortunately."

"It's up to you, sir."

"Thank you very much. I'm not interested."

When I was leaving, she gave me her card.

"If you change your mind, please let me know."

"I won't change my mind. If you change your mind, you can let me know, madam."

In the evening, I cooked a nice meal for myself and watched a comedy on television.

My telephone rang.

"Hello, Goldash, this is Rachel from the recruitment agency. When you left our office this afternoon, I looked at your CV again. I have an offer for you."

"Thank you for giving me good news. Is it twenty pounds per hour?"

"Yes, it is. Would you be happy to clean my house, iron my clothes, give me reflexology and a massage, and cook a nice steak for dinner this Saturday?"

"Yes, I would be happy to serve you. If you text me your address, I'll be at your house on Saturday morning at nine o'clock."

"See you Saturday."

"See you then."

I cleaned her house in the morning and ironed her clothes in the early afternoon. While I was doing the cleaning, she did the shopping. I gave her reflexology and a massage in the late afternoon. She had a shower, and I prepared dinner. After eating, I cleaned the table and the kitchen.

"I hope everything has been satisfactory, Rachel."

"Thank you so much. Everything has been splendid. I'm well pampered and relaxed. You're amazing. Would you like to watch the film Stir Crazy with me?"

"Thank you for the offer. Perhaps we can watch it another time."

She gave me two hundred and twenty pounds and looked at me strangely.

"It isn't late. Why are you going home early? Do you have a girlfriend?"

"No, I don't have a girlfriend at present. I want to read and go to sleep early."

"You have healing hands. I have been dripping since you touched my body. It would be a crime not to make love to me tonight."

She dropped her bathrobe, and I was speechless. Her wonderfully well-balanced body and attitude would make all top models useless. I was surprised that such an extremely beautiful lady hadn't been taken away by the cyclone of city life. She was standing there like a golden-girl statue. Under those unusual circumstances, I couldn't say no to her. I had to accept her offer, do my delicate and delightful duty, and show her my lovemaking skills.

I said, "Yes, you're right. It would be a crime if I left you alone tonight."

She was overjoyed and kissed me passionately. I made fresh coffee for both of us. After watching the film, she took me to her temple of happiness. I had better leave it to your imagination what we did there. I woke up about nine o'clock and had a shower. I washed her Bondi blue BMW and bought her the Sunday newspapers. It was about eleven o'clock when I knocked on the door of her bedroom.

"Good morning, my lady. I'm having a cup of coffee, would you like one?"

"Yes, my tiger."

I made a cup of coffee for her.

"When would you like to have breakfast, my lady?"

"We can have breakfast later. Would you like to be my bull before breakfast?"

I wasn't expecting anything like that. She had made me speechless again.

"Yes, my darling."

I was her bull, and she was soon on the planet of pleasure again. After breakfast, she asked me to drive her car. She said her car had an "any driver" insurance policy. Sometimes her parents and her brothers used her car, and she used theirs. We went to Epping Forest for a walk, and she told me about her parents and brothers. Her mother was a recruitment consultant too. Her father and two brothers were martial arts experts. They had their own security company.

"My darling Goldash, you wouldn't challenge three men, would you?"

"No, I wouldn't challenge three men, but I would challenge four men."

Before I could say that I would challenge four men intellectually, she said:

"I'm so happy to hear this. I know my tiger will protect me at all times."

"Yes, Rachel. Your tiger will protect and please you all the time."

When we came back from Epping Forest, she asked me to cook a vegetarian meal.

After dinner, I thanked her for a wonderful weekend. I wanted to go home.

She looked me in the eye and said, "I would like to spring the tiger trap early tonight. You're not going home, are you?"

I realised her tiger was going to be on duty again, and stayed in her temple of happiness a second night.

"Enjoy holding the tail of the tiger," I said.

For the following months, I went to her place at the weekends, *and she took me out every Thursday night. She received a job offer in New York and went there. When she had settled there, she sent me an air ticket. I caught terrible influenza and couldn't go to New York. She sent me an air ticket a second time. I had terrible back pain and couldn't go again. She sent me an air ticket a third time. It was an early flight. I took a taxi. On my way to Heathrow Airport, the taxi got a flat tyre. The driver fitted a new tyre and then had an accident. I felt that something didn't want me to go to New York on that day, and so I didn't go. It was late afternoon. She phoned me. I told her what had happened in the morning. She didn't believe what I said. She was angry with me, and I was angry with her.*

"Why didn't you buy an air ticket with your money and visit her in New York? Were you expecting an invitation from the President?" asked Susanna.

"No, I wasn't expecting an invitation from the President, though that would have been nice. I'm sure you would be delighted to join me at the White House, wouldn't you, Susanna?"

"Yes, Goldash. I would love to be there with you. I wonder what you would say to the President."

"I would say, 'Let's work together for peace and prosperity, dear President.' I wanted to go to New York, so when I had saved enough money, I phoned Rachel and sent her text messages many times. I had no reply from her. When I checked my emails, there was an email from her: 'You are a bloody bastard. Good luck for a good fuck.' That was the end of our fabulous friendship."

"I'm sorry your friendship with her ended like that. You didn't make your young lady jealous of me, but you have made me jealous of Rachel. You turned me on. You have been a very naughty boy."

He gave her reflexology and a massage. While she had a

shower, he did twenty minutes of the Alexander technique. They had dinner and played acey-deucey for the best of three.

"It's interesting that I couldn't find anybody to play acey-deucey with. I only play it with you. I'm glad you taught me how to play," said Susanna.

"I'm pleased that you didn't forget it. You beat me fair and square. Congratulations!"

They went to bed together. She got what she had longed for after thirteen years. He woke up early and washed her Mercedes-Benz and Rolls-Royce.

"Good morning, Goldash."

"Good morning, my lady. How are you feeling this morning?"

"I feel overjoyed. That was the best sex I ever had. I would love to learn more about sex."

"I thought you knew all about the art of sex. You've seduced many wealthy men, haven't you?"

"Yes, I seduced them, but none of those men seduced me. I learn from my students more than they learn from me. I didn't know anything about the splitting bamboo position until last night. I felt I was out of this world."

"Perhaps you were on the planet of pleasure."

"When would you like to take me there again, my gorgeous Goldash?"

"I think it's better if we have an orgasmic trip to the planet of pleasure before breakfast."

She smiled. "I would love to have that splitting bamboo position again and again. It simply drives me crazy."

"Yes, you can have it many times."

It was late morning, and Goldash prepared an omelette for breakfast.

"I haven't had ostrich meat, duck egg omelette, dragon fruit and sweet granadilla before. You've been spoiling me, my darling."

"You're right. We haven't done many things together. I cleaned your Rolls-Royce this morning. It was dusty. How often do you use it?"

"Only special occasions, my birthday, family birthdays, wedding anniversaries and whenever my grandmother visits me. The last time I used it was about six weeks ago."

"I wonder if we will use your Rolls-Royce tonight. It's in your garage. Nobody would see us if we made love in it. I haven't done that before and bet you haven't either."

"You are a very naughty boy indeed. I bet you thought about that when you were cleaning my Rolls-Royce."

"Yes, you're right again."

The phone rang. Susanna excused herself and went to the next room. When she returned, she was very pale.

"What's the matter with you, Susanna? You look bewildered."

"A lady phoned me. I don't know anything about her, but she knows everything about me. I haven't been declaring all my rental income. She knows what I declare and what I don't. She told me what to do for the next seven days. I wrote down everything she said."

"Did she tell you her name?"

"Yes, she did. Her name is LL. L for love, and L for love."

"The same lady sent me a text message yesterday. This is her text message. I think it should be L for love and L for lust. We have both of them at the same time."

"I don't understand how she knows what I keep in my safe," she wondered.

"I don't understand either. It would be better if there were nothing in your safe, Susanna. Let me read what she told you to do."

- Give Goldash the three thousand four hundred pounds that you keep in your safe. Take a long walk with him in the park this afternoon. Fulfil one of his fantasies in the evening. He would love to make you scream in your Rolls-Royce.
- On Monday, add him to your Rolls-Royce car insurance. Instruct your solicitor to buy the shop you saw last Thursday. A property developer will buy it from you after eighteen months, and you will make about three hundred thousand pounds' gain. After deducting capital gains tax, give twenty-five per cent to Goldash, and twenty-five per cent to your neighbour, who has an individual voluntary arrangement. Goldash must clean your house. Make sure he doesn't go to that shop during the week. That young lady is in charge there from Monday to Friday. Her parents are not working this week. She is a lustful lioness. If he goes there, she will lock the front door of the shop and have a steamy session with him in the back. They have done that a few times in the past.
- On Tuesday, take him to your sister's house. He must clean her house too.
- On Wednesday, take him to Moss Bros and buy him a few suits.
- On Thursday, take him to Mrs Ozana Tokkan, who lives in Hampstead. Her address will be texted to you. He must give reflexology to her and two of her friends. Take him to your favourite restaurant in the evening.
- On Friday, have a day off. He must go home in the

morning. His landlord will take him to La Lune, the French restaurant in Highgate, in the evening.

- On Saturday, go to his flat. He will be your chauffeur and take you to the Cotswold Wildlife Park and Gardens. Stay in the bed and breakfast that is for sale. It will be a good investment for you if you buy a B&B there. You could let it to a nice couple who live in the area.
- On Sunday, enjoy the countryside, and return to London.

"I've never been to the Cotswold Wildlife Park and Gardens. Have you been there?" asked Susanna.

"Yes, I've been there twice. The first time I was there with my dream lady, Oya. The second time I was there with my close Canadian friend, Gail the graceful. I guess you were busy making money and making love to your marvellous men, and didn't have time to see some places in beautiful Britain."

"We should go to some of those places together."

"Well, well, well, Susanna, our secrets have been revealed. I know one of your secrets, and you know one of mine. Let's be honest with each other in the future, shall we?"

"You're right, Goldash. This LL will inform the taxman if I don't declare all my income in my next tax return."

He nodded. "You've been a very naughty girl, cheating on your sleeping partner, the taxman. That isn't fair, is it? Taxmen and taxwomen are our sleeping partners: they must have their shares of our income."

"Do you declare all your income?"

"Yes, I do. I always make the taxwoman happy."

"I hope that doesn't make the taxman jealous."

He laughed. "I think the taxman would enjoy watching us."

"What do you know about taxation?"

"I passed my tax exam with distinction, and worked for a chartered tax adviser for about two years. I can teach you all about taxation. Would you like to be my tax student, my dear English teacher?"

"Yes, I am your tax student now. Can I have my first lesson please?"

"Young and old, we all pay taxes. For example, when a schoolboy or a schoolgirl buys a fizzy drink, they pay value added tax or sales tax, which is an indirect tax. If they don't buy anything like that, they don't need to pay indirect tax. Let's talk about your rental income tax, which is a direct tax, and compare it with the taxes of other taxpayers. Assume four different taxpayers have the same amount of income:

"Taxpayer A only has an employment income. Taxpayer B only has a self-employment income. Taxpayer C only has a rental income. Taxpayer D has both a rental income and capital gains.

"Taxpayer A pays tax after the personal allowance, and National Insurance contributions after the National Insurance threshold.

"Taxpayer B pays tax after the personal allowance, and National Insurance contributions after the National Insurance threshold. The National Insurance contribution rate for self-employed taxpayers is lower than for employed taxpayers. So, a self-employed taxpayer pays less in National Insurance contributions than an employed taxpayer.

"Taxpayer C pays tax after the personal allowance, and no National Insurance contributions.

"Taxpayer D pays tax on rental income after the personal allowance, tax on capital gains after the capital gains annual exemption, and no National Insurance contributions.

"The four taxpayers have the same amount of income and

pay different amounts of tax. The National Insurance contribution is another direct tax. It's a deduction from a taxpayer's income, and the taxpayer has to pay National Insurance contributions by law.

"If we had a single tax allowance for every taxpayer, and simplified taxation; let's say twenty per cent tax, and a ten per cent National Insurance contribution; all taxpayers would pay the same amount of tax, and our beloved government would collect more taxes.

"This simple explanation clearly shows that our government would be better off using a simplified taxation system. I think some people wouldn't agree with me and would argue over what I say. Some people would agree and wouldn't argue over what the figures say. When big corporations practise price discrimination, they make more profit. When our government practises income discrimination, the tax office collects less tax."

"Now I have a better understanding how it works. Do you think we need a taxpayers' revolution?" asked Susanna.

"I'm not sure about that. We definitely need proper tax reform. You can talk to your Member of Parliament about simplified taxation."

"Yes, I will. It sounds like every taxpayer should get in touch with their MP about a justification in taxation."

"In theory, the desire of every government is to collect taxes fairly and spend taxes wisely. In practice, the faces of many governments are turned in the right direction, but their legs are turned in the wrong direction. This is a trick used by many politicians, and many ordinary voters don't notice it. I think every modern government needs a four-year rotation of politicians, and a simplification and justification in taxation. Donations from individuals and corporations to political parties should not be above the personal allowance."

"Thank you for enlightening me. I never knew any of this."

"My dear English teacher, of course you wouldn't know about this. You are another ordinary voter in our wonderful society."

"Would you stop calling me 'English teacher'? You have forgotten that I am your tax student now. You can teach me everything you know about tax and sex. There is always some secrecy in tax affairs and sex affairs."

"You were once my English teacher and always will be. You are a terrific teacher. I still learn English from you. You told me to study the dictionary. I started studying it a long time ago and haven't finished it yet."

"You were a super student. If you haven't finished studying the dictionary by now, I'm sure you will finish it by the end of the decade."

"I'm going to be a good student and listen to you. Let's go to the park. You can tell me all about your adventures and affairs."

It was a cold and windy afternoon, and as they were walking in the park Susanna told him about her affairs passionately, while he listened to her patiently.

"I don't understand those men in power. They are well educated and make the right decisions to run their organisations smoothly, but sometimes they do crazy things that schoolboys wouldn't do. Perhaps they are bored with being in power and want to do something different," said Susanna.

"I guess they can afford to do those sorts of crazy things that some people can't afford to do. So, how many relationships with men have you had so far?"

"Come on, Goldash! Do you think I count them? I don't even remember some of the men's names."

"I'm sorry, Susanna. I was just intrigued by your affairs."

"How many women have you been with so far?"

"I stopped counting after reaching my century break. Once, I was lost in the city jungle and encountered many lustful lionesses there."

"I wish I could believe that. You are boasting, aren't you?

"You don't need to believe me this time either."

It was Thursday morning. Susanna received a text message with Ozana's address.

"Your appointment with Mrs Tokkan is at two o'clock. We can go to Hampstead early and have our lunch there. We can't afford to get there late. Today I am your chauffeur, and you will be my chauffeur at the weekend," said Susanna.

Goldash put his reflexology chair into her Rolls-Royce, and they headed for Hampstead.

He wondered about what had been going on in his life so far.

"What are you thinking about?" asked Susanna.

"I feel as if I'm having another dream. The last ten days have been so interesting and exciting. I can't believe what has happened."

She nodded. "I can't believe it either. I thought I would never find you. My dream has come true. I have been so happy over the last few days. If I had dreamt about this, I wouldn't have believed it. I enjoy every second of my time with you. I don't care what happens tomorrow or after tomorrow. Let's enjoy ourselves today."

"Yes, Susanna. Let's continue beating the drum."

Goldash arrived at Ozana's house just before two o'clock. A lady in her late fifties opened the door.

"Good afternoon, madam. I am Goldash. I was told to come here this afternoon."

"Good afternoon, Goldash. Please come in. I'm so happy to meet you. Oya told me about you. She and her parents were my good friends. I knew what a dilemma the both of you were facing. I always had sympathy for you."

"Thank you, madam. That's very kind of you."

"My friend, Mrs Gulizar Gulbar, will come here at half past three, and then another friend, Mrs Rina Reismann, will come at five o'clock. Is that all right with you?"

"Yes, that's fine. I haven't seen Mrs Gulbar for a long time. I'm excited to see her again."

"She is a lovely lady. Everybody loves her in our neighbourhood. Would you like to have something to drink before we start?"

"No, thank you. It would be better if we started now."

He gave reflexology to Ozana, and later to Gulizar and Rina. The three women were draped over sofas in the sitting room, their faces glowing. Goldash stood nearby, smiling at them.

"That was the best reflexology I've ever had. How much do we owe you?" asked Ozana.

"I was paid in advance. You don't need to pay me today. These are my phone numbers. Would you like to take them?"

"Thank you so much, Goldash. This is my mobile phone number. You can call me at any time. Would you like to have dinner with us this evening?"

"I would like to, but one of my friends is taking me to a restaurant this evening. Perhaps we can have dinner all together another time."

"Goldash, my dear, I met your English teacher and tax student Susanna Smith at the café this afternoon," said Gulizar.

"I'm pleased you've met Susanna."

She smiled. "I was at the café when you were having lunch with her. You didn't see me there. After you left the café, I talked to Susanna. She said she would like to talk to you about various things tonight."

"I can talk with Susanna about anything and everything."

"She is a lovely and lustful lioness. You know how to pamper lustful lionesses, don't you, Goldash?"

He winked. "Well, they can be deeply delightful and dangerous."

"Make sure they are not angry with you and not hungry for you. Good luck, and have lots of fun with her."

"I will treasure your advice, Mrs Gulbar."

"That was the first time I'd had reflexology. I enjoyed it very much. I felt as if I were walking on air. You are our treasure, Goldash," said Gulizar.

"Thank you very much, ladies. I hope to see you again soon."

He returned to his flat on Friday morning and visited his landlord.

"Good morning, Mr Barnaby."

"Good morning, Goldash. You look tired. I was told you were entertaining your English teacher."

"On the contrary, she entertained me. How do you know I've been with her for the last few days?"

"Your friend LL was here last Saturday afternoon. We had a long conversation about you. She was frank with me and told me all about you. I'm so proud of you, son."

"Surely you can't be serious about adopting me as your son. I am a grown man and don't need an adopted father. Would you stop calling me 'son'?"

"Yes, I agree with you. It isn't a good idea. I misunderstood her. I should adopt you as a son spiritually, not legally. She asked me to make a will. You will inherit what I own."

"Thank you very much, Mr Barnaby. It makes more sense now. I am so confused. Who is this lady, LL?"

"You thought she was an angel and was going to take your breath away. She isn't an angel. She is a human being just like us, and a psychic. Her name is Leyla Lovebird, and sometimes she uses her initials. She is a gifted person and has a good heart. We went to La Lune. It was one of her friends' engagement party. She is a vivacious violinist. She played her violin for about two hours and made everybody happy. I had dinner with your friend Barbara and her assistant. Barbara sent her kind regards to you. I'm not your landlord any more. We can have a father-and-son relationship. When you go away, would you let me know please? If Leyla hadn't told me that you were with Susanna, I would have called you."

"Yes, sir. You're right. I should adopt good habits. Leyla told me she would be going away. How come she is still in London?"

"I took her to the airport last Monday. She flew to the USA. Would you take me to La Lune at half past six please?"

"Of course, see you then."

Goldash had lunch, and then had a nap in the afternoon. He thought about Susanna, wrote a poem, and emailed it to her.

LADY ON THE OTHER SIDE OF THE RIVER

I was in Greenwich last weekend,
Hoping to meet one of my friends.
I was let down once again.
Another friend is another time waster.
While I was on my way over to the other side of the river,
Somebody called my name.

She was my English teacher.
What a sweet surprise it was.
After we said hello to each other,
She asked me to take a walk in the park,
To have dinner together
And to have a long conversation
As we did thirteen years ago.
A good student must be a good listener.
So I kept quiet and listened to her.
She told me all about her adventures and affairs.
She used to ride a bicycle.
Recently she bought a Rolls-Royce.
Surely, she must know
How to handle men and money.
After all those years she hadn't changed.
She had the same young-looking face and figure.
I wondered about it.
She said she had been very passionate for
Life, love and lust.
What a lover of living she was!
I wish she had told me all about it thirteen years ago!

Bernie and Goldash went to the restaurant. When they arrived, Goldash noticed two ladies were sitting at his favourite table.

"Do you know those ladies, Mr Barnaby?"

"The elder one is my girlfriend, Felicity, and the younger one is her daughter, Fiona. Felicity was supposed to be working this evening. I have no idea why they are here."

"Do you think it's another of Leyla's tricks?"

"Let's find out what's going on."

Bernie introduced Goldash to Felicity and Fiona.

"You look surprised, Bernie. We've been waiting for you. I

didn't know you would come here with your son. Why didn't you tell me about him?" asked Felicity.

"Goldash isn't my son. He is my tenant. I'm surprised to see you here. Why aren't you working tonight?"

"Something happened in the restaurant, and it has been closed for three days. I received a text message this morning. I couldn't help but come here this evening. Fiona and I would love to have a delicious dinner and a bottle of special wine."

"That's splendid. I'm so happy to see you here," said Bernie.

"I like your piano tie, Goldash. Are you a pianist?" asked Felicity.

"No, I'm not."

"He is a playboy," said Bernie.

"I thought you were a playboy, Bernie," said Felicity.

"I haven't seen any ladies coming to his house during the last few years. I don't think he is a playboy. Mr Barnaby is right. I'm an unemployed and penniless playboy. Many ladies are trying to stay away from me. Perhaps one day I will strike it lucky," said Goldash.

"Bernie usually comes to my place, and sometimes he gets my name wrong," said Felicity.

"You must forgive my landlord. Sometimes he gets my name wrong too," said Goldash.

"I like your honesty, Goldash. I am a trainee architect and like classical music. Would you like to go to a concert with me on Sunday?" asked Fiona.

"Yes, it would be very nice to go out with an attractive architect. Unfortunately, I'm not available this weekend. I'm going to the Cotswold Wildlife Park and Gardens with an investor, and will be chauffeuring her and earning my pocket money."

They had dinner like a family. When they had finished their

meals, Felicity and Fiona left the restaurant. Bernie and Goldash stayed behind.

"What do you think of Felicity and Fiona?" asked Bernie.

"They seem to be lovely ladies. I like them very much and enjoyed having dinner with them. Perhaps we can all come here once a week."

"Are you crazy, Goldash? Our bill tonight is more than Felicity's weekly earnings."

"That's perfectly all right as long as you can afford it."

"You say that because you fancy Fiona, don't you?"

"Yes, I fancy her, and she fancies me. Nothing wrong with that. If you take me to Felicity's house next time, Fiona the fabulous won't feel lonely."

"All right, we'll go to her house together next time."

"Thank you, sir."

Susanna came to his flat on Saturday morning at half past seven.

"I would like to introduce you to my landlord and surprise him. I'll cook special omelettes for us. Is it all right if we have breakfast at his place?"

"Yes, let's surprise him."

He introduced Susanna to Bernie, and they had breakfast. Susanna gave Goldash the key to her Rolls-Royce.

"I guess you know the best route to get there."

"Yes, my lady. I have driven there twice. You can relax and enjoy the journey."

He took his time and drove carefully. After about two and a half hours, they arrived at the Cotswold Wildlife Park and Gardens. They looked for the B&B for sale. There were a few of them available.

"Which B&B is the right one?" he asked.

"If I buy a B&B for a low price, my builders can add some value, and it will be a presentable B&B in this area."

"Certainly, you know it better than me. Let's find out which one is up for the lowest price."

After checking the prices and conditions of each one, they decided to stay at the one they liked the best. Once they had made the necessary arrangements for a night, they walked around the area and in the park. When they returned, they found the owners of the B&B, and Susanna talked with them. It was a peaceful and pleasurable night, and both of them enjoyed being there.

In the morning Susanna asked him, "What do you think about this place? Should I buy it or not?"

"I feel comfortable here. If I were you, I would buy it."

She paused. "I feel the same way, but I am concerned that I won't come here as often as I would wish to."

"These days, people invest abroad too. It shouldn't be a problem at all. For any kind of investment, the right information is very important. It is common sense. I think Leyla knows something that we don't know, otherwise she wouldn't have suggested it to you. She mentioned a nice couple in this area who might be able to run it. It would be a good investment for you, and good employment for them."

"Yes, I'll buy it. I'll talk to the owners and instruct my solicitor tomorrow."

"Congratulations! I'm very happy for you."

"You are a good cook, cleaner and lover, and above all, a true friend. Would you like to be my full-time assistant? I will pay you well."

"Yes, I'd love to, but I'm going to start studying accountancy next month. You may employ me in the future."

"Good luck with your studies. Let's enjoy driving around before going back to London."

He had been studying for a few days. It was a Thursday afternoon, and he was reading his book on auditing when his phone rang.

"Hello, Goldash, this is Lorna. Do you remember me?"

"Hello, Lorna, I'll always remember you."

"I miss you so much. Can I visit you today please?"

"Yes, you can. How do you know my phone number?"

"Araks gave it to me. I am a doctor now. Araks and I live in the same house."

"I'm so excited! After eleven years, it would be so nice to see you. What time are you coming?"

"I know where you live. I'll be at your place in about forty-five minutes."

"See you soon, then."

He hung up and thought about Lorna. She had been nineteen the last time he saw her.

"She became a doctor, and here I am still studying to become an accountant," he sighed, and felt pity for himself.

She came to his door. He welcomed her and offered her a cup of coffee.

"How are things with you and your family? Tell me everything," he said.

"Before I start talking, can I show you something?"

"Yes, of course."

"This is the cue that you gave to my father. I have been practising snooker with it since my father gave it to me. I always feel this cue is a part of you. Whenever I remember your hat-trick night, I feel so proud of you. Sometimes I wonder whether anybody else has ever done anything like that. My father told me you had named the cue GG, your initials. You always treated your cue as your friend. You kissed the cue before you gave it to my father. After what happened on the twenty-eighth of August 1989, my father never went back to our snooker club. My mother sold the club in September that year. I wanted to see you and went to 147 Mentmore Terrace in October. Your landlady told me that you and Oya had gone on a world tour and wouldn't be back for a long time. I was so sad. When I told my father about you, he gave the cue to me. I promised myself I would study hard and become a doctor. I visualised your face and felt you had spoken with me. I promised you that I would train myself to become an ambidextrous snooker player just like you. I kept my promises. I became a doctor and an ambidextrous snooker player."

His face breaking into a wide smile, he said, "I am so proud of you. You are simply the best."

"It was the thirtieth of July 1989. You gave me reflexology and a massage. Before I went on holiday to Australia, you wrote a poem for me."

"I don't remember it exactly. I'm sorry. My memory isn't very good these days."

"It was called *Your Guiding Star*. You've been my guiding star since I read the poem, and you always will be. I often visualise your face and hear your voice. Sometimes you make me laugh or cry. You are amazing. I love you so much, Goldash."

"I love you too, Lorna."

"Do you remember what you promised me?" she asked.

"Yes, I remember. I said I would examine every inch of your body when you became a doctor. Honestly, I didn't mean it. I just wanted to motivate you and didn't think you would take it seriously."

"I took it very seriously. I'm so grateful you motivated me."

"How is your snooker playing? Have you got a maximum break yet?"

"Yes, I got a maximum break a long time ago. My father has

a parrot. His name is Mr One-Four-Seven. When I say, 'Hello, Mr One-Four-Seven' to him, he says, 'Hello, Miss One-Four-Seven' to me. He can recite your poem too."

MR ONE-FOUR-SEVEN

My snooker-playing style is like a sensual storm.
I play it with my right hand and left hand.
It is soft and strong.
It is short and long.
The target is getting a maximum break.
No interference and no wrong.

"Do you remember your ex-employer Samuel and his wife Sylvia?" she asked.

"Yes, I remember them. They were our good friends, and we had lots of fun together."

"I hoped you would have returned from your world tour. I went to 147 Mentmore Terrace again in October the following year. The Jamiesons were there. Your landlady had retired and moved to Kent. They had bought the building and wanted to keep the ground floor as it had been, in memory of you and Oya. They told me how Oya had died. I didn't stop crying for the whole day."

Goldash looked away. "How are your parents and your brother?"

"After selling the snooker club, my parents bought a farm in Essex. They've been doing well. Lewis became a chartered surveyor. He got married two years ago. His wife is a midwife. They have a baby girl, and her name is Oya."

"Do you see the Jamiesons these days?"

"Yes, I see them on a regular basis. Their house isn't far away from my parents' place. Sometimes they visit us and we play acey-deucey. You taught Samuel how to play it, and we learned it from him. We've been celebrating your birthday on the twenty-eighth of August every year since 1990, and watching your maximum breaks. Sometimes my father gets emotional and cries."

"Bless you all, Lorna. I haven't celebrated my birthday for ten years. It's unbelievable other people celebrate it and I don't."

"We all love you and admire you, Goldash."

Bernie came to the door.

"Mr Barnaby! Please come in." He gestured towards Lorna. "This is Dr Lorna Hothorn. Her other name is Miss One-Four-Seven. Lorna, this is my landlord, Mr Bernie Barnaby."

"I am so happy to meet you, Lorna. Goldash told me all about you."

"Mr Barnaby has been trying to get his first century break. Perhaps one day we'll go to a snooker club and you'll show him your snooker skills."

"Yes, it would be very nice. Playing snooker has become a big part of my life. Of course we can show him how to get a maximum break, for the right price," said Lorna.

"How much would it cost?" asked Bernie.

"It would be five thousand pounds," replied Lorna.

"I'm sure Mr Barnaby can afford it and will remember the show for the rest of his life," said Goldash.

"It's a deal. Let's do it on the twenty-eighth of December," confirmed Bernie.

"Thank you very much," said Lorna.

"I'm going to visit Felicity this evening. She and Fiona are expecting you as well."

"Thank you, Mr Barnaby, but I can't make it this evening. I haven't seen Lorna for eleven years and want to cook something special for her. Would you give my kind regards to them? Perhaps I'll join you another time."

"I understand, Goldash. See you tomorrow."

"Have a nice evening, sir."

Lorna smiled as she watched him leave. "I wasn't expecting anything like that. I will be five thousand pounds richer in the new year."

"My dear Lorna, I gave you ten per cent of my winnings. Have you forgotten your snooker partner's share?"

"I'm sorry, Goldash. I was so excited. I was joking with Mr Barnaby and he accepted it."

"It's fine with him. He can afford it and accepts it. I can't afford it and don't accept it. When I met Oya for the first time, I cooked monkfish for her. Can I cook it for you this evening?"

"Yes, I will have whatever you cook."

After enjoying dinner, Lorna said, "I should be heading off. What is your plan for tomorrow?"

He smiled. "I have no plans for tomorrow or the day after."

"Can I take you to a special place tomorrow? I have to go somewhere this evening."

"I thought you would stay here tonight. Have you forgotten what I promised you?"

She smiled. "I would never forget your promise, my guiding star. We will talk about your promise when the right time comes. Can I see you tomorrow afternoon at three o'clock?"

"Yes, that sounds good. I look forward to seeing you."

"Thank you so much for dinner. Have a nice evening."

Lorna arrived right on time the next day.

"Good afternoon, Goldash."

"Good afternoon, my double delight."

"Shall we go to my office today? I thought you might like to do a role play with me."

"I used to do that with Oya. I haven't done it for eleven years."

With a shy smile she said, "I've never done a role play before. Please be patient with me, and don't ask me where my office is."

"Yes, my double-delight doctor. I would love to be your patient."

She winked. "I would love to be your patient too. Would you examine every inch of my body in my office?"

"Oh yes, my double delight. It's getting seductively serious now."

She brought him to his old flat on Mentmore Terrace and glanced at him, blushing slightly.

"This used to be your place. Now I use it sometimes. Please come in. The Jamiesons call this place the Goldash Shelter. You see, everything is here as you left it eleven years ago. Your sewing machine, your scissors, your sofa bed, your acey-deucey set, your apron and other things; they are all here. They painted the place and took the drawings of Oya, her parents, your mother, and Pigeon Pelin & Company. These drawings are duplicates. My parents have duplicates too. Samuel lets the first and second floors of this building to students and gives them a twenty-eight per cent discount. Sometimes he and Sylvia stay here for a night, especially on the twenty-eighth of each month, as it's a kind of ritual. They keep their wine bottles under the sofa bed. When I told Samuel I intended visiting you, he suggested I bring you here. I had to go to his place to get the key last night. Sylvia told me to buy one hundred red roses, ninety-nine of them for the bed and one of them for the dinner table. She said she had got the idea from you. When I was here this morning, I had mixed feelings about you and Oya. First, I was sad and cried, and then I remembered Samuel telling me how you became a naked chef for her, and how she bit your bum. That cheered me up and made me laugh."

He was quiet and she noticed it.

"Are you all right, Goldash?"

"Yes, I'm all right. I'm suddenly lost for words. I don't know what to say."

She kissed him.

"I remember the drawings of Oya and her parents here were not the originals," he said.

"I understand. We shouldn't worry about who owns the originals."

"Yes, I agree."

"Well, Goldash, first I want to have reflexology and a massage. We can have dinner and play acey-deucey later. I did the shopping for my charming chef this morning. I want to have venison steak for dinner and a duck egg omelette for breakfast. Tonight, we are staying here and will spread red rose petals on the sofa bed."

"Yes, doctor. I am ready for you."

It was late morning. Goldash and Lorna sat around the table enjoying their breakfast as sunlight streamed through the open curtains.

"Would you like to go to my parents' house today? Both of them are dying to see you. The Jamiesons are also visiting my parents this evening. We can have dinner all together," she said.

"Yes, that would be very nice, but I don't feel comfortable seeing them today. I'm still trying to get my confidence back. I would love to visit them one day, though."

"I'm sorry to hear that. I stand by you and would love you to get your confidence back soon. You were very confident last night. It was magical and mysterious spending a night here. It was the best night I've ever had. I feel ten years younger today and just wish we could have done it ten years ago."

"If we had done it ten years ago, you wouldn't have felt ten years younger."

She laughed. "You're right. I was only twenty then."

"I received this text message," he said.

Araks and Lorna live at Samuel's house in Bethnal Green. You should clean the house, iron their clothes and prepare dinner for them next Thursday. LL

"Who sent this message?"

"She was a friend of Oya. I wasn't well, and she visited me on the twenty-eighth of November and nursed me back to health. I have no idea how she knows all about me and the people I meet. Sometimes she instructs me on what to do."

"How fascinating! I've received a text message too," she said.

Hi Lorna, you are bisexual, aren't you? Would you take Goldash to his flat today?

"Is that true, Lorna?"

"Yes, it's true. You're the first man I've ever slept with."

Lorna took him to his flat. He had a nap in the afternoon. When he woke up, he wrote a poem.

A ROLE PLAY

My dearest soulmate,
Yesterday I met a delightful doctor
And later we did a role play in her office.
I was her doctor.

She was my patient.
I examined her body and wrote a prescription for her.
"Nothing is wrong with you.
You need some excitement."
She read it and laughed at me.
She said she was a real doctor, not a con.
She examined my body and wrote a prescription for me.
"You, poor poet!
Nothing is wrong with you either.
You need some action to ease your tension."

On Thursday morning, he drove to Araks and Lorna's house. Araks opened the door and was delighted to see him.

"Good morning, Araks."

"Good morning, Goldash. Lorna isn't in this morning. She left some money for the shopping. She said you would cook trout for dinner. Before you start cleaning the house, would you give me reflexology please?"

"Yes, of course."

He brought his chair from his car and gave her reflexology.

"Thank you so much. That was so relaxing. I wish I could have it every week. I'm going to a meeting this afternoon and will be here by seven o'clock. This is a spare key to the house. See you later, Goldash."

"See you later, Araks."

First he did the shopping for dinner, then cleaned the house and ironed their clothes.

"These doctors work too hard, and they have no time to look after their house," he thought.

Lorna and Araks arrived home just before seven to find the dinner ready for them. After dinner, he cleaned the table and the kitchen.

"Thank you so much, Goldash. That was the best trout I've ever had," said Lorna.

"It was a great pleasure to be here today. I enjoyed it very much."

Lorna smiled and gave him two digital versatile discs.

"There are two videos on each DVD. One is your hat-trick of one-four-sevens on the twenty-eighth of July 1989, and the other one is my maximum break, which I achieved when we were celebrating your birthday on the twenty-eighth of August last year. Can you give one of them to Mr Barnaby please?"

"Thank you so much. I haven't watched my own maximum break. Mr Barnaby and I will watch it together tonight."

"I haven't given the key back to Samuel. Shall we spend another night at 147 Mentmore Terrace this Saturday?"

"Yes, that would be fun. I'll be there on Saturday afternoon."

"Goldash," said Lorna slowly, hesitating.

"Lorna, my dear, do you want to say something?"

"If you don't mind, can I ask you a question?"

"Yes, you can ask me whatever you like."

"Would you mind if Araks joined us on Saturday?"

He grinned. "Of course she can join us. Sometimes a patient needs more than one doctor. I'm sure I'll be your perfect patient and enjoy the company of the double-delight doctors."

"Yes, Goldash. We will treat you very well, with three hundred and thirty-three red roses."

"Now I understand why Araks has the letters L and A on her right hip: L for Lorna, and A for Araks. Both of you are fascinating. You surpass my expectations."

"You're very clever and worked it out quickly," said Araks.

He winked at Araks, span on his heel and made for the door.

"See you on Saturday, doctors."

It was the twenty-eighth of December. Lorna and Araks came to Goldash's place in the afternoon. They were well dressed for the occasion. After complimenting one another, they set off for Bernie's house.

"You don't look happy, Mr Barnaby. Aren't you excited about my show this evening?" asked Lorna.

"I thought you were joking about the maximum break and the price. After watching your videos, I realised it was a mistake."

"We make jokes about sex, not about snooker and sensitive subjects. Snooker is a serious business for us. You regret you accepted the price. It wouldn't be a good idea to change your mind now. We all love you, Mr Barnaby. You were free not to accept it, but you accepted it. I'm sure you will have a free show on the twenty-eighth of January and the twenty-eighth of February. Sometimes you have to buy one to get two free. Lorna is my well-disciplined disciple and our magical Miss One-Four-Seven. Next time you won't mess with a lioness, will you?" asked Goldash.

"You're right. It has been very educational for me."

"What time shall we go to the snooker club, Mr Barnaby?" asked Lorna.

"The show is at seven, and we can go there at six. Mr Richard Ridgard, the owner of the snooker club, watched your videos and told all the members of the club about your maximum breaks. He admires you and has been as excited as a schoolboy. He is dying to see you."

Goldash drove them to the snooker club, and Bernie introduced them to Richard, who was a well-built, well-dressed, middle-aged gentleman.

"I watched your videos and analysed them carefully. I haven't seen anything like them before. It was a pure pleasure to watch. I call them magical maximums. I didn't know there was a genius female snooker player. Goldash and Lorna, you are a perfect ambidextrous snooker couple," said Richard.

"Which snooker table are we using this evening? I want to clean the table before the show," asked Goldash.

"I cleaned the table myself. It's ready for Lorna," said Richard.

"I'm not playing snooker this evening. As a matter of principle, I must clean the snooker table and balls myself. We can't afford a margin of error this evening."

"I understand, Goldash," said Richard.

He strode away from the group towards the table. With great care, he polished each ball and cleaned the baize. When he was done, he took a step back, surveying his work.

"It is ready, Richard."

It was a male-dominated club. All the members could talk about was this mysterious Lorna, this magical Miss One-Four-Seven.

Araks stood behind a camera on the far side of the room and pressed her eye against the viewfinder as Richard hushed the audience.

"Good evening, guests and members. We are going to witness something extraordinary. We are going to watch another magical maximum from Miss One-Four-Seven. This is a show 'once seen, never forgotten'. After the show until closing time, everything will be free. I am honoured and proud to present her to you. Here she is, the magical Miss One-Four-Seven."

Lorna greeted the assembled audience majestically, curtsying carefully before taking her place at the table. The cheers of the men faded, and the atmosphere in the club became tense and tantalising. It looked like a lioness was amongst wolves. They all knew challenging her would be easy and defeating her difficult. Goldash whispered to her, "I wish you the best of luck, Lorna. I know you are at your best when you are under pressure."

That was all Lorna needed to hear from him. She potted each ball with one hundred per cent concentration and a wide smile on her face, and achieved an inch-perfect position after potting each one. He re-spotted the black ball. She took her time, switched hands repeatedly and finished her maximum break in style. The guests and members were frantic and congratulated her.

"Mr Barnaby, shall we go to the restaurant before these people get drunk? Rodrigue is waiting for us," said Goldash.

"Yes, let's get out of here, they've all gone crazy. They're celebrating as if they had got their own maximum break for the first time. Lorna made them very happy. Nobody has got a maximum break in this club before. I guess they will talk about it for a long time," he chuckled.

Richard thanked Bernie for sponsoring the show and said, "I hope to see you all again soon."

"We'll be here on the twenty-eighth of January and the twenty-eighth of February. We owe you and your club two magical maximums," said Goldash.

"That's fantastic," said Richard.

Goldash drove them to La Lune, where they had a special dinner and special wine.

"That was a very enjoyable evening. Now I know how to get a maximum break. Thank you so much, Lorna."

"It's my pleasure, Mr Barnaby. We want to see your century break on the twenty-eighth of February. I'll be re-spotting the coloured balls for you."

"I'll clean the snooker table for you, Mr Barnaby. I'm sure you will break your century break duck," said Goldash.

"When can I have my cheque for five thousand pounds, Mr Barnaby?" asked Lorna.

"Goodness me, Lorna. I've been enjoying the whole evening and had forgotten all about it. I have my chequebook on me. I'll write you a cheque. After all, you deserve it."

"I received a text message for Lorna," said Araks.

Lorna should pay the bill tonight. LL

"Rodrigue, can we have our bill please?" asked Goldash.

He brought the bill and gave it to Goldash, who handed it to Lorna.

"This must be a kind of practical joke. This bill is for one thousand pounds."

"No, madam, it isn't a joke. You pay one hundred pounds for the dinner and nine hundred pounds for the wine," said Rodrigue.

"My dear Lorna, you should know there is always a special price for something special. I paid five thousand pounds to witness your fifteen-minute magical maximum. I'm sure you can afford to pay one thousand pounds for a special dinner and special wine. We all enjoyed it very much tonight, didn't we?"

"Ten per cent of that five thousand pounds is my share. Would you give a cheque for three thousand five hundred pounds to Lorna, a cheque for five hundred pounds to me, and a cheque for one thousand pounds to the restaurant? We should get on well with our magical Miss One-Four-Seven," said Goldash.

"Yes, all right. I'll do that straight away," said Bernie.

Goldash brought them all back to Bernie's house. Araks and Lorna said their farewells and departed quickly.

"What's going on between you, Lorna and Araks?" asked Bernie once they had gone.

"Nothing is going on between them and me."

"Something was different between you and them."

"I beg your pardon, sir?"

"Come on, Goldash. They kissed me on the cheek and kissed you on the lips."

"I'm surprised you can't work it out. You're a veteran playboy, aren't you?"

"No."

"Sometimes I have threesomes with them."

"You are joking, aren't you?"

"No, I'm not. Otherwise only one of them would have kissed me on the lips, not both of them."

"I have never had a threesome. How did you persuade them?"

He smiled. "I didn't need to persuade them. They wanted it."

"A penniless playboy has struck lucky again."

"Yes, indeed. I've hit the jackpot."

"Yes, Goldash, you certainly have."

In early January, he enrolled on his accountancy courses and received his textbooks. He enjoyed attending the classes and studying at home. One evening, he pondered on what had been happening in his life so far.

"There have been lots of ups and downs in my life. I was hopeless and useless just a few months ago. These days, I have no money problems. I am studying accountancy and having fun with three lovely ladies. It may go in the right direction or in the wrong direction, but no matter what, I am ready and will enjoy it for the rest of my life," he thought. He grabbed a pen along with his notebook and wrote a poem.

POET'S DESTINY

My dearest soulmate,
One day I live in luxury.
One day I live in poverty.
One day I am a high-flyer.
One day I am a poor player.
One day I am proud of myself.
One day I pity myself.
I try very hard,
Things are not in harmony.
That is all.
It is a poet's destiny.

As he finished writing the poem, his phone rang.

"Hello, Goldash, this is Barbara, your barrister friend. I wish you a Happy New Year."

"Hello, Barbara, Happy New Year to you too."

"I was wondering when you can come to our office. Our accounts assistant is on maternity leave. We need to update our books, and prepare the VAT return and our annual accounts."

"I go to college three days a week, but I'm available on Thursdays and Fridays."

"Very well, see you next Thursday. I will text you my office address."

"All right, see you then, Barbara."

On Thursday morning, he got up early. Barbara's office was on Chancery Lane, so he would have to take a bus to Seven Sisters

Tube station, the Tube to Holborn and then walk to Chancery Lane. It was nine o'clock by the time he arrived. Barbara was at reception and introduced him to her assistant, Debra.

"She'll show you our invoices, books and bank statements. You know what to do. I'm going to court today and have a meeting later. See you tomorrow."

"See you tomorrow, Mrs Bigsby."

Debra led him to the accounts office and showed him the daybooks, the petty cash book and the cash book. He hoped to update the books and reconcile the accounts by the end of Friday.

The next day, it was just before lunchtime when there was a knock at the door. He looked up.

"Excuse me, Goldash," said Barbara.

"Yes, Mrs Bigsby?"

"Debra and I have enjoyed watching you for the last ten minutes. You use the calculator with your right hand without looking at it, and write with your left hand. I wish I could do the same thing. It is amazing."

"Thank you, Mrs Bigsby."

"We are going for lunch. Would you like to join us?"

He smiled and stood. "Yes, that sounds lovely."

It was just after four o'clock by the time he finished reconciling the accounts. He headed to Barbara's office and knocked twice.

"Come in please."

He walked in and noticed there was a framed photo of a man, and a painting of four roses next to the photo, on the wall behind her chair.

"I've updated the books and prepared the VAT return. I will prepare your annual accounts and do your tax computation next week."

"You're incredible. Our accounts assistant couldn't finish updating our accounts in four days. You've finished it in less than two."

"It's a great pleasure to work with you, Mrs Bigsby."

"Please call me Barbara. Debra calls me by my first name when there are no clients in the office."

"Is that a photo of your husband, Brandon?"

"Yes, it is."

"I like that painting of the four roses. It looks like it represents parents and two children."

She smiled. "I like the way you describe the painting. One of my artist friends painted it for me. I'm taking my sons to La Lune next Tuesday evening. If you're available, would you like to join us?"

"Thank you, Barbara. I would love to meet your beloved sons."

The following Thursday, he enjoyed working in the office and achieved his target by four o'clock on Friday. He knocked on Barbara's door.

"I've prepared your annual accounts and done your tax computation. There is a six-digit tax sum payable."

"Here is your cheque for this month. I doubled your hourly rate. You're fast and fantastic. Perhaps you'll come here on the last Thursday and Friday of each month to update our books."

"Yes, that would be fun. I enjoy working here."

"My sons like you very much. They think you are a funny man."

"I like them too. They're cute and clever boys. I think they are right, I can be funny sometimes."

"You are funny and fantastic. Can I see you at La Lune next Wednesday evening?"

"Yes, I'll be there. Have a wonderful weekend."

On the last Thursday of February, he finished updating the books in the late afternoon and went to Barbara's office.

"I have updated all the books and reconciled all the bank accounts. There is no point in me coming here tomorrow."

Barbara smiled up at him. "Great. This is your cheque for this month. Do you have any plans for the Easter break?"

"No, I'm not going anywhere."

"I'm thinking of going to Mexico for sixteen days."

"That sounds lovely. I wish you a nice holiday."

"Would you like to join me there?"

"No, thank you. I've been to Mexico."

"Where would you like to go on holiday?"

"London."

"Come on, Goldash. You live in London."

"You don't understand me, do you? I don't want to go on holiday these days. Once I had a wonderful time travelling the world with my beloved Oya. We went to many countries and interesting places, and met many fascinating people. I have unfinished business that I need to finish before it finishes me."

"I think you say that because you don't want to go on holiday with me."

He shook his head and said, "I would love to go on holiday with you one day, just not at present."

With a pondering look on her face, Barbara asked, "If you don't mind, can I ask you a personal question?"

"Yes, of course. Please feel free to ask me anything you like."

"When was the last time you slept with a woman?"

"I had a threesome with the double-delight doctors last weekend."

"What? You're joking, aren't you?"

"No, I'm not joking. You asked me a question, and I

answered it. I don't see any problem. Now, if you don't mind, can I ask you a personal question?"

"Yes, you can."

"Your body language tells me you need an orgasm. Would you like to have one this weekend?"

"I beg your pardon? I didn't expect a question like that from a gentleman."

"You are right, Barbara. A gentleman shouldn't speak to a lady like that. I can be naughty sometimes. I am a qualified massage therapist and reflexologist. When you have my healing hands all over your body, you will feel completely relaxed, as if you have been on a long holiday. Would you like to come to my place this Saturday afternoon? You will be treated like a princess at the poet's place. If you're not completely satisfied, I will be your humble servant for the rest of my life."

"Well, you are very nice and naughty. That sounds interesting. You have made me curious now."

"When I met you for the first time, I said I liked curious and creative ladies, didn't I?"

"Yes, you did. That wasn't a joke about the massage, was it?"

"No, it wasn't. I was very serious. If I wasn't good at it, I wouldn't have suggested it to you in the first place. So, do you accept my offer?"

"Yes, I do. If I'm satisfied with your treatment, what would you like in return?"

"I would like you to sponsor me. I need a sponsor for publishing and promoting my poems. Do you think that is a fair deal?"

"Yes, it is. I will sponsor you when you write one hundred and one poems. It will be nice to visit you on Saturday."

"I look forward to your visit. I'm also good at cooking and want to cook something special for you. Would you bring me a bottle of forty-year-old red wine? We can talk all about the necessity of love and law in our society, and have intellectual intercourse and intellectual orgasms too."

"What are you talking about? I've never bought a bottle of forty-year-old red wine. Do you know where I could buy such a special wine, and how much it costs?"

"You can ask Rodrigue about it. He is a wine expert. The quality of my wine must match the quality of my woman."

She looked at him strangely.

"What's the matter, Barbara?"

"Nothing. I think I may have underestimated you."

"I hope you won't overestimate me after Saturday."

"No, I doubt if I will underestimate or overestimate you."

"Very well. See you Saturday, Barbara."

On Saturday morning, he cleaned his flat and bought the things he needed for cooking.

"Everything must be in good order for Barbara," he thought.

Early in the afternoon, she arrived at his flat.

"Rodrigue suggested I get these two bottles of wine. I wouldn't know the quality of them without opening them. They're forty-two years old and match my age."

"Thank you so much. I'm sure their quality is to our taste."

While having reflexology, she fell asleep on the chair. He covered her with a blanket and let her sleep. He lay down on his bed and thought about his reflexology teacher.

"Whoever has reflexology from me falls asleep on the chair. The last time I had reflexology from my teacher, it was very relaxing, and I slept on the chair. I wish she were here now to give me reflexology."

He tried to remember the teacher's name and fell asleep for a while. He woke up when he heard Barbara calling him.

"Goldash, where are you?"

"I'm lying down on my bed."

"Can you come here please? I had a delightful dream."

He stood up and went to her. "Please tell me all about it."

"We were in a small aircraft. You were my pilot, and I was your navigator. We flew over Mexico and landed in a beautiful place. You gave me reflexology. Frida Kahlo played the guitar for us."

"That's very interesting. I had the same dream. She was wearing a pink dress, a pearl bracelet, necklace and earrings. I said to her, 'I thought you were a painter, not a guitarist.' She smiled at us and said, 'I am a guitarist too.'"

"That's amazing. Yes, Goldash, you said that. I was there too. Can you remember the colour of her shoes?" asked Barbara.

"She wasn't wearing shoes. She was standing on sand," answered Goldash.

"You're right."

"She said she wanted to take us somewhere. Can you tell me the name of that place?" asked Goldash.

"El Castillo," answered Barbara.

"Yes, that's correct. It's the same dream we had simultaneously. We were in Yucatán. I was once there with Oya."

Goldash helped her up and set up the massage couch.

"What's the matter with you, Barbara? You're looking at me like a teenage girl."

"You are amazing, Goldash."

He smiled. "You fascinate me, Barbara. The massage couch is ready for you. Would you get undressed and lie down on your stomach please?"

He gave her a massage for about ninety minutes. She slept again. He had a shower and wanted to start cooking. He heard Barbara speaking again.

"Goldash, I had another dream."

"You look very happy. You must be very relaxed."

"I am completely relaxed. You must be a magician, my darling. Can I have a kiss please?"

He kissed her.

"Well, Barbara, are you going to tell me about your dream?"

"We were on the same aircraft. This time we flew over India and landed somewhere in Agra. We visited the Taj Mahal, and you gave me a head massage in the garden there. And then we flew over China and landed somewhere near to the Great Wall. While we were walking on the Great Wall, a Chinese man recognised you. He showed us a photo of you and Oya. In the photo, you and Oya were playing acey-deucey. He said he was a translator and wanted to translate your poem *Acey-Deucey* into Chinese. You said to him, 'Yes, you can translate my poem into Chinese if you beat me at acey-deucey.' He smiled at you and said, 'Nobody can beat me at acey-deucey.' You smiled at him and said, 'You have won it. Congratulations!' And then we flew over Japan and landed somewhere in Tokyo. I had a beauty treatment in a spa. You talked to a Japanese translator who wanted to translate your poems into Japanese. And then we flew over Russia and landed somewhere in Moscow. We met a Russian translator in front of the Bolshoi Theatre. She said her father was a poet and wanted to have dinner with you at his house. You went with her and left me there. I wanted to watch *Swan Lake* and entered the theatre. The show was *Black Swan* instead of *Swan Lake*. After the show, I was offered ice cream with black mulberries and white strawberries."

"How fascinating! I gave Oya a head massage in the garden of the Taj Mahal. Oya and I played acey-deucey in the garden of a hotel when we were in China. She had a beauty treatment when we were in Tokyo. We watched *Swan Lake* at the Bolshoi

Theatre when we were in Moscow. We didn't watch *Black Swan* or have ice cream, though."

"I've never seen a black swan. Have you ever seen one?"

"Yes, when Oya took me to Leeds Castle in Kent, I saw black swans there."

"I haven't had black mulberries and white strawberries either, have you?"

"Yes, my parents used to grow both fruit. I miss them, as I haven't had them for a long time."

"This is amazing. I feel as if I've been on a long holiday. I'm having dreams and connecting to your past. What's happening to me, Goldash?"

"I wish I knew, Barbara. I'm doing my very best to entertain you."

"This is much better than going on holiday."

"It's my pleasure. I want to cook sultan's delight for you. It's my mother's favourite meal. I learned how to cook it from her. You had better have a shower, and in the meantime I'll start cooking."

"Yes, my chef."

They had dinner and played acey-deucey for the best of three.

"You beat me. Congratulations! You're very good at playing this game. Perhaps we'll have a rematch when you visit me next time," said Goldash.

"Yes, if you like."

After having a peaceful and pleasurable night with her, he woke up about nine o'clock. He had a shave and a shower. While he was doing the Alexander technique, he heard Barbara crying. He went to the bedroom immediately.

"Are you all right, Barbara? You were crying."

"I had a dream about your mother. Is her name Güldem?"

"Yes, it is."

"Your parents have a cat. Is his name Meslan?"

"Yes, it is. Come on, Barbara. You don't need to cry because you had a dream about my mother. I would like to see you happy all the time."

"You didn't tell me about your parents and their cat. This means my dream was real. In my dream, I visited your parents' house. I met your mother. Your father wasn't there. She cooked cornbread in a *pileki*[1] and told me about you and Oya. A nurse and her husband from London visited your parents in August 1991. The nurse told your mother that you and Oya had died in a traffic accident. That couple has been visiting your parents and celebrating your birthday on the twenty-eighth of August since then. She and I cried."

"I understand now why you were crying. Oya never told me about her nurse friend. I wonder who that nurse is, and why she has been visiting my parents."

"Come on, Goldash. Why don't you call your mother and find out?"

"I haven't spoken with her since the accident in August 1990. I'll call her when the right time comes."

"My poor darling, now I understand what you mean when you talk about unfinished business."

He thought she wouldn't have had a full Turkish breakfast before and carefully prepared it for her.

"That was extraordinary. I haven't had anything like that before. I won't forget it for the rest of my life. Thank you so much, my darling," said Barbara.

"I am honoured to have you here."

At that moment, the phone rang.

---

[1] Clay cookware for cooking cornbread.

"Hello, Goldash, this is Leyla. Can I talk to Barbara please? While I'm talking to her, will you take a walk until you receive my text message?"

"Yes, Leyla. Let me pass the phone to her."

He left the flat. Barbara talked to her. After forty minutes, he received a text message from Leyla:

You can go to your flat, naughty boy.

He returned home. Barbara looked flabbergasted.

"This Leyla is an amazing lady. She knows all about me," said Barbara.

"She knows all about me too. We must be careful when we talk about her."

"According to her, I had experienced astral travel yesterday and last night. I didn't know anything about it. According to her, it can only happen to a person who has a good heart and positive energy. She asked me to take you to the John Lewis store on Thursday and will send me an email about the shopping. She wants you to write a poem for Debra. Her mother is a florist, and her shop is in Muswell Hill."

"I'm surprised she wants me to write a poem for Debra, rather than for you. I haven't done any astral travel yet, so your heart must be more tender than mine."

"Come on, Goldash. You are a loving man."

"You are a loving woman too. In a relationship between a man and a woman, love is essential, and lust is complementary."

"Yes, I agree with you. When Arsenal plays against Tottenham, I'm going to take my sons to the match. Would my loving man join us?"

He paused. "Yes, I'll join you there, on one condition. If Tottenham beats Arsenal, you won't beat me, will you?"

"No, I won't beat you. Why would you say something like that?"

"My mother bought me a match ticket as a present for my seventeenth birthday. It was the seventh of September 1980; the match was between Bursa and Beşiktaş.[2] My mother was a fan of Bursa, and my father was a fan of Beşiktaş. I went to the match with one of our neighbours who was a fan of Beşiktaş. The result was Bursa five, Beşiktaş nil. After the match, I was happy and shouting, 'Bursa, Bursa, Bursa is a great team.' Our neighbour got angry, and he punched my face. I had a big bruised eye for a while. I never told my parents about what he did."

"My darling Goldash, if Tottenham beats Arsenal, I will kiss you."

"I take that as a promise. If Arsenal beats Tottenham, I will kiss you, and if it is a draw, we will kiss each other. Is it a deal?"

"Yes, it is. That's the best arbitrage I have ever had. Whatever the result, my lips will touch your lips."

"I'm hoping for a draw!"

"Do you bet, Goldash?"

"Yes, I do. Sometimes I bet for my life. It is advisable for you to stay away from such ventures, though. When it is vital, it can be fatal too."

"I see, sometimes Goldash is a risk taker too. My husband was a fan of Chelsea and used to take my sons to the match once a month. You are a fan of Tottenham; would you be happy to take my sons to the match once a month?"

"Yes, I would. Tottenham Hotspur always needs young tigers like them."

"I'm sure my three tigers will have lots of fun together. I'll text you the address of the flower shop tomorrow. See you on Thursday."

---

[2] Beşiktaş – Beshiktash.

After receiving the address of the flower shop, he visited it on Tuesday afternoon. He looked at the flowers and remembered Oya. When he had bought a bunch of flowers for her for the first time, he had written a poem for her.

UNFADED FLOWER

You are my unfaded flower.
Every morning,
Every evening,
I want to smell you.
I want to look after you.
When I have my dinner,
I want you to be in front of me.
When I sleep,
I want you beside me.

He heard the voice of the shop owner.

"Excuse me, sir. You've been thinking a lot. Can I help you?"

"Yes, madam. Can I have one of those beautiful blue roses please?"

"Certainly."

She wrapped a blue rose and gave it to him.

"I would like to order a big beautiful bouquet for Thursday. I can pay you all together now."

She smiled at him. "I remember you. I am good at remembering faces. You used to live somewhere near Mare Street in Hackney in 1989. Those days, I worked in a flower shop on Mare Street. We had a beautiful woman who was a regular customer. She always smiled at me. Whenever she smiled, I felt happy. I'll always remember her face. I saw you and her walking together a few times. One day in August, you came to the flower shop and ordered one thousand one hundred red roses. My employer took your order, and the roses were delivered to your address on the twenty-eighth of August."

"Thank you for remembering both of us. You are incredible."

"I'll prepare a bouquet for you. I'm sure she will like it."

"See you on Thursday."

Late on Thursday morning, he prepared his favourite sandwiches, took a black cab and went to the flower shop, picked up the bouquet and headed to Barbara's office on Chancery Lane.

"Good afternoon, Debra the delightful. These are for you."

"I'm sure Barbara will like these beautiful flowers."

"This bouquet is for you, not Barbara."

"What a sweet surprise. Thank you so much, Goldash."

"It's my pleasure. I've brought sandwiches. Let's go to Barbara's office."

Barbara greeted them with a smile, and they had their sandwiches.

"We're going shopping and won't be coming back today. See you tomorrow morning, Debra," said Barbara.

"Debra, I wonder if you would like to have lunch with me tomorrow?" asked Goldash.

She didn't know what to say and looked at Barbara.

"Debra, my dear, if I were you, I would say yes to Goldash."

"Very well, Debra. See you tomorrow," said Goldash.

"Leyla must be keen on clothes. She emailed me a long shopping list for you."

"Bless Leyla. She has been spoiling me recently."

"I would like you to be smart and strong, Goldash. Today, I will choose clothes for you. Next time, you will choose clothes for me. Let's enjoy shopping together."

On Friday, Goldash and Debra went to a nearby café for their lunch.

"Barbara has been very happy this week. I haven't seen her like that before. She told me she had visited you last Saturday and that you are a terrific therapist. I haven't had either reflexology or a massage before. If you are available, can I visit you tomorrow please?"

"Yes, I am. You can come to my place tomorrow afternoon, say around three. I'm going to give Barbara a head massage in her office this afternoon. If you like, I can give you a head massage afterwards. I'll tell her about it. I'm sure she won't mind."

"Thank you, Goldash."

He gave both Barbara and Debra a head massage at the office.

"Debra liked it very much. She fell asleep on the chair," said Barbara.

"I didn't know it was so relaxing. Why didn't you tell us about your massage skills before?" asked Debra when she woke up.

"If I had told you about it, you wouldn't have believed me, would you? You would have thought an accounting technician wouldn't know anything about massage."

"Yes, Goldash. You're right. I believe you now, though."

"You said you would write a poem for Debra. Did you write one for my adorable assistant?"

"Yes, I did. I forgot to give it to her when we were having lunch. It's in my pocket. Thank you for reminding me, Barbara."

He took the poem from his pocket and gave it to Debra to read.

THE DAUGHTER OF THE FLORIST

Like a flower, the daughter of the florist,
She takes so much delight.
Because nobody gives her flowers,
But I do.

She thanked him.

"I'm glad you like my poem. It was all Leyla's idea. She told me about your mother and her flower shop. I bought those flowers from there yesterday. She is a lovely lady."

"It's amazing. You're an accounting technician, reflexologist, massage therapist and poet."

"I'm studying to become an accountant. Do you have any qualifications?"

"Yes, I'm a legal secretary."

"You're an intelligent, beautiful and delightful lady. Why don't you study law and become a fully fledged lawyer?" asked Goldash.

"I think she could, if she wanted to," said Barbara.

"Perhaps we will talk about it when you visit me tomorrow, Debra," said Goldash.

On Saturday afternoon, Debra came to Goldash's flat as arranged.

"After you left the office yesterday, Barbara told me all about you. I understand why you are studying accountancy after all these years. I've made up my mind and am going to study law. You've inspired me, Goldash."

"Yes, Debra. You inspired me too."

"I told my mother you bought those flowers for me. She laughed and said, 'Goldash must be a naughty boy.'"

"She is right. Sometimes I can't help being a naughty boy.

Perhaps I'll be her regular customer and buy flowers for her daughter. What is your mother's name?"

"Her name is Debbie. I am sure she will be happy to see you at the shop. She still wonders what you did with those one thousand one hundred red roses."

"She must be a curious lady. The thousand roses were for my birthday celebration, and the hundred roses were for our best friends, the Jamiesons. Oya and I used to spread rose petals on our bed before we made love on our birthdays. That year was my best birthday celebration."

"How exciting! My mother's birthday is in May. I think it would be better if I left my parents alone and stayed at my sister's place on her birthday."

"You are a delightful daughter and understand your parents very well."

He gave her reflexology and a massage, and afterwards she had a shower.

"Last Saturday, I cooked sultan's delight for Barbara. She liked it very much. I want to cook it for you as well. I hope you'll like it too."

"That would be nice. I haven't had sultan's delight before. I had a dream when you were giving me the massage."

"You had better tell me about it before I start cooking."

"In my dream, I was in a big garden. There were so many roses, and a round building in the middle. I walked through the garden and entered the building. Barbara was there. She said it was our new office and I was her business partner. We looked at the garden from the second floor of our office. It was a beautiful garden of roses."

"I think Barbara wants you to be her business partner. You must study hard and become a lawyer in record time."

She nodded. "I will do my very best."

"I'm convinced you will do it. If you like, you can watch me and learn how to cook sultan's delight."

"Great!"

She received a text message.

"Goldash, somebody sent me a text message for you."

Susanna isn't well. She has a terrible cold. Goldash must visit her immediately. LL

"Who is LL?" asked Debra.

"She is Leyla Lovebird, the vivacious violinist. She played the violin at the restaurant."

"Yes, I remember her. Who is Susanna?"

"She is my extraordinary English teacher. I am sorry. I must go to Susanna now. I'll see you next week."

Susanna and Goldash went to her newly acquired B&B in the Cotswolds during the Easter break. They travelled around the countryside. He wondered about Leyla, as he hadn't heard from her for more than six weeks. He asked Susanna about her.

"Have you heard from Leyla recently?"

"Last time I received a text message from her was in February. She gave me the names and phone number of the couple who run my B&B."

"I haven't heard from her for a while either. I'm trying to understand what kind of woman she is. When I met her for the first time, she wanted to seduce me. She knows what I've been doing with other women and isn't bothered by it."

"Come on, Goldash. You don't need to complain about her. She wants you to enjoy yourself. We've been enjoying ourselves since December, haven't we? I've been so happy with you and with her. Bless her."

"You're right, Susanna. Bless Ms Leyla Lovebird."

After coming back from the Easter break, he was in his flat, lying awake, picturing Leyla's naked body. She held her violin, the strains of *Romance* echoing around her.

He received a text message.

Hi Goldash, would you like to visit us on Saturday, the twenty-first of April, at 2 p.m.? My husband and I want to have reflexology. My daughter wants to meet you. If you like, we can play acey-deucey and have dinner all together in the evening. Ozana.

He replied:

Yes, great. See you then.

On Saturday afternoon, he arrived at Ozana's house.

"Good afternoon, Mrs Tokkan."

"Good afternoon, Goldash. Come on in."

She introduced Goldash to her husband, Osman, and her daughter, Mili.

"Mrs Tokkan, I met Mili last November. She said her name was Leyla."

"Her name is Mili. She is also known as Leyla. We call her Mili; however, other people call her Leyla."

"Mr Tokkan, I like your American accent. Your name is familiar to me. I'm not sure why, though."

"My parents moved to New York when I was eleven. I made my fortune there and have enjoyed living in London for many years. I don't think we've met before."

"Remember, Goldash, you issued an invoice to my father," said Mili.

"Yes, I remember it now. You took some tax advice from Ms Georgina Green, didn't you?"

"That was a long time ago," said Osman.

"I think it was about three years ago."

"Are you a chartered tax adviser too?"

"No, I'm studying accountancy."

"You are a late starter, aren't you?"

"Yes, you are right, sir."

Then Goldash turned to Mili.

"Thank you for reminding me about the invoice. I like your double-knotted braids hairstyle, it makes you look like a country girl."

"Thank you, Goldash. I am glad you like my hair."

"Sometimes she changes her hairstyle. Never mind that now. Shall we go into the kitchen?" asked Ozana.

Nicole was already there, filling the kettle.

"What a sweet surprise. I was supposed to meet you at Greenwich Market, not in Mrs Tokkan's kitchen."

"It wasn't meant to be. When I was in the car park, I realised I had forgotten my mobile phone, so I went home. There were two text messages. I had better show them to you. Here's the first message."

Hi Nicole, I am sorry to disappoint you. I don't want to sell my café. Good luck.

"And here's the second message."

Goldash is entertaining his English teacher. If I were you, I wouldn't worry about him. LL

After reading the text messages, Goldash said, "I

understand, Nicole. Perhaps I will give you reflexology and a massage next week."

Ozana took a step forward, separating the two. "I have known Nicole for more than six years. She is an excellent cook. When we have guests, she cooks for us."

Nicole smiled and said, "Let me take the tray into the sitting room."

When they had finished having their tea, Goldash said, "Well, Mr and Mrs Tokkan, shall we begin reflexology?"

Afterwards he stood in the sitting room, peering down at the reclining couple.

"How are you feeling, Mr Tokkan?" asked Goldash.

"It was so relaxing that I fell asleep on your reflexology chair. I had a dream about my tax adviser, Georgina, and you. In my dream, she and you were playing golf. You were happy, and she looked upset. Do you play golf?"

"I used to play golf with her. I haven't played for more than two years, though."

Osman was curious about Georgina and Goldash, and asked him, "Would you tell us how you met Georgina?"

"It's a long story..."

When I had surgery on my fingers, I was staying with Doctors Nigel and Narine Nesbitt. I had an accident in October 1990, and lost my memory and my confidence. The Nesbitts suggested I stay with one of their friends, Dr Kenneth Kavanagh. I moved to his place and worked for him for about six years. He was a dedicated heart surgeon and a talented pianist. He always brought two different ladies to his place at the weekends. I had no idea where he found those lovely ladies. I used to prepare our dinner. After the meal, he liked to play the piano with his pyjamas on. He would sleep with the most attractive lady while I was left with the other one.

Anyway, one Saturday morning Kenneth said, "I'm visiting my parents today. Two ladies are coming here this afternoon. You can give them a massage and prepare dinner for seven o'clock. I'll be here by then."

"Yes, sir. I'll do that."

One of those ladies was Georgina. She had a stiff neck, and I gave her a massage. After having a shower, she looked at me strangely, and I asked her, "How are you feeling, Georgina?"

"I feel fresh and free. You must be a magician. Thank you so much, my darling. Do you have cuddly toys in your room?"

"Yes, I do."

"Are their names Teddy Tulin and Bunny Benny?"

"Yes, they are. I haven't told Dr Kavanagh about them. How do you know their names?"

"When you were giving me the massage, I had a dream about you. I haven't had any dreams like that before. I want to see your toys. Would you take me to your room please?"

I showed her Teddy Tulin and Bunny Benny.

"You go to sleep with them, don't you?" she asked.

"Yes, I do. They were gifts from Oya. I treat them as my good friends."

"I would love to sleep with you tonight. Wouldn't it be nice if the four of us slept in the same bed?"

"We have to ask Dr Kavanagh about it first. This is his house. He might want to sleep with you."

"Don't worry about Dr Kavanagh. Leave it to me, I'll sort it out."

"I don't wish to have any problems with Dr Kavanagh. Do you understand me?"

"Of course I do, my darling. I don't want to have any problems with him either."

Kenneth came in just before seven o'clock, and we had dinner together. He was a good talker, had a good sense of humour and *made us laugh a lot. He went to his room, put on his pyjamas and started to play the piano. As he improvised his music, Georgina and I were dancing, and she started kissing me. He noticed and stopped playing the piano. He had a word with her in private and was angry with her. He asked me, "Do you want to sleep with Georgina or not?"*

"I wouldn't mind, Dr Kavanagh. She is a beautiful and intelligent lady."

It was a red card offence in his house. I had committed myself and couldn't step back. He went to his room and came back to the sitting room, gave me a cheque for five thousand pounds and fifty pounds in cash, and asked me to leave his place within half an hour. I prepared my luggage and thanked him for the six years of our friendship. He asked me to go to his room with him. He gave me another cheque for five thousand pounds.

"My parents will ask us why you left here. You should tell them you needed a change and left this place by choice. Is that understood?"

"Yes, I understand. Your parents have always treated me as their son. I respect them very much. We don't need to upset them."

"Very well, Goldash. You can take one of my expensive wines with you. Good luck, my friend."

"Thank you, sir."

I left his house immediately. I went outside and thought about what I had done. Was it worth ending my friendship with Kenneth just like that for the sake of a woman? I heard Georgina's voice.

"Hello, handsome, I understand you want to go to a hotel."

"Yes, I need to now more than anything else."

"I know a very nice hotel. Shall we go there in my car?"

I wasn't expecting anything like that and followed her. We didn't talk during the journey. She stopped in front of a house and said, "This is the Georgina Green hotel. You can stay here as long as you want. The first night is always free for you."

"Thank you, Georgina. This is an expensive wine. It's a gift from your guest."

She, Teddy Tulin, Bunny Benny and I slept in the same bed that night. In the morning, after breakfast, I received my job description. I was her cook, cleaner, chauffeur, bookkeeper, caddy and lover. I was interested in playing golf and bought a Teach Yourself Golf book. Her mother had just undergone a hip operation. After work she stayed at her mother's place, for about two months. I was bored on my own and practised golf every day. One day, she asked me to clean her parents' house and stay there at the weekend. When I returned to her place on Sunday evening, she was tipsy and was boasting about herself.

"No man can beat me at golf at our club."

"If no man can beat you at your club, no one can beat me there either."

"Are you challenging me, Goldash?"

"Yes, I am. I want to show you my golf skills."

"I know you have ten thousand pounds. If you like, I'll beat you and take your money happily. Do you want to bet?"

"Yes, you are on. We'll find out who is the better golfer. If you beat me, I'll be your humble servant for the rest of my life. If I beat you, I would like to have ten thousand pounds from you."

"It's a deal. After next Saturday, I'll have a free servant for the rest of my life."

"I wish you the best of luck."

"Thank you, Goldash. You need it, I don't."

On Friday evening, I prepared dinner for her. After eating, she teased me.

"A good golfer needs good sex before playing golf."

"Yes, a good golfer needs good sex all the time. We've been having good sex, haven't we? Tonight, you will be given special treatment."

On Saturday morning, we went to the golf club. I wanted to play a psychological game with her.

"Can I introduce Goldash to you, Georgina? Goldash, this is Georgina. She is the most attractive lady at this club. Georgina, this is Goldash. He is the only ambidextrous golf player at this club."

"You must be joking! He isn't an ambidextrous golfer, is he?"

"Yes, he is. Goldash, would you like to show her your golf skills please?"

I demonstrated two shots with my right hand and two shots with my left hand. Her body language told me she had lost the game before it had started. When she lost, she wanted to have a rematch. I demanded twenty thousand pounds for the rematch, and she accepted it. When she lost the second time, she called me a lucky bastard. I demanded a sincere apology from her. She didn't apologise, and I wasn't happy with her attitude.

"It's unfair. You lost twice and called me a lucky bastard. I am not a bastard. I have an offer for you. If you beat me, you'll have your thirty thousand pounds back. If I beat you a third time, you will apologise. Is it a deal?"

"Yes, it's a deal."

When she lost the third time, she apologised, and I accepted her sincere apology. After that Saturday, we neither played golf together nor talked about it again. She wasn't happy about losing thirty thousand pounds and wanted to have a short break. I was happy to pay for our short break, and we went to Snowdonia. While we were having dinner in a hotel, she said,

"I'm thinking of writing a book about taxation. Would you like to be my co-author?"

"Yes, Georgina. That would be beyond my wildest dreams."

"If you want to be my co-author, you must study the Advanced Diploma in International Taxation."

"You know it better than me. You have a master's degree in

taxation, and you are a Fellow of the Chartered Institute of Taxation. Whatever you say, I would be happy to follow your instructions."

I enrolled on the course and received my textbooks. One evening, I thought of buying a new car and getting a special number plate for it. I searched for it on the Internet and found an interesting number plate. It was Y4 TAX. I bought it for two hundred and fifty pounds. When I bought my car, we visited Georgina's parents on a Saturday. I cleaned their house, gave them reflexology, and prepared dinner in the evening. When we were coming back to her house on Sunday afternoon, I stopped at a red traffic light. A policewoman saw my number plate and said, "I like your number plate."

"Thank you, madam. I have another interesting number plate."

"What is it?"

"It is GO4 SEX."

She laughed and said, "That's even better than this one."

When we came back to her house, Georgina said, "Many people liked your number plate. Some of them gave you a thumbs-up sign. Some of them sounded their horn at you. Would you consider selling it to me for three thousand pounds?"

"No, thank you. I would consider selling it to you for thirty thousand pounds."

After a few weeks, she wanted to buy my number plate for thirty thousand pounds, and I demanded sixty thousand pounds. She said it was expensive. After a few weeks, she wanted to buy it for sixty thousand pounds, and I demanded one hundred and twenty thousand pounds. She was angry with me and called me a stubborn bastard. I demanded a sincere apology from her. She didn't apologise. I was angry with her and left her house for good. After a few weeks she phoned me.

"Hello, my darling. I miss you so much. I sent you an email. Did you read it?"

"I'm not interested in reading your email and don't want to receive any further emails from you."

"You really are a stubborn bastard, aren't you?"

After that short phone conversation, I was curious and read her email. She offered two hundred and forty thousand pounds for my car number plate and wanted to have my bank details. I realised it was a genuine offer from her. I felt I had been unfair and prejudiced against her. I missed a golden opportunity and wasn't happy about what I had done to her. I paid the price for being prejudiced and wrote this poem from her point of view about me.

PREJUDICED

Dear Sir,
You are prejudiced.
Don't you see the colourful flowers
In the garden of my heart?
Are you blind?
Are you colour blind?
You never said so.

"How interesting! So, you were playing a game with my tax adviser. You really are a son of a bitch," said Osman.

"I beg your pardon, sir. I am not a son of a bitch. My mother is a well-respected lady. I demand a sincere apology from you."

Osman stood up. "I don't apologise to anybody."

There was silence in the sitting room. Ozana and Mili were staring at Osman.

"Come on, Osman. You asked Goldash about Georgina, and he frankly told us everything. You must apologise."

"I agree with my mother. You must apologise, Father."

Osman didn't have any other choice but to apologise.

Goldash accepted his apology. Osman was humiliated in front of his family and went out to the garden to have a cigarette.

"Well done, Goldash. You made my father apologise for the first time."

"I am sorry, Mrs Tokkan. I didn't want to humiliate your husband in front of his family, but it was very important and necessary for me to ask him for an apology."

"That's perfect, Goldash. If I were you, I would have done the same thing."

"Excuse me, ladies, I want to have a cigarette as well."

He went out to the garden.

"Excuse me, Mr Tokkan. Can I have a cigarette please?"

"Here you are. I didn't know you smoked."

"I have cigarettes a few times in a week, just as I have sex a few times in a week."

Osman laughed. They didn't talk again until they had finished their cigarettes.

"Do you play snooker, Goldash?"

"I used to play and was very good at it. I haven't played in more than eleven years."

"We have a snooker room. Would you like to play snooker with me?"

"Yes, sir."

They went to the snooker room and started to play. After the first game, Mili came into the room.

"Are you enjoying playing snooker together?" she asked.

"He isn't as good at snooker as he is at golf. He lost the first game," said Osman.

"I haven't played for a long time. People used to call me Mr One-Four-Seven."

"You don't need to boast, Goldash."

"I'm telling you the truth."

"Father, we must give Goldash a chance. This is a brand new cue. You can practise for half an hour with it. If you get a century break with your right hand, I'll give you five hundred pounds, and if you get a century break with your left hand, another five hundred."

"If you do it, I will make the same offer as Mili," said Osman.

"Yes, I'll try it. The name of my first cue was GG. Can I call this cue GG the Second?"

"We don't care what you call the cue as long as you show us two century breaks," said Mili.

He practised with his right hand for ten minutes, and for another ten minutes with his left hand. He practised again, alternating between either hand for the remaining ten minutes. Mili and Osman watched him practising. He made a century break with his right hand and then a century break with his left hand. First Mili congratulated him, and then Osman did the same.

"You are a genius, Goldash. You did it again. You're a son of a b.... You're a son of a bard."

"Mr Tokkan, you have a habit of saying 'a son of a bitch', don't you? You say it, but you don't mean it. I wish I had known that; I wouldn't have humiliated you in front of your family."

"I understand, Goldash. I know it's a bad habit. Let's have our dinner."

After dinner, Ozana and Goldash played acey-deucey. Mili watched them. Goldash wasn't concentrating on the game, and Ozana noticed.

"Goldash, what's the matter with you? You're thinking a lot. I want to have a good game with you."

"I remembered that I had promised Oya never to play snooker again, so I can't accept these cheques."

"That's all right. Oya told me you could play snooker," said Mili.

"Excuse me, Mili. Can I have a word with you in private please?"

"Yes, of course. Shall we go out to the garden?"

When they were in the garden, she asked, "What would you like to tell me?"

"You intrigue me. Would you tell me who you are please?"

"I am a doctor of finance, a doctor of information, a member of the Securities Institute,[3] a violinist and a psychic. I think I'm a blessed person."

"You are indeed. You are a double doctor and a double delight."

She smiled and said, "You are a double delight too. You are a bilingual poet and write poems in English and Turkish. Shall we go inside? My mother wants to continue playing acey-deucey with you."

"I would like to have another cigarette. Would you get one for me from your father please?"

"You really are a naughty boy. You told my father you have cigarettes only a few times in a week."

"Yes, you're right. I couldn't tell your father that sometimes I have both cigarettes and sex a few times in a day."

"If you told my father that, he would admire you more. I'll tell him what you told me."

She brought him a cigarette. He smoked it with Mili at his side.

"You are a heartbreaker, Goldash. You were unfair to Georgina. She always loved you. No man at that golf club, including my father, wanted to beat her at golf; nevertheless,

---

[3] The former name of the Chartered Institute for Securities & Investment.

they all wanted to be intimate with her. You were lucky to sleep with her. Your reality was their dream."

"I agree with you. I was unfair to her and hope she will forgive me."

She nodded. "I'm sure she will forgive you. Come on, let's go back inside."

He continued playing acey-deucey with Ozana.

"Well done, Mrs Tokkan. You're a very good player. Who else do you play with?"

"Sometimes I play with Gulizar and Rina."

"That explains it then!" He stood up. "Well, I should really be going. Thank you all for your hospitality."

"It was a very interesting day. We all enjoyed it very much. Thank you, Goldash," said Osman.

"Yes, I enjoyed it very much too. I hope to see you again soon."

He went to his car and was ready to go when he heard Mili calling him.

"Excuse me, Goldash. Just a moment please."

"Yes, your ladyship. Should I call you Mili or Leyla?"

"You can call me either Mili or Leyla, it depends on the context. Last night, I remembered your poem *I Want To Write All About You*, so I wrote all about you. This is the story of your life so far. You can read it when you are at home tonight. My birthday is on Monday. Debbie and her husband will deliver one thousand red roses to your old flat on Mentmore Terrace tomorrow afternoon at three. Would you be there to receive them please? I'll be there on Monday morning at eight."

She gave him the manuscript and the key to the flat.

"Yes, of course. Everything will be ready, just as Leyla wishes. See you there."

I WANT TO WRITE ALL ABOUT YOU

I WANT TO WRITE ALL ABOUT YOU

My dearest,
Tonight, I want to listen to you.
While I am listening to you,
I want to cry.
While I am listening to you,
I want to laugh.
The story of everyone's life is a book,
If it is written.
Tonight, I want to write all about you,
Pages and pages.

It was the twenty-eighth of November 1988. Goldash didn't have anything to do on the ground floor of 147 Mentmore Terrace, where he lived and worked as an outdoor machinist. He cleaned his flat and had a shave, a shower and breakfast. It was raining gently. He took his umbrella and went walking in London Fields. Leaves were falling gracefully from ageing branches and recycling themselves happily. He walked around the park, stood under a plane tree and looked at the branches. He was enjoying the falling of the leaves when he realised a puppy was pulling at his trousers. He was scared and stood quite still. An elderly man approached him calmly and tapped him on the shoulder.

"Don't worry, son. She is a vegetarian."

That was the turning point in Goldash's life. When the puppy pulled at his trousers, he remembered to go to Dillons bookshop and buy a copy of the book *Reflexology: The Definitive Guide*. He immediately walked to Graham Road, took the number 38 bus, and got off at Holborn before heading to the bookshop on Gower Street. He found the book in the basement of the shop and checked its price, realised he had forgotten to bring his wallet, and looked a bit strange checking all his trouser and jacket pockets again and again. He heard the voice of a woman.

"Excuse me, sir."

When he saw her face, he was mesmerised and dropped the book from his hand. Both of them crouched down to pick it up at the same time, and he hit his nose against her knee. His nose started to bleed. She took a tissue from her handbag and gave it to him.

"I'm a doctor. My name is Oya Oydash."

He couldn't say anything and just stood there, holding the tissue to his nose. She held his hand and took him to the nearest café. She bought coffee for both of them and waited for him to say something. When he had finished his coffee, he finally started to speak.

"I'm sorry, doctor. I was having a poet's tragedy and couldn't speak for a while."

"Are you a poet?"

"Yes, I am."

"Where do you come from?"

"I come from Gulistan."

"Unbelievable! Can you recite some of your poems to me please?"

"This is very strange, doctor. Suddenly, I don't remember any of my poems. My memory has failed me for the first time."

He stood up and checked his jacket pockets.

"Yes, I've found my notebook. These are my recent poems. Would you like to read them for me? I like it when somebody reads my poems."

He gave her his notebook, and she opened it and read two poems.

A CONQUEROR

This fertile land has a golden field
On the left-hand side.
Many enthusiastic volunteers
Were dying to be the owners.
Unfortunately,
All of them failed to get it.
Though they knew
Keeping it would be more difficult
Than getting it.
This fertile land needs a conqueror
Who knows how to get it
And how to keep it.

IF SHE HAS

If she has the combination of
A beautiful body and a brilliant brain,
She will be in charge all the time.
So never try to compete with her.
It is more than enough
To be her humble worker.

"I like them very much. Can I have your name please?"

"My name is Goldash Goldadash."

"Are you studying medicine?"

"No, I'm studying accountancy. I am a qualified reflexologist and massage therapist, though."

"You were at the medical books section in the bookshop. I thought you might be studying medicine and was going to buy that book for you."

"That's very kind of you. I give reflexology and massages to my landlady, her parents and her friends. In return she doesn't take any rent from me. I don't have any other clients at present. I do a cleaning job in a snooker club in the mornings, and work part-time as an outdoor machinist. I don't go to college on Mondays and have no work today."

"Unbelievable!"

"What is unbelievable, doctor? You've said that twice. I'm not lying to you. I would never lie to you. You are a doctor."

"I believe what you say, you seem to be an honest person. Somebody told me once that one day I would meet a poet from Gulistan who had healing hands. I thought she was joking and didn't believe her. That is unbelievable, isn't it?"

"Yes, doctor. I'm beginning to understand you. Somebody told me that one day I would meet a delightful doctor. Her birthday would be on the twenty-third of April. I thought she was joking and didn't believe her either."

"My birthday is on the twenty-third of April. This is truly incredible."

He stared at her. "You're not joking, are you?"

"No, I am not joking. Here, have a look at my driving licence."

He looked at it and said, "It is the twenty-third of April. This truly is like a dream."

"Some dreams do come true after all. I know Gulistan means 'the land of roses'. I am told people give and receive lots of roses there. Is that true?"

"Yes, it might be true. I haven't had any experiences like that yet though."

She smiled at him. "I knew you wouldn't have had experiences like that. When you were a teenager, you had a stomach operation, didn't you?"

"Yes, I did. How do you know that?"

"I am both a medical doctor and a medical psychic. When I look at you, I also know your body's medical condition."

"I've never heard of a medical psychic before. I am so happy to meet you."

"So am I."

"Where do you come from, doctor?"

"I come from Lovistan."

"I know Lovistan means 'the land of lovely people'. You must be the princess of that lovely land."

"You're right. I haven't had either reflexology or a massage before. I would really like to enjoy your healing hands today."

"I'm not sure if I have healing hands, although my landlady and her parents say I have."

"I know you have no money on you. Would you take this twenty-pound note and buy that book from the bookshop? I'm going to make a phone call."

"That's very kind of you. Thank you, doctor."

"Please call me Oya. I am your friend now."

"Yes, you are my dearest friend."

He bought the book and came back to the café.

"Where do you live, Goldash?"

"I live in Hackney. Let me hail a black cab."

They took a black cab and went to 147 Mentmore Terrace. He turned the heater on, prepared the chair and started giving her reflexology.

"Oya, you are not relaxed. Are you all right?"

"I didn't expect to meet a poet and have reflexology today. I am excited."

"You will be all right. Just relax and enjoy the treatment."

Goldash told her what had happened when he was sixteen:

The day before I went to hospital for my operation, I was very scared and nervous. I was sixteen at the time. I saw a pigeon on the tree near to our house and felt I should talk to that pigeon.

"Hello, pretty pigeon. I'm going to hospital tomorrow. When I come back, I will give you lots of nice food."

I felt as if the pigeon were speaking to me. "Don't worry, my friend. Everything will be all right," it said.

"My name is Goldash. What's your name?"

"My name is Pelin. Good luck for your operation. See you soon, my friend."

She flew away. I felt happy and relaxed. When I went to hospital, a nurse called Oya took my blood pressure.

"You're very relaxed. I haven't seen a patient as relaxed as you are before an operation."

"When I see a beautiful nurse, I am always relaxed."

She laughed at me and said, "You are a baby. I am much older than you."

"Yes, nurse. You are older than me. This baby needs breastfeeding."

She laughed again and said, "You are a very naughty boy. Good luck for your operation."

While I was in hospital, Nurse Oya kissed me on the cheek every morning and whispered to me, "My baby is doing very well."

After eighteen days, I was discharged and wanted to see Pigeon Pelin. Whenever possible, I looked at that tree and hoped to see her, but I never saw her again. I bought a bouquet for Nurse Oya and went to the hospital and was told she had left the hospital. I never saw Nurse Oya again either.

Oya sighed. "Goldash, it's so relaxing. I feel sleepy."

"Yes, I should shut up and concentrate on reflexology."

When he finished, she was asleep. He went to the shop and bought some vegetables and fruit. When he returned, she was sitting up on the chair.

"Where have you been, Goldash?"

"I went to the shop. How are you feeling after having reflexology?"

"It was fantastic. I feel completely relaxed. You do have healing hands indeed. I had a dream about Pigeon Pelin. In my dream, I was in a high place called Tepetarla in SP Village. I was sitting on a chair. There was a big eagle on my right and another one on my left. There were lots of different birds. They were all in a line, and flying about two metres off the ground. They were singing and saluting me. At the end of the line there were two pigeons. They slowly came closer, and one of them said, 'My name is Pelin the Second, and this is my daughter Pelin the Third. My mother couldn't make it this time. She is unable to fly long distances these days. This is our seasonal parade. Perhaps Goldash will join you next time. Would you give our love to him please?'"

"That's an interesting dream. I know Tepetarla means 'high field', but I've never heard of SP Village."

"My grandmother and my mother stayed there for about two years during the Second World War. The name of the village is Soğukpınar. For some reason my grandmother and her associates used to call it SP Village. They used to say it stood for 'safe and protected village'."

"Have you been there?" asked Goldash.

"My parents took me there a few times. Last year my parents, my uncle, his wife and I visited the village."

He prepared the massage couch and gave her a relaxing massage.

"Thank you so much, Goldash. You're a magician. I felt as if a sensual storm from Mount Olympus had taken me to Atlantis. I wish I could have a massage from you every day."

"It's my pleasure. I'm glad you enjoyed it. While you are having a shower, I'm going to prepare dinner."

He cooked monkfish and rice with saffron. She prepared salad.

"Do you have a dinner suit?"

"No, I don't have a dinner suit, or any other suit in fact. Why do you ask?"

"My father always wears a dinner suit when we have guests."

"I'm sorry, Oya. I forgot you're the princess of Lovistan. Would the princess forgive this poor poet please? I'm sure he will be better prepared for your highness' next visit."

"She forgives her precious poet. Do you drink wine?"

"Yes, but only if it's over forty years old. In Gulistan, people drink rosehip wine on special occasions, and it must be at least forty years old. I'm not sure if that is real wine. Women make rosehip wine; men are not allowed to make it there. I have white grape juice for dinner."

As they were having dinner, she smiled and started talking.

"I was supposed to meet one of my friends at the bookshop this afternoon. For some reason, she didn't turn up at the arranged time, and I went to the medical books section. While I was passing my time there, I saw you. It's strange how things happen. If she had arrived, I wouldn't have met you."

"I'm delighted your friend didn't turn up."

"Yes, we should be grateful to her and thank her for that."

After they had eaten, she smiled at him from across the table. "How much do I owe you for today?"

"It's free for your highness."

"Thank you very much. It's getting late. Can you call a black cab for me please?"

"My landlady is a black cab driver. Let me call her to see if she is available. Where do you live?

"I live with my parents in Hampstead Heath."

He phoned his landlady and asked her to take Oya home.

"She will be here in ten minutes."

"Your body language tells me you would like to see me every day. I would like to see you again as soon as possible. You are an imaginative person and can visualise that I'm always here with you."

"Yes, Oya. You'll always be in my heart."

She kissed him on the cheek and left his flat.

He was restless after she had gone and remembered what his mother had once told him: "You must study and obtain a qualification, my son."

His mother had had a dream about a medical student when he was in hospital. Oya perfectly matched his mother's description. After nine years, her dream had come true. He lay down on his bed and visualised her. First, he pictured her beautiful green eyes, then her eyebrows, nose, lips, chin, cheeks, ears, forehead, hair, and her smiling face. She was like a beautiful bird hovering in the air. Her lips said, "Good night, my beloved poet. Sleep well."

"Good night, my princess."

He awoke early the next morning and went straight to the snooker club. He could feel Oya's presence the entire time he was there. He cleaned the place immaculately.

"I'm sure Oya would like everything clean and tidy," he thought.

He usually practised snooker for thirty minutes after cleaning. He visualised Oya watching him. She winked at him with her right eye. Suddenly, he dropped the cue and picked it up with his left hand; she winked at him with her left eye. He held the cue with his right hand; she winked at him with her right eye. He held the cue with his left hand, and once again she winked at him with her left eye.

"Yes, princess. I understand you very well. You want me to play with my right hand and then with my left hand. Let me do a few shots using both hands."

He practised, alternating his hands.

"This is amazing. I can use both my hands equally well. Thank you so much, princess. You helped me to discover myself. I am an ambidextrous snooker player now. You're always with me. You are my guiding star indeed."

Afterwards, he went back home to prepare breakfast. He put out an empty plate for Oya and visualised her again. Her lips said, "*Bon appétit.*"

His life had been changed forever. From that moment on, he enjoyed everything he did. His final level of Association of Accounting Technicians exams were in December. He didn't do any sewing work and focused on studying. After his exams he received a letter from Oya.

My dearest Goldash,

I miss you so much and think of you all the time. You are my healer. I wish I could enjoy your healing hands every day.

Please accept this cheque for £200. Perhaps you will buy a dinner suit for yourself.

It would be nice to see you in a suit.

Lots of love!

Oya

On Friday evening, Goldash went to the snooker club to collect his wages. There was an announcement on the noticeboard.

DEAR MEMBERS,
£1,000 PRIZE FOR MAXIMUM BREAKS EACH MONTH IN THE NEW YEAR.
WE WISH YOU A HAPPY AND SUCCESSFUL NEW YEAR. GOOD LUCK TO YOU ALL!

He thought about getting a maximum break and winning the prize money. Oya's face appeared on the noticeboard, and she winked at him. Her lips said, "Yes, you can do it, Goldash."

He needed to be a member of the club, and to have a good cue and a three-piece suit for that. He went to the club's office and talked to the wife of the club owner.

"Good evening, Mrs Hothorn. Can I become a member of the club please?"

"Yes, you can. Just fill in this form please. As you work here, you'll get a twenty per cent discount."

He filled in the form and gave it back to her.

"Mrs Hothorn, I want to get a new cue. Would you choose one for me please?"

She carefully chose a cue. "I think this will be the best one for you."

"Thank you. I don't think I have enough money to pay for my membership fees and my new cue right now. Is it all right with you to deduct it from my wages?"

"No problem at all. Enjoy the evening."

On Christmas Day, he went to the snooker club. After cleaning up the mess from Christmas Eve, he named his cue.

"Your name is GG now. We'll get many maximum breaks together, my friend."

He practised snooker Christmas Day and Boxing Day. On the twenty-eighth of December, after finishing the cleaning in the morning, he got his first maximum break. It was a happy monthiversary for him: he had met Oya on the twenty-eighth of November.

"I'll buy a suit next week, and get my next maximum break on the twenty-eighth of January," he thought.

He received a Happy New Year card from Oya and thought of the nice meals he would cook for her during her future visits.

"It would be nice if I learned how to cook properly. I'm sure she would like to have delicious meals. I'll wear my suit and serve my princess. She is very beautiful," he thought.

That same afternoon, he enrolled on a cooking course.

On the twenty-seventh of January 1989, a Friday evening, he donned his suit and headed to the snooker club. As he entered, he spotted the club owner's daughter leaning against the bar.

"Good evening, Lorna."

"Good evening, Goldash. You look very smart. Do you have a date tonight?"

"Yes, I have an appointment with Lorna the lovely."

"What can I do for you?"

"I'm going to get a maximum break tomorrow evening. Would you be happy to be my snooker partner and re-spot the black ball for me please?"

"You must be joking! No member of this club has ever got a maximum break, and I doubt if anybody ever will."

"I'll give you ten per cent of my winnings, if you're happy with that. Here you are, fifty pounds now and fifty pounds after our show."

"Yes, I would be very happy to take a hundred pounds from you. Frankly, I don't care if you get a maximum break or not."

"Thank you, Lorna. You are gorgeous. I knew you would be my snooker partner. See you tomorrow evening."

On Saturday morning he went to his cleaning job, then later finished his sewing job, had dinner, and was at the snooker club by eight o'clock. He cleaned his snooker table and called Lorna to re-spot the black ball. He was nervous in front of all the guests and members of the club. He visualised Oya's face and saw her first wink of the evening. He took his time and enjoyed his show. When he had potted fifteen red balls and the black ball fifteen times, everybody stopped their whispering and watched him. They all wanted him to get a maximum break even more than he did. He calmly potted the yellow, green, brown, blue and pink balls in order and waited for Oya's wink. There it was. "Well done, Goldash," her lips said. He potted the black ball and completed his maximum break. Everybody cheered and applauded him. Lorna hugged and kissed him.

"You've done it! You surprise me, Goldash."

He laughed. "You surprise me too, Lorna. You kissed me. I hope your parents don't mind. You forget I'm just a cleaner at this club."

"Let me kiss you again and again. You're our cleaner and our Mr One-Four-Seven at this club. I am so proud of you. Can I have my fifty pounds please?"

"I'm sorry, Lorna. I was so excited that I forgot about it. Here is your money. You can have one hundred pounds each month if you agree to be my snooker partner on the twenty-eighth of every month."

"Yes, I would like that. You're my partner in pleasure."

It was the fourteenth of February. Goldash hoped to finish his sewing work before noon. His phone rang.

"Hello, Goldash, this is Oya. I've been missing you so much. I feel that you are my magician and my best medicine."

"Hello, Oya. I'm very flattered. Are you trying to be the second flatterer after Shakespeare?"

"No, I'm not. Can I visit you within an hour please?"

"I'm working now and still need to clean my flat. Can you come this afternoon?"

"It's fine with me. I would like to watch you while you're sewing and help you to clean your flat."

"See you soon then."

He looked at the mirror and realised he hadn't had a shave or shower that morning.

"I must be presentable for my princess," he thought as he headed to the bathroom.

After an hour, Oya came to his door.

"There is something for you in my car. Can you help me with it please?" she asked.

They went to her car.

"I bought this drawing when I was in Milan. It's called *Trinity*, but I call it *Pigeon Pelin & Company*."

"It's beautiful. Did you buy the drawing from the artist?"

"Yes, I bought it from her. She is extraordinary, her name is Bruna X."

"When I was at secondary school, I wanted to be an artist and did a few drawings of my mother, but soon realised I wasn't good enough. I admire artists," said Goldash.

"I also visited my uncle in Istanbul and bought an acey-deucey set for you. Do you know how to play it?"

"Yes, I used to play acey-deucey and bridge during my high-school days."

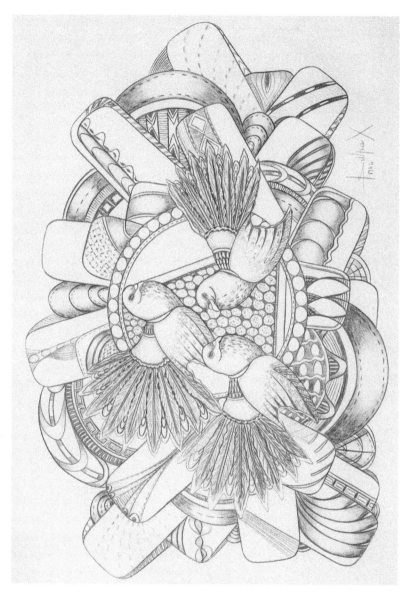

Pigeon Pelin & Company

"I am glad you know the rules of acey-deucey."

"Thank you so much for all these pretty presents. I must finish my work before noon. I'm making gents trousers. It's called piecing-up work."

She watched him sew a few pairs of trousers, then went shopping while he finished his work.

When she returned, she said, "Happy Valentine's Day, Goldash. I bought a dozen red roses and a vase for you."

"Happy Valentine's Day, Oya. I was focusing on my work and forgot all about it."

"Have you written any new poems recently?"

"Yes, I have. One of them is written in my notebook. You can read it if you like."

LIKE A TURKISH DELIGHT

You are sweet and seductive
Like a Turkish delight.
I dream of having you tonight
Like a Turkish delight.
It is said that speeding is a crime
When you travel on the highway of love.
But baby,
You increase my speed
And my heart rate will double.
Oh yes,
You are that sweet trouble.
I dream of having you tonight
Like a Turkish delight.

"Well done, Goldash. Now I'm your muse and Turkish delight. Keep writing lovely poems."

She put the notebook down on the table. "Did you buy a dinner suit?"

"Yes, I bought a suit that I can convert into a dinner suit if I wear it with a bow tie."

"I want to buy a dinner suit for you. Let's go to that menswear shop on Mare Street."

He paused and said, "I was planning on buying a dinner suit at the beginning of next month, as I am expecting some money at the end of this month."

"Goldash, my darling, you don't need to worry about that. I want to buy it for you as a Valentine's Day present."

"That's very sweet of you. Let's go to the shop, then."

When they were in the shop, she chose a dinner suit, a shirt, a bow tie, a few pairs of socks, a pair of shoes and an overcoat for him.

"Excuse me, sir. I am a doctor. I understand you have migraines on a regular basis. Is that right?" she asked the shop owner.

"Yes, it is. How do you know that?"

"Never mind how I know. My friend Goldash is a healer. If he gives you a head massage on the chair, you won't have migraines for a while. Now, I'm just going to pop across to the Marks & Spencer store. See both of you later."

The shop owner locked the door, and Goldash gave him a head massage. Just as he was finishing, Oya returned.

"How are you feeling now, sir?" she asked the shop owner.

"That was amazing. I feel good. He is a healer indeed. How much do I owe you, Goldash?"

"It was my pleasure. I give head massages when Oya asks me to. She knew you needed it. I enjoyed giving you the massage."

"Thank you, Goldash. Would you put your suit on please?"

He put his suit on, and the shop owner looked at him.

"I think you need a scarf, a hat, a briefcase and an umbrella. These are from me. You look like a proper gentleman now. Both of you can come to my shop at any time. Have a lovely day."

"You certainly know what is best for me. Thank you very much, sir."

They went back to his flat and had tea.

"When I visualise you, I read your lips and know what you say to me. As we were coming back from the shop, I read some people's lips. When they saw you, some of them said, 'Oh my God!' Have you heard the saying about the vicar and his daughter?"

"No, I haven't."

"The vicar says, 'When people see me, they say, "Hello, Father." When they see my daughter, they say, "Oh my God!"'"

She laughed and said, "I don't know about your parents. Both my parents are professors."

"That's interesting. Both my parents are peasants."

"My paternal grandparents were peasants, and my maternal grandparents were secret agents. If you had been wearing a suit when I first met you, I would have thought you were the son of wealthy parents. It suits you very well. Are you going to give me reflexology and a massage today?"

"Yes, Oya. Let me wear my green trousers and white T-shirt, which are the colours of my favourite football club."

After having reflexology, Oya lay back and sighed. "I don't know what you do to me. When you touch my feet, I feel fabulous and go to my dreamland. I had another dream. This time I was riding a big eagle. We flew over Nigeria and landed in a protected area of the River Niger. I was bathing with Goddess Oya, and your nurse friend Oya was serving us in the river. Both of them sent their love to you. Did Nurse Oya have a mole on the right side of her neck?"

"Yes, she did."

"This is incredible. It means she was the same Nurse Oya you met."

"Who is Goddess Oya? I've never heard of her."

"She is a beautiful and blessed African lady."

"I want to cook sultan's delight for you. It is my mother's favourite meal," said Goldash.

"It's my mother's favourite meal too. I don't know how to cook it, though."

He smiled. "My mother taught me."

When he was cleaning the dinner table, he heard a noise in the backyard of the flat and opened the rear door. His peace rose in a big pot had bloomed, and it was snowing gently.

"Oya, can you come here please?" he called softly.

"What is it, Goldash?"

"Look at my lovely peace rose. It has bloomed, and it's snowing. I haven't seen anything like that before."

"It's beautiful. Would you like to dance with me in the snow?" asked Oya.

"Yes, I would love to."

The poet of Gulistan and the princess of Lovistan danced until it became too cold to bear.

"Today has been wonderful. I've enjoyed every minute of it. Can I visit you next Saturday?" asked Oya.

"Yes, of course you can. I'm very happy to see you at any time."

Oya was ready to go and noticed Goldash wanted to say something.

"Do you want to say something to me?" she asked gently.

"Yes, I do, but I don't know how to start."

"Come on, Goldash. You can tell me anything you like."

"When I was in hospital for my operation, my mother had a dream about a medical student. Your green eyes, long hair, smile and date of birth match her description. She can't have been wrong."

"That's unbelievable. How did she know about me nine years ago?"

"I don't know. It is unbelievable. I always thought it was one of my mother's stories. Can I verify something with you?"

"Yes, of course."

"In her dream, that medical student told my mother she had an eleven-year-old sister whose name was Ayla. When both of them were going to school one day, her sister was hit by a car and died before she could be taken to hospital. The student thought if she had known first aid, she might have saved her sister. That was the reason she wanted to study medicine. Was Ayla your sister?"

Oya couldn't say anything and started to cry. He hugged her until she stopped.

"My mother is a polyglot, a professor of languages and a member of the Institute of Linguists.[4] She used to work as a conference interpreter and wanted me to study languages at university. I didn't tell anybody the reason I wanted to study medicine. I want to meet your mother. When will you take me to her, my dearest Goldash?"

"I can't go to our village at present. I promised my mother I wouldn't return without a qualification. You can go there whenever you want to. I'm sure she would be delighted to see you. However, it isn't advisable for a lady to go there alone. My

---

[4] The former name of the Chartered Institute of Linguists.

mother's birthday is on the twenty-first of March. We celebrate her birthday and Nowruz.[5] Your birthday is on the twenty-third of April. We celebrate your birthday and Children's Day. My sister's birthday is on the first of May. We celebrate her birthday and Labour Day. It would be better if you went there on my sister's birthday."

"I understand your dilemma. If we went to your village together, your mother would understand, wouldn't she?"

"No, she would never forgive me."

"I'll go there with one of my cousins. Both of them are bodybuilders and live in Istanbul."

"Thank you for understanding."

"You make me happy and sad. You make me laugh and cry. What am I going to do with you, Goldash?"

"I wish I knew! At present, I am your patient and you are my doctor."

"My patients usually get two kisses from me. As you are my very special patient, you will get three."

She hugged him and kissed him on the cheeks and on the lips.

He was so happy when he lay down on his bed. He visualised Oya and his mother together.

"Now I understand why my mother wants me to have a qualification. She thinks if I have a qualification, I will be eligible for Oya. Perhaps it isn't important to her, though I think it is important to her parents and my parents," he thought.

He went to the backyard of his flat and pictured himself dancing with her in the snow. He felt he was the luckiest person in the world, and wrote a poem.

---

[5] A celebration at the beginning of spring.

THE BEAUTY OF HER BRAIN

I had an unusual experience tonight.
I was so engaged with
The beauty of her brain,
And I forgot all about
The beauty of her body.

On Saturday, at lunchtime, she came to his door.

"Good afternoon, Goldash. I brought sandwiches for lunch. Would you make fresh coffee for us please?"

"Of course I will. I bought a recipe book. What can I cook for you this evening?"

"I fancy something vegetarian. I'm going to do the shopping and will come back in about two hours. When I come back, can I have my treatment please?"

"Yes, of course."

By the time she came back with some shopping bags and flowers, he had managed to sew ten pairs of trousers.

"I went to the market and found some tiger nuts. It's enjoyable walking around the market. It's amazing what can be found in London these days."

"I haven't had tiger nuts before and will enjoy having them."

He gave her reflexology. She relaxed and fell asleep on the chair. He read the recipe book, thinking about what to cook for her. Then he heard the voice of his mother: "GG!" He thought she was outside and went out of his flat. Nobody was there. He continued reading his book and heard the voice of his mother again: "GG!" He hoped to see her and went out of his flat a second time. Again, he didn't see anybody there. He was a little bit scared and sat down next to Oya, holding her right hand.

"Are you all right? Why are you holding my hand?"

"Something strange happened. I heard my mother call me twice. No other person calls me GG."

"Your mother wouldn't be here. That was me calling you. I don't usually have dreams, but when you touch my feet, you send me to my dreamland, and I meet whomever I want to. You are my magician. Why didn't you tell me your mother called you GG? I know it means 'pretty'. Come on, give me a hug and kiss me, GG Boy!"

"Would you tell me about your dream please?"

"In my dream, we met your mother at Highbury and Islington Tube station. You drove my car and brought us to your flat. You went to that Vietnamese shop on Mare Street to buy carambola, dragon fruit, mangosteen and rambutan. She spoke English without an accent. We talked about a few things. She said she would be going to visit her friends in France and Germany. When you came back from the shop, we had those exotic fruit together. She asked when we would get engaged."

"My mother doesn't know a word of English. It's amazing how things can be so different in our dreams. As you know, the middle fingers and ring fingers of both my hands are joined, so I am unable to wear an engagement ring."

"I think you should have an operation on your right hand first. You can ask your general practitioner to make a hospital appointment for you. When I was with Bruna X, she showed me some of her drawings. There was a drawing of a lady. She looked like your mother. I must call Bruna X about that drawing. Can I use your phone please?"

She phoned Bruna X and spoke to the artist in Italian.

"I'm going to Milan next week. I must buy that drawing for you."

"How many languages do you speak, Oya?"

"In addition to English and Turkish, I am fluent in French,

German, Italian and Spanish. Also, I can speak basic Arabic, Hebrew and Russian."

"Bless you, Oya. You know many languages. I've been struggling to master one language and express myself as a poet."

"There are many ways you can express yourself. When I met you for the first time, you didn't say anything for the first twenty minutes, and yet you expressed yourself very well."

"How do you know Bruna X?"

"My mother knows her. She did drawings of my parents and me. My photographer friend is going to make duplicates of those drawings for my room. If you like, she can make duplicates of them for your flat too."

"It would be great to have drawings of you and your parents here."

"Do you drive, Goldash?"

"Yes, I passed my driving test last October."

She smiled. "In that case, I will add your name to my car insurance."

"I understand your ladyship needs a chauffeur."

She grinned and said softly, "I've been thinking of us having each other this evening. After having a dream about your mother, I think we should do it on my birthday. It is better if we order a sofa bed for your flat. We must keep one red rose on the dinner table and spread the petals of ninety-nine red roses over our bed on my birthday."

"Yes, my dearest Oya. It sounds romantic."

Two weeks later, she phoned him from Milan.

"Hello, Goldash. I bought the drawing from Bruna X. It's beautiful. Its name is *Will You*. I call it *Marvellous Mother*. Bruna said when she started drawing it, there was an image of a lady in front of her. Although she had no idea who that lady was, she drew it as if the lady were posing for her. I'm so happy to get the drawing for you. I'm flying to London tomorrow morning. Would you meet me at Heathrow Airport please?"

"Yes, I'll be there. I'm dying to see the drawing of my mother."

"See you then, my love."

After Goldash met Oya at the airport, they took the Piccadilly line to Holborn, and then the Central line to Bethnal Green.

"If I'm going to meet your mother on your sister's birthday, we should have a duplicate of this drawing made for her as well."

"I'm sure my mother would like it. Let's call her and surprise her on her birthday."

"What a wonderful idea. I'm so excited to talk to her."

"My mother has been waiting to talk to you for more than nine years."

She held his hand tightly. They got off the bus near Hackney Town Hall and walked the rest of the way to Goldash's flat. As they approached it, somebody called his name.

"Hello, Goldash. You were not in. I was just about to go back to the factory."

"I'm sorry, Mr Jamieson. I forgot all about the delivery this morning. I went to Heathrow Airport to meet my friend. I should have let you know."

"It isn't a problem. My assistant has just become a father again and is off for a few days, so I have to do some deliveries this week. Who is your beautiful friend?"

"This is Dr Oya Oydash. Oya, this is my employer, Mr Samuel Jamieson."

"It's so lovely to meet you, Mr Jamieson. Would you like to join us for a cup of tea?" asked Oya.

"Yes, that would be nice. This is my last delivery today."

Marvellous Mother

When they got to the flat, Goldash took two bags of materials from the van to his flat and made three cups of tea.

"Are you really a doctor? You're so beautiful. I thought you were a model."

"Yes, I am a doctor. My poor poet Goldash can't afford a model. You're a businessman. Maybe you can afford a model. You had a polyp in your intestine, didn't you, Mr Jamieson?"

"Yes, it was removed recently. How did you know that?"

"I am a doctor and a medical psychic. You're not relaxed. Goldash must give you reflexology today. After having a treatment from him, you'll feel lighter and younger."

"I never heard of a medical psychic before, and had no idea that Goldash did reflexology."

"Yes, he is my healer. When he gives me reflexology, he takes me out of this world."

"Very well, I must call my wife and let her know. Can I use your phone please?"

"Yes, of course," answered Goldash.

After having tea, she said, "I fancy a salmon sandwich for lunch and some exotic fruit. I'm going to do some shopping. See both of you shortly."

During the reflexology session, Samuel relaxed and fell asleep on the chair. While he was sleeping, Oya returned. She and Goldash had their sandwiches in the garden and played acey-deucey. Samuel sprang awake when the phone rang.

"That was Mrs Jamieson. She wanted to make sure everything was all right with you," said Goldash.

"What time is it?"

"It's almost three o'clock."

"I can't believe that I've slept for that long."

"Believe it or not, you were sleeping and snoring for about two hours. Let me help you up."

He offered Samuel a glass of water.

"How are you feeling, sir?" asked Goldash.

"That was amazing. I am so relaxed. I haven't experienced anything like that before. How much do I owe you?"

"First time, it's free for you, Mr Jamieson."

"I usually give fifty pounds to Goldash," said Oya.

"If Oya said five hundred pounds, I would give it to you. You are marvellous."

"Thank you, sir."

"When I came back, you were sleeping like a baby. Your body language tells me you're going to be an action man tonight. I'm sure Mrs Jamieson will be very happy with your performance," said Oya.

"Bless you, Oya. You read my mind too."

"I would like to meet your wife. I'm coming here again next week. Perhaps we can have lunch together. Goldash makes nice sandwiches."

"Yes, I'm sure my wife would be delighted to meet you and have reflexology too."

"Definitely, she would enjoy being pampered as well. See you next week," said Oya.

The following week, one lunchtime, the Jamiesons arrived at Goldash's flat, and Samuel introduced Sylvia to Oya. Goldash prepared the sandwiches.

"I've brought a bottle of wine. Would you open it for us, Goldash?" asked Samuel.

"Goldash drinks wine only if it is at least forty years old," said Oya.

"Yes, it's forty years old. We don't drink wine if it's younger than that either," confirmed Samuel.

"Goldash comes from Gulistan. It's a tradition there for people to only drink forty-year-old rosehip wine," said Oya.

"My grandfather saved a French soldier's life during the First World War. They became good friends. That French soldier invited my grandfather to his birthday and gave him a few bottles of forty-year-old wine. When he visited his friend a second time, he met his friend's sister. He fell in love with her and eventually they got married. His friend became his brother-in-law. Every year he bought one hundred bottles of French wine and kept them in his cellar. It became a custom in our family to drink forty-year-old wine. My grandmother was French, my mother was English, my father was Scottish, and my wife is Italian," said Samuel.

"How are your French and Italian?" asked Oya.

"I am fluent in both languages."

Oya talked to Samuel in Italian about the drawings on the wall.

"You are amazing people. The more I get to know you, the more I like you."

"Thank you, Samuel."

After lunch, Sylvia said, "We must go back to the factory."

"Perhaps you can come here for dinner next time," said Oya.

Sylvia smiled at Samuel and nodded.

"Yes, we would like to come here again and again," he said and followed his wife towards the door.

It was the twenty-first of March. Oya came to Goldash's flat in the morning.

"In the old days, there was only one phone line in our village. I used to call the village office to talk to my parents. These days, every house there has a phone line. My mother's name is Güldem, which means 'an unfaded rose'. My sister's name is Güliz, which means 'as impressive as a rose'. If you're ready, I can call my mother," said Goldash.

"Yes, I would love to hear her voice."

"She is expecting my call, but she doesn't know you are with me. Let's surprise her now."

He dialled the number.

"Hello, Mother. I wish you a very happy birthday."

"Thank you, my son."

"Mother, there is somebody next to me, and she would love to talk to you. Just a second please."

Oya talked to her for more than half an hour. During their conversation, she started crying, and he comforted her.

"When you're happy you cry, and when you're sad you cry. Whenever you laugh or cry, your eyes become greener and greener. Perhaps all the politicians, preachers and people of our world will follow you. We will finally have a greener environment," said Goldash.

"Will you stop teasing me? I was so happy to talk to your mother. She told me about her dream, and I told her about mine. It was very emotional, and we cried. When I asked her if we could visit her together in May, she said no. My poor poet can't go to his village without a qualification. We must go to that jewellery shop on Mare Street and buy our engagement rings. I know you can't wear it at the moment, but you will be able to when the right time comes."

She sat up suddenly. "I was so excited about talking to your mother and forgot about the drawings in my car. Let's bring them in. My photographer friend did some excellent work. They look as good as the originals."

They took the drawings into his flat.

"This is the drawing of my parents, Belkis and Barlas. Its title is *The Two of Us*. This is the drawing of me. It's called *The Secret Toast*."

She realised she had left the bottle of forty-year-old wine in her car. She fetched it, and he opened it.

The Two of Us

The Secret Toast

"Let's toast our engagement and your mother's birthday," said Oya.

They said together, "Happy birthday, Mother."

Later they went to the jewellery shop and bought their engagement rings. When they came back, Oya had mixed feelings about their situation. She wasn't able to wear her ring either, as she hadn't told her parents about him.

"Goldash, my love, I think you understand why I am unable to introduce you to my parents."

"Yes, I understand very well. It would be problematic. Both of your parents are professors. They wouldn't be happy with their doctor daughter going out with a part-time cleaner, machinist and student. You understand why my mother wants me to have a qualification?"

"Yes, I do, my love. Now I understand what you have been going through. Would you give me reflexology? I wish to go to my dreamland and forget the problems of this world."

"When I give you reflexology, I am at peace and hear every beat of your heart. It's so enjoyable and entertaining."

After reflexology, she lay back and smiled at him.

"Come here, my magician, and kiss me. I'll tell you about the dream I had. I was riding a big eagle again. This time, we flew over Brazil and landed in an area of the River Amazon. My guides were a native couple. We were on a boat, and two boys and two girls were rowing for us. I saw different birds and animals. My guides saw a goat. They said they hadn't seen any goat like that before. She had big udders and an identification tag on her neck. It said 'MELTEM'."

"She was my favourite goat. My mother showed me how to milk her. I enjoyed milking her and making yogurt."

Oya smiled. "I'm going to meet one of my friends for lunch

at Whitechapel. When I come back, we can go to La Lune, the French restaurant in Highgate. Would you be happy to be my chauffeur this evening?"

"Yes, your ladyship. I am always at your service."

It was mid-April. Goldash was trying to finish his sewing job early, as he wanted to read a book for his cooking course. Samuel came to his door.

"Good afternoon, Goldash."

"Good afternoon, Samuel. You don't look happy. Is everything all right?"

"I'm fine. There was an accident at the factory. I took one of our machinists to hospital. Oya was working in the accident and emergency department and treated our machinist very well. When my employee saw her smiling face, he said he felt better. She asked me to visit you this afternoon to have reflexology."

"Yes, I enjoy giving reflexology."

Once again, Samuel fell asleep on the chair.

"Thank you, Goldash. You made me feel lighter and younger again," he said when he awoke.

"Samuel, if you don't mind, can I ask you to do me a favour please?"

"Of course, Goldash. I would be very happy to help my healer."

"Oya's birthday is on the twenty-third of April, and my sister's birthday is on the first of May. She is going to visit my family. I want to buy presents for Oya, my sister and my parents. Can you lend me one thousand pounds for a month please? I'm expecting some money in May."

"What do you want to buy for them?"

"Pearl sets for Oya, my sister and my mother, and a watch for my father."

"We can go to the jewellery shop on Mare Street. The owner is my friend, and he always gives me a five per cent discount. I will buy them for you. In return, you can give my wife and me reflexology. My two sons play football. If you think reflexology helps footballers, you can give it to them as well."

"Yes, it would help them. I think every footballer should have reflexology on a regular basis."

"It's a deal, then."

"Thank you, Samuel. I'm very grateful."

They went to the jewellers, and Samuel introduced Goldash to the owner.

"I'm so happy to meet you, Goldash. The owner of the menswear shop told me about you a few days ago. I've been wondering where I could find you, but you found me first. It must be my lucky day. My wife has been having regular headaches recently."

"I see. She needs a head massage."

The man nodded. "She works for Hackney council. Are you available after five o'clock.?"

"Sure, I'll be here at around half past five. You can let her know."

"Goldash wants to buy some presents for his family but doesn't have enough money. I am going to buy them for him. What discount would you give to our healer?" asked Samuel.

"I would give him ten per cent discount."

"Thank you, my friend."

It was Saturday the twenty-second of April. Oya was lounging on Goldash's sofa.

"Let's go to the flower shop and buy our red roses for tomorrow," she suggested.

"The Jamiesons are coming for dinner. Sylvia wants to learn

how to cook sultan's delight, and Samuel wants to play acey-deucey with you."

"I didn't know he played."

"He was a quick learner when I taught him. After buying the roses, shall we do the rest of the shopping?"

"Yes, of course. My photographer friend is coming here tomorrow afternoon at three o'clock. Her mother lives in Hackney. After taking a photo of *Marvellous Mother*, she will take you to her mother's house, and you can give them both reflexology."

"I do sewing less these days and spend more of my time giving reflexology and head massages."

Oya smiled. "I'm so happy for you, my healer. My parents are going to have a barbecue tomorrow afternoon. We're expecting some guests for my birthday. I'll be here tomorrow morning at eight o'clock and must leave before eleven. Do you think three hours are enough to spend with each other on my birthday?"

"Yes, I think so."

On Sunday morning, the twenty-third of April 1989, the two lovers fulfilled what they had desired. His flat became a temple of happiness. He was overjoyed and wrote a poem.

HAPPINESS

After an interesting journey,
The two lovers are in their temple of happiness.
There is no limit to their happiness,
And all they want is
For all lovers to be as happy as they are.

Oya visited Goldash on Thursday evening.

"Your photographer friend brought a duplicate of

Marvellous Mother this afternoon. She said it was free for us. She wants to have duplicates of the drawing for herself and her mother," said Goldash.

"I talked to her yesterday. She and her mother liked you very much. You can give them reflexology whenever it is necessary. I told my friends Doctors Nigel and Narine Nesbitt about you. They know my parents and my uncle in Istanbul. They would like to have reflexology this Saturday."

"Your friends are my friends. I would be happy to meet them. I have wrapped the drawing and presents for my sister and parents."

Oya nodded. "My mother is taking me to the airport on Saturday morning. I told her about the drawing and a therapist from Gulistan."

"Very well, my darling. You know what to do. I'll talk to you on my sister's birthday. Have a safe journey."

Oya stayed for a night at her uncle's house in Istanbul, and the following day one of her cousins took her to Gulistan, a journey of about two hundred kilometres. She was as excited as a teenage girl. Goldash's parents and sister were so happy to see her.

On the first of May, he phoned his parents. His sister answered the phone.

"Happy birthday, my dearest *abla*![6] How have you been keeping?"

"I am so happy, my dearest brother. Thank you so much for the present."

"It's my pleasure. Let me talk to my mother please."

The phone was handed to his mother, his father, and finally to Oya.

---

[6] 'Elder sister' in Turkish.

"1 wish you were here, Goldash. We came here yesterday afternoon and are going back to Istanbul this evening. Güliz showed me how to milk your favourite goat. Meltem is so cute," said Oya.

"I'm so happy you visited my family. You've made me the happiest man in the world."

After a short pause she said, "I'm flying back to London tomorrow evening. Shall we meet at the airport."

"Yes, I'll be there. Can you bring two bottles of rosehip wine? One of them is for my birthday, and the other one is for the Jamiesons."

"Of course 1 can."

When Oya returned, she and Goldash decided to visit a few historic places in the south of England. They visited Leeds Castle in Kent, and Bodiam Castle in East Sussex. At the end of May, they spent a day at Kew Gardens. As they wandered through the gardens, he composed a poem.

THE BEE OF ALL SEASONS
Thousands and thousands of flowers grow
At Kew Gardens from all over the world.
Each of them has a different colour
And a different shape,
Like the girls in a world beauty parade.
Flowers of friends, flowers of foes,
All flowers are beautiful, aren't they?

When they came back from Kew Gardens, Oya phoned her friends in Paris.

"My friends in Paris are a very nice couple. Annabelle is an artist, and Albert is a doctor. 1 told them about you. They are very interested in meeting you and have invited us over for a few days. If you like, you can go to Paris a few days earlier and give reflexology to them and their friends."

"That would be very nice. I haven't been to Paris before. I don't know French, though. Do they know English?"

"They both speak English well. It won't be a problem. Let me call them again."

She talked to Annabelle again.

"You can go to Paris on Monday the nineteenth of June. They will visit Albert's parents in Troyes on Friday and will come back to Paris on Sunday. I'll go to Paris on Friday morning and will stay with Francine and Fernand, a couple of family friends. They always treat me as one of their own daughters, and I treat them as my parents. They have two daughters. The younger one, Monique, will meet me at the airport. The elder one, Mélodie, is married. I will come back to London on the twenty-sixth."

"Shall we come back to London together?"

"I'm thinking of telling Francine and Fernand about you. It would be nice if you visited them and gave them reflexology on either the twenty-sixth or the twenty-seventh."

"That's fine with me, but I must come back to London by the twenty-eighth of June."

Oya bought air tickets for both of them. They visited Warwick Castle on the seventh of June, and Sir Isaac Newton's house, Woolsthorpe Manor and Lincoln Castle on the tenth.

His landlady took him to Heathrow Airport on the morning of the nineteenth of June. Annabelle met him at Roissy Airport.

"We live in the 7th arrondissement. Albert asked me to drive around Paris and show you some of the beauties of the city."

"That was very thoughtful of him. I didn't expect to have a chauffeur and a tour guide today."

"Oya told us to look after her healer very well. She is one of our best friends. When we were in London, she showed us around, and we stayed at her parents' place."

The couple's flat was on the top floor of an apartment building. In the evening, Goldash gave reflexology to both Annabelle and Albert.

"Thank you so much, Goldash. That was extraordinary. I've had reflexology a few times before, but I didn't feel this good. This is the first time I have felt that I've had proper reflexology. You are exceptionally good."

"It's my pleasure, Albert. It was very thoughtful of you to have bought a reflexology chair and a massage couch."

"You'll be very busy for the next few days. I'm sure my friends would be delighted to enjoy your healing hands too."

For three days, Goldash worked as a therapist and gave massages to Annabelle and Albert and reflexology to their friends. On the twenty-third of June, he had breakfast with his hosts before they went to Troyes. Later he walked the streets of the 7th arrondissement and went to the Eiffel Tower. While he was enjoying a cup of coffee there, he saw a long rainbow and an image of Oya's face. It looked as if tears were showering down from her eyes. He looked at the rainbow and her image again and again, and wrote a poem.

OVER THE RAINBOW

My dearest darling,
This afternoon
I had my dream journey to
The garden of roses over the rainbow.
Four girls welcomed me.
They all smelled of love and lust.

They offered me a glass of oldest wine
And a hot bubble bath.
They cleansed my body and my soul.
I felt that
It was the heaven everybody talks about.
I looked at the world from
The garden of roses over the rainbow.
I saw your face.
You were crying.
Your tears were like heavy rain.
As the rainbow was disappearing from the sky,
They all said,
"Sir,
Without her
Heaven would be Hell for you!
Please go back to her.
She has been longing for you!"

He walked the streets again. He did some shopping, returned to the flat in the evening, and wanted to cook something nice for dinner. The phone rang.

"Hello, my love, how have you been doing?" asked Oya.

"It has been very enjoyable. I feel fantastic."

"I'm at my friends' house. They live in the 8th arrondissement, on the other side of the River Seine. We're going to play bridge after dinner and will do some shopping tomorrow morning. I hope to see you tomorrow afternoon."

"Excellent. I'll have dinner too, and will try to visualise you at your friends' house."

"That sounds like fun. Have a nice evening, my love."

He cooked a nice meal and wore his dinner suit. He imagined she was there with him.

While having his dinner, he visualised Oya and her friends. He enjoyed every minute of it and slept peacefully.

The following day, Goldash woke up early, had breakfast, cleaned the flat and waited for Oya to arrive.

"*Bonjour, monsieur.*"

"*Bonjour, madame.*"

"Are you learning any new French words, Goldash?"

"Yes, I've been doing my very best to impress our French friends."

"I have no doubt about that. How are our friends?"

"They are an incredible couple. I've been enjoying being their guest. Albert is a generous man. He gave me lots of money for the shopping. Yesterday, I walked the streets and wrote a poem at the Eiffel Tower. Would you like to read it?"

"Yes, of course."

She read his poem and looked up into his eyes.

"I wish I could compose music for this poem. I feel that it would be the best love song ever written," said Oya.

"I hope one day somebody will compose music for it."

"You've been very imaginative, my love."

"Imagination, inspiration and perspiration are the daily life of your poet. Last night, I visualised you at your friends' house. The four of you were playing bridge, and a young boy was sleeping on the sofa. He had oddly large ears. Well, Francine and Fernand were excellent bridge players. However, they allowed you and Monique to win. Congratulations!"

"That boy is the son of their neighbour. Francine looks after him when his parents go out some evenings. You are amazing, my love. How did you visualise me?"

"I am full of love and wish everybody could be as happy as I am. My life has been a dream since I met you, Oya."

"This is real, my love. It isn't a dream."

"I feel pleasure, no pain. Whatever happens to me, I will only feel pleasure."

"Let me bite your hand and wake you up."

She bit the side of his hand.

"As you see, I feel no pain."

"Yes, your body language tells me. This is incredible."

She looked away as her eyes filled with tears.

"What's wrong, my darling?" he asked and hugged her.

"Because no dream lasts very long."

"Let's enjoy ourselves today. Nobody knows what will happen tomorrow. I bought one hundred red roses for tonight. Samuel's relative in Paris brought two bottles of forty-year-old red wine for us. I'm going to give you reflexology and a massage, then I will cook a nice meal. We'll make love for the whole night. When lovers are in their temple of happiness, the night is always bright. I am sure you will feel this place is a little paradise in Paris."

On Sunday morning, they woke up late and went to the nearest café.

Oya sighed. "It's so nice being in Paris with you."

"I've been thinking of studying nursing instead of accountancy. When I become a nurse, we can work together. Do you think that is a good idea?"

"You must be joking! You're a doctor of love and don't need to study nursing. It was incredible the way you treated me last night. I'll never forget it. When you make love to me, you take me to the planet of love. I feel you come from there. You should study accountancy, become a company doctor and help companies have a healthy balance sheet."

"Excellent! I would never have thought of it like that."

In the afternoon, Annabelle and Albert came back from Troyes. Annabelle took a photo of Oya and Goldash, and showed them some of her artwork. It was mainly paintings and drawings.

"I want to do a painting of both of you to scale. Can I measure your heights please?" asked Annabelle.

"You surprise us, Annabelle. You are amazing," said Oya.

"Sometimes I surprise myself," laughed Annabelle.

Oya and Albert spoke to one another in French while Annabelle and Goldash prepared dinner. That night, the conversation was long, lively and almost entirely in French. Goldash didn't understand what they were talking about, although somehow he felt he did.

On Monday morning, while Oya and Goldash sat in the back seat of the car, Annabelle took Oya to the airport.

"Monique will pick you up this afternoon. You can give reflexology to Francine and Fernand today, Mélodie and Monique tomorrow. Francine would like to cook nice meals for you today and tomorrow. Perhaps you'll learn some French-style cooking from her."

"Yes, I would love to learn a few French recipes."

Goldash kissed Oya and said, "*Bon voyage, mon amour.*"

He got back to his flat in the afternoon on the twenty-eighth of June. He rested for a few hours and then went to the snooker club to get his maximum break. Lorna was waiting for him.

"Hello, Goldash. My father told me you were in Paris. Did you have a nice holiday?"

"Yes, I did. My friends there treated me very well."

"I'm going to Australia for five weeks in August. My auntie lives there."

"Who will be my snooker partner when you are away?"

"My father or my mother will be your partner. They know what we've been doing, so there won't be any problem. Can I tell you something?"

"Yes, of course."

"I studied very hard and hope to get three good Advanced-level results. I want to study medicine next academic year. Would you give me fifty per cent of your winnings for my holiday please?"

"No, Lorna, I won't."

"I thought you would want me to have a nice holiday."

"Yes, I do. That's why I'm going to give you ninety per cent of my winnings in July."

Lorna almost jumped for joy. "You are so generous! You like to surprise me, don't you?"

"Let's get our maximum break this evening and collect our cheques from your parents."

"Yes, Mr One-Four-Seven."

It was a beautiful July day. Goldash wanted to do more sewing and make as much money as he could. He received two bags of material for making trousers. When he opened them, he realised the white cotton needed for making the hip pockets was missing. He went to the factory to get the cotton he needed.

Sylvia was in the factory office sorting out some invoices. He knocked once before stepping into the office.

"Good morning, Mrs Jamieson. There was no white cotton in the bags I received this morning."

"Good morning, Goldash. All right, let me fetch some for you."

She left the office, returned with some of the material and handed it to him.

"Are you all right, Goldash?"

"Yes, I'm very well. Thank you for asking, Mrs Jamieson."

"I noticed some of our staff members were looking at you strangely."

"You should ask them about it. I don't know them. See you later on, Mrs Jamieson."

He went back to his flat and started sewing. After he had made a few hip pockets, the phone rang.

"Hello, Goldash, this is Samuel. Can you come to the factory immediately please?"

"Is everything all right, Mr Jamieson?"

"Will you stop questioning me and come to the factory?"

"Yes, sir. I'll be there in ten minutes."

He went to the factory again and knocked on Samuel's office door.

"Come in."

"Hello, Mr Jamieson. You called me."

"I did, Mr One-Four-Seven. Would you like to have a cup of tea?"

"Yes please."

"Why didn't you tell me you played snooker? We're good friends, aren't we?"

"Yes, sir. I didn't know you liked snooker."

"Look at these trophies. We are the Jamiesons pool team and have been invincible at our venue for the last eleven years."

"I thought all these trophies were for success in business! Now I understand why you're not happy with me. Do you want me to join your opponent's team?"

"No, I want you to join our team, Mr One-Four-Seven."

"If I joined your opponent's team, you would have a taste of defeat at your venue after all these years. Wouldn't that be exciting, Mr Jamieson?"

"Would you please stop teasing me and tell me when you will join our team?"

"I'm sorry. I won't join your team. I have my own snooker show once a month, which I enjoy every minute of. That's more than enough for me."

"Those who like snooker in this factory admire you very much. I am told that on the twenty-eighth of each month you get a maximum break. They all think your sexy snooker partner is your girlfriend."

"She is just my snooker partner. I only see her at the snooker club."

"If you performed your show once a week, they would be happy to pay you one thousand pounds for each show."

"Who are 'they'?"

"Your admirers, who else do you think?"

"No, sir. I only have my show on the twenty-eighth of each month. I met Oya on the twenty-eighth of November. It's like a happy monthiversary celebration for me. I wouldn't think of playing anywhere else."

"Come on, Goldash. There are seventeen admirers of yours in this factory. Don't you want to make them happy?"

"Yes, of course. I think it will be better if I get a hat-trick of one-four-sevens on the twenty-eighth of this month. It will be one for the snooker club, one for my admirers and one for you."

"Excellent. I would be happy to pay you one thousand pounds too."

"Thank you so much, Mr Jamieson. I would like to dedicate a trick shot to you and another one to your wife after getting my first hat-trick of one-four-sevens. Does Mrs Jamieson like snooker?"

"Yes, she likes it very much. She is a member of our pool team."

"Oya has no idea about snooker, and I haven't told her about my show yet. I'll tell her about it when the right time comes. For now, please keep it between you and me."

"Yes, Goldash, of course."

It was a hot day on the twenty-second of July. Oya and Goldash drove to the Cotswold Gardens in her car. After strolling around the gardens hand in hand, they found a shady spot for a picnic. After enjoying their food, they lay down, and she read some cynical quotations to him from a book.

"These quotations are nice, they make me laugh," said Goldash.

"Let me find a quotation about accountants."

"I don't think there will be any quotations about my fellow professionals."

After turning a few pages, she smiled. "Well, I've found two for you."

"Please read them to me."

"Of course, my love."

Economists are people who work with numbers but don't have the personality to be accountants. Anonymous

An actuary is someone who moved out of accountancy because he couldn't stand the excitement. Anonymous

As she finished reading, he laughed and said, "We need good economists, actuaries, accountants and managers in the modern economy. When I am with you, I always get excited. You take care of me like my beloved mother, talk with me about anything and everything like a true friend, and make love to me like a perfect lover. You are my everything, and I love you very much, my dearest Oya."

"I love you very much too, Goldash. When I am with you, I always feel peaceful and totally relaxed. It's your turn to read.

Come on, my love, read some interesting quotations to me please."

He took his time, turned some pages, found interesting quotations and read them to her.

A professor is a man whose job is to tell students how to solve the problems of life which he himself has tried to avoid by becoming a professor. Anonymous

A professional is a person who tells you what you know already, but in a way that you wouldn't understand. Anonymous

Poetry is the stuff in books that doesn't quite reach the margins. Anonymous

After reading the quotations, he didn't hear her laugh. He turned his head to his right side and noticed she was having a nap. Just by looking at her, he felt inspired. He rolled over and reached for his pen and notebook.

A ROMANTIC MESSAGE

My dearest,
All great philosophers and poets wish to have
Rightness, richness,
Love and lust.
I do too.
Don't you?

THIS GAME OF LOVE

No loser, no winner;
We are the players
And the referees in
This game of love.

The Jamiesons came to his flat on the twenty-eighth of July in the evening. After having dinner, they went to the snooker club all together. He bought drinks for Sylvia and Samuel and went to the office.

"Good evening, Lorna."

She smiled at him. "Good evening. I am excited about getting ninety per cent of your winnings this evening."

"No, Lorna. You're not going to get ninety per cent of my winnings this evening."

"What are you talking about? You promised me, didn't you?"

"Yes, I did. After careful consideration, I changed my mind. You can have one thousand pounds of my winnings this evening."

"Goodness! You do enjoy teasing me, don't you?"

"I'm allowed to make jokes with my sweet snooker partner. I want to get a hat-trick of one-four-sevens this evening. We can make three thousand pounds easily. You can have one thousand, and I will have two thousand."

"That's so lovely. I'll kiss you three times this evening."

He laughed. "No interference and no interruptions until I finish my job. After the hat-trick, I will dedicate two trick shots to my friends. You can kiss me after my trick shots. Is it a deal?"

"Yes, Goldash."

"The club is full of people this evening, and they are all waiting for us. I am ready for our big show. I like your sweet and seductive voice. Would you do the introduction please?"

"Of course, follow me." He followed her to the snooker table.

"Good evening, guests and members. Our Mr One-Four-Seven is going to get a hat-trick of one-four-sevens for the first time this evening. It'll be the show 'once seen, never forgotten'. Can we all keep quiet during the show please? There will be free drinks afterwards. Let's enjoy the work of a genius. Thank you very much."

Goldash saluted everybody and focused on the snooker balls. He visualised Oya's face and read her lips: "I love you very much, Goldash." He was simply unstoppable and finished his hat-trick within an hour. Everybody was overjoyed at what they had just witnessed and applauded him. When the applause died down, he beckoned the Jamiesons to come closer.

"It is dedication time for my wonderful friends. My first trick shot is for Sylvia. I am going to pot the black ball with my right hand, and after touching three cushions the white ball will go into the same pocket. My second one is for Samuel. It will be the same shot but with my left hand."

He did his trick shots. Sylvia and Samuel congratulated him.

"I've never seen anything like that before. I'll remember this show for the rest of my life. Thank you for entertaining us this evening," said Sylvia.

"I couldn't have done it without you. Thank you for coming to my show. Oya is coming to my place tomorrow lunchtime, and I would love it if you would join us. Now, enjoy the rest of the evening."

"We will. See you, genius," said Samuel.

He went back to the office, put on his jacket, took his cue and looked at the people in the hall through the glass. They were all happy and enjoying the evening.

"It's so nice to see everybody happy at this club. Bless them all," he thought.

He came out of the club and saw Lorna standing outside.

"They didn't give me a chance to kiss you."

"I'm sorry. You're only allowed to kiss me in front of people at the club after our show."

"Where is your car?"

"I don't have a car. Why do you ask?"

"You are so silly. Why don't you have a car?"

"Thank you very much. I give you one thousand pounds of my winnings and you call me silly. I thought you were my sincere snooker partner."

"You don't understand me, do you? I'm wet and wicked. I'm dying to make love to you this evening. Can I come to your place please?"

"No, you can't. I'm engaged to a doctor."

"You're a joker. You say you're engaged to a doctor and don't wear an engagement ring."

"You know my fingers are joined on both of my hands. I'm on the waiting list to have my fingers separated. I don't want to have any problems with your parents or my fiancée. I respect your parents very much. I love Oya, and she loves me. Do you understand me?"

"Yes, I do. What is her surname?"

"Her surname is Oydash."

"That's unbelievable. I wouldn't have thought my snooker partner would be engaged to Dr Oya Oydash. My brother Lewis is crazy about her. The walls of his room are full of her photos."

"Well, Oya is a delightful doctor and must have some crazy admirers. She is coming to my place tomorrow lunchtime. If you like, you can visit us tomorrow. I'm sure she would be delighted to meet you. I live on the ground floor of 147 Mentmore Terrace."

Lorna was disappointed and said, "See you tomorrow, Goldash."

Oya came to his flat in the late morning.

"The Jamiesons are coming here for lunch. Lorna Hothorn, the daughter of the snooker club owner, is coming here as well.

She wants to study medicine. Apparently her brother Lewis is crazy about you and has put your photos on the walls of his room. Do you know the boy?" asked Goldash.

"Yes, I remember him. He had an injured arm, and his father brought him to hospital. I treated him a few times, and he asked if he could take some photos of me. He is a nice boy."

"Do you know anything about snooker?"

"I've seen it a few times on television, but have no idea how the game is played."

"Perhaps Samuel can explain it to you this afternoon."

There was a knock on the door. Goldash opened it to see the Jamiesons smiling at him.

"Good afternoon, Mr One-Four-Seven. I'm still so excited about what happened last night. You were unbelievable. Everybody went crazy and put lots of money into this carrier bag. I haven't counted it yet, so let's do it, shall we?" asked Samuel.

"Can somebody tell me what is going on here?" asked Oya.

"Samuel, can you explain to Oya the game of snooker please?" asked Goldash.

While Goldash and Sylvia were counting the money, there was another knock at the door. Goldash let Lorna in and introduced her to Oya.

"We've counted the money. There is one thousand and seventy pounds" said Sylvia.

"This is the cheque for two thousand pounds, as I promised," said Samuel.

"I didn't know my gorgeous Goldash was a snooker genius. I am so proud of him," said Oya, and she kissed him.

They had lunch together. Lorna was nervous and started biting her lips.

"Lorna, my dear, you keep biting your lips. If you'd like to come here tomorrow afternoon, Goldash will give you reflexology and a relaxing massage," said Oya.

Late Sunday afternoon, Lorna came to his flat.

"Oya is an amazing lady. You're so lucky, Goldash."

"Yes, I am very lucky indeed. Oya asked me to write a poem for you. She wants to make my snooker partner happy. Here is the poem."

Lorna read it.

YOUR GUIDING STAR

My dear lady,
Every star in the sky
Has its own freedom and fire.
Let me be your guiding star
And make you a happy high-flyer.

"Thank you so much. Both you and Oya have made me very happy."

"Oya always treats her admirers nicely."

He gave her reflexology and a relaxing massage. After he had finished the massage, she sighed.

"I am so relaxed. You're amazing. Oya knew I needed this, didn't she?"

"She is a medical psychic too and reads people well. She told me that when you saw her you forgot all about me. Is it true, Lorna?"

"Yes, it is. Her face mesmerised me instantly."

"I was lost for words when I saw her for the first time in the bookshop."

She looked at him strangely and said, "I had an interesting dream when you were giving me the massage. In my dream, I was at my auntie's house in Australia. You and Oya were in the garden. You were examining her beautiful breasts with a stethoscope."

"That is an interesting dream. Sometimes we do role play. I become her doctor and examine every inch of her body."

"When would you like to examine my body?"

"I would like to examine your body when you become a fully fledged doctor. You're an intelligent lady. I'm sure you will study hard and become a doctor."

"I will achieve that, my guiding star."

"When are you flying to Australia?"

"Next Tuesday. What shall I bring back for you?"

"You can bring me a kangaroo."

"Yes, I'll bring you a toy kangaroo."

"You're a clever girl and have worked it out quickly. I think it would be better if you just sent me a postcard of a kangaroo."

"Yes, I will."

"Have a nice holiday, Lorna."

Oya and Goldash visited the Jamiesons on the sixth of August.

"We're going to Italy next week. My nephew is getting married. Are you going anywhere next week?" asked Sylvia.

"We're going to Dartmoor National Park and staying at the Manor House Hotel[7] for two nights next weekend. The manageress of the hotel, Mrs Gloria Goodenough, is my friend. Her husband is a chef at the hotel. Both of them want to have reflexology from Goldash. When I was in Milan, I met a nice American couple. They are coming to London next week and want to go to Stonehenge and Devon. She is a music teacher and professional violinist. He is a doctor. We will go there all together," said Oya.

---

[7] The former name of Bovey Castle Hotel.

"That's very interesting. We go to the Manor House Hotel every September," said Samuel.

"Why do you go there every September?" asked Goldash.

"Mr William Henry Smith, the founder of WHSmith, bought the land. His son built the manor house. My great-grandfather worked as a builder during the construction of the manor house. It became a hotel in the early 1930s. My grandfather liked the hotel and the area. It became a custom for our family to go there once a year."

After their long weekend in Devon, Goldash had been working every day. It was Saturday morning and the phone rang.

"Good morning, Goldash. If you're available this afternoon, Sylvia and I would like to have reflexology," said Samuel.

"Yes, I'm available. Oya is coming here later. If you like, we can have dinner together as well."

"That would be nice. See you later."

When Oya arrived, he told her about the Jamiesons' visit.

"I need to go shopping. Would you like to join me?" asked Goldash.

"No, I'm going to call one of my friends. You can do the shopping, my love."

When he came back, he noticed she didn't look happy.

"Is everything all right, my darling?"

"I'm very disappointed. I don't know what I am going to do with you."

He was puzzled. "I don't understand. What are you talking about, Oya?"

"You left your exam results on the table. Auditing: Five; Business management: Absent; Financial Accounting: Absent. You said you were studying hard to pass your exams, and now I've found out you didn't even bother to take two of them! I want you to be a member of the Association of International Accountants in the near future."

He sighed. "Let me explain to you what happened. When I was taking my auditing exam, I read all the questions and knew all the answers. While I was answering the first question, I suddenly visualised you and forgot all about my exam. You were swimming in a lake and calling me. I left the exam hall and went to the park. In the afternoon, I was ready for my second exam. While I was going to the exam hall, your image appeared in front of the building. You were in an apple tree. There were different apples on the tree. You were throwing them at me, and I was jumping and catching them. When somebody said 'Are you all right, sir?' I realised I was in front of the exam hall but hadn't entered."

"I've been thinking of introducing you to my parents as a healer and telling them about you."

"That was something I couldn't help. I am very sorry. I've been doing my very best for the two women I love so much."

She said in a high-pitched voice, "That's great! You have another woman in your life! Who is she?"

He laughed. "She is my mother. I love her very much. She is always my unfaded rose. You know it very well, don't you?"

"I'm sorry. I didn't realise you meant your mother."

"You thought I meant another woman? You are funny. There are two women in my life, you and my mother. You are my dream lady. My life has become a dream since I met you."

"Come on, my love. Give me a hug."

He hugged and kissed her.

"How about being my naked chef and making pancakes for me?" she asked.

"Yes, my princess. Whatever you wish, I will do it for you."

He undressed and put on his green and white striped apron.

"How do you fancy your naked chef?"

She looked at him and laughed. "Come here, GG Boy, and let me bite your bum."

"That's a good choice, my lioness. My bum is the biggest muscle in my body."

When they were having their pancakes and coffee, the doorbell rang.

He gasped. "We forgot all about the Jamiesons. Let me get my overcoat on and open the door."

"Come on, Goldash. You shouldn't open the door for them like that."

"They are our best friends. Let me make them laugh."

He put on his coat and opened the door.

"Good afternoon, Sylvia and Samuel. Welcome to the pancake party."

Both of them laughed at him.

"What is going on here, Goldash?" asked Sylvia.

"A non-political party is going on here. My lioness has bitten my bum, and she is completely satisfied. Would you like to have some pancakes?"

"You're the happiest couple I've ever met. You are incredible," said Samuel.

On the twenty-sixth of August, Oya and Goldash went to Sherwood Forest and had a long walk.

"Yesterday, I visited Mrs Gulizar Gulbar. She is a psychic and a teacher. My parents have known her and her husband for many years. They don't have any children. She is my godmother and always treats me very well. Somebody sponsored them to join the Golden Guide Group and go on a world tour for nine months. They aren't able to go at this time, and she wants both of us to go on a world tour and write a book about it," said Oya.

"That would be incredible. We can meet different people and see different places of the world and write a book about our experiences. It would be nice if we sent postcards to our parents from the different countries we visit."

"Yes, my love. Let's do this adventure together. It's a once-in-a-lifetime opportunity."

He thought about Robin Hood and similar legends of different countries, and looked at a tree. Somebody had engraved the bark. It said "LEGENDS LIVE FOREVER."

He pondered about the desire and destiny of a legend, and wrote a poem.

MR SOLO

You have faced reality.
You are now a daydreamer no longer.
So say goodbye to the past.
Dream of something that you can make.
Think of something that you can take.
Say hello to a new beginning.
Say hello to a new challenge.
Love the job you do.
Love the place you live in.
There is a wild world outside.
There are bad people outside.
They are all looking for a new name.
They are all waiting for a new game.
In a wild world
You can have a place at the top.
Among bad people
You can be a real hero,
If only you can become Mr Solo.

Goldash went to the snooker club on the twenty-seventh of August.

"Good evening, Mr Hothorn. Lorna told me you'll be my snooker partner for my show tomorrow. If you like, you can have fifty per cent of my winnings. However, I'm not available tomorrow evening. Can we do it at lunchtime please?"

"Everybody wants to see your show in the evening. What's the problem?"

"There is no problem. It's my birthday tomorrow, and I want to have a quiet evening with my fiancée."

"I thought you were going out with Lorna."

"No, I wouldn't go out with your daughter without your permission."

"Lorna has our permission to go out with you. Your fiancée must be more attractive than Lorna. Who is she, anyway?"

"I thought Lorna would have told you about her."

"No, she didn't."

"My fiancée is Dr Oya Oydash. She wants to watch my maximum break tomorrow."

"You must be joking! She is a doctor and wouldn't get engaged to a cleaner!"

"I agree with you. She is engaged to Mr One-Four-Seven, not a cleaner. The Jamiesons are coming to our show as well. Lorna told Oya all about your family. She wants your wife and your son to join us. We can all have lunch together."

"Yes, Mr One-Four-Seven. Let's have fun together."

The next day, Goldash's birthday, Oya came round early, and together they left for the factory.

"Happy birthday, Goldash," said Samuel.

Sylvia stepped forwards and gave him a hug "Your admirers in this factory want to have a photo taken with you."

"Let's make them happy, then," said Oya.

After Goldash had posed for photos with some of the snooker lovers in the factory, Samuel drove them to the snooker club in his amber Audi. The Hothorns were all there waiting for them. Oya spotted Lewis.

"Hello, Lewis, my handsome admirer. Lorna told me you're crazy about me. That's so sweet of you."

Lewis muttered something and didn't meet her eyes. Oya kissed him on the cheek.

"I'm not the only one who is crazy about you," he managed to say at last, blushing. "My father is too."

"That's even better! A father and his son both admire me."

Hazel, Lewis' mother, stepped forward. "I don't blame Henry and Lewis. We're all crazy about you, Oya."

"I'm so flattered. Parents and children of the same family admire me."

"It's nice to be loved. We all love you, Oya," said Goldash.

"There is something I must tell you, Goldash," said Henry.

"What is it, sir?"

"Some of our members are very envious of you. They've been thinking of breaking your arms. It would be better for you if you stopped playing snooker at this club."

"That's terrible. I would never allow something like that to happen to my healer. Goldash, my love, promise me you won't play any more snooker after getting your maximum break today," requested Oya.

"Yes, Oya. You know I can't say no to you. I promise you this will be my last show."

Hazel filmed the show, and Henry re-spotted the black ball. Goldash enjoyed every shot of the show and finished his maximum break in style. He dedicated one trick shot to Hazel and another to Henry.

"I started playing snooker at this club, and stopped playing here. Thank you so much for everything. I treated my cue as a friend and want to give it to you, Mr Hothorn. Would you look after my friend please?"

He kissed his cue and left it on the snooker table. Suddenly, Henry started to cry.

"I killed a genius. I lied to you. Please forgive me, Goldash. Everybody loves you at this club."

"Thank you very much, Henry. I'm glad you lied to us. Goldash has promised me he won't play snooker or come to this club any more. Now he'll have more time to play with me," said Oya.

"It was a very entertaining show. I will never forget it. I'm so proud of filming this show and will show it to everybody this evening. We will celebrate your birthday today and every twenty-eighth of August. Here is a cheque for two thousand pounds. Happy birthday, Goldash," said Hazel.

"Let's go to the café and have lunch," said Oya.

After lunch, they went to the flat. Samuel and Oya played acey-deucey while Sylvia and Goldash prepared dinner. The doorbell rang.

"The florist brought one thousand one hundred red roses for us. Can you help me bring them in please?" asked Goldash.

Sylvia gasped. "One thousand one hundred? Goodness me!"

By the time they had got them all in, half of the flat was full of red roses.

She was very curious. "What are you going to do with all these roses?"

"Oya and I will spread the petals of nine hundred and ninety-nine of the roses on our bed and put one rose on our table. We're going to have a jolly good time tonight. You can take these one hundred roses and spread the petals of ninety-nine of them on your bed and put one of them on your table. I'm sure you'll enjoy it."

"You forgot the forty-year-old wine."

"Yes, Sylvia. You can have that too."

Oya and Goldash visited Gulizar on the third of September. She told them all about the Golden Guide Group and the details of the world tour. They flew to Glasgow on the twelfth of September. The following day, they hired a car, drove to Inverewe Garden and stayed in a cosy cottage for two nights. He was inspired by the beauty of the Highlands and wrote a poem.

REFLECTION

While we were driving in the Highlands,
The harvest moon was shining.
I didn't want the moonlight that night.
I wanted the moon itself.
My beloved,
I wish I could take you to the moon
And make love to you,
Then the whole universe would know
What good lovers we are.

After coming back from the Highlands, they flew to New York on the twenty-first of September 1989 and met some members of the Golden Guide Group.

During the two hundred and seventy-four days of their world tour, Goldash and Oya wrote their dairies on a daily basis. It widened their vision and horizons to be in different countries and continents and to understand the cultures and customs of different people and places, witnessing how some people of the world live in luxury while others live in poverty in different and difficult conditions and climates.

They enjoyed every minute of their world tour and returned to London on the twenty-first of June 1990. They had so many sweet memories of their adventure and wanted to incorporate all of their writings and photos into a book.

"When I go through our writings and look at these photos, I feel excited about our world tour," said Goldash.

"I feel the same thing, my love. I'm glad we trotted the globe. We'll talk about it for the rest of our lives."

He smiled at her and said, "I'm going to buy a typewriter and type up our diaries. I think the title of the book can be *In the Footsteps of Oya and Goldash*."

She looked at him and said, "It would take you ages to do them with your joined fingers. I know somebody who can type them up for us."

"You are right, my darling."

The following day, he visited his landlady and gave her fifty-two necklace and earring sets, which he had bought from fifty-two different places, and a few T-shirts for her son and daughter. She had been good to him for the last few years and hadn't even taken rent from him during his world tour. There was always a mutual respect and understanding between them. Her husband had had a cardiac arrest and passed away on a Sunday afternoon in front of his family before the ambulance arrived. Goldash felt sympathy for her and had been treating her as his adopted mother, and she had been treating him as her adopted son.

The following eight days he was busy giving massages and

reflexology to his landlady and her son, daughter, parents and friends, and talking with them about his world tour with Oya. Of course, he didn't forget his employer and friend Samuel and his wife and sons.

On the first of July 1990, he woke up early and had his breakfast. There were so many thoughts on his mind. It was the fourth anniversary of his coming to London. He felt he was still an underachiever, although he had met his dream lady and enjoyed a world tour with her. His mother had sold all her jewellery to finance his education. He could have finished his studies during the previous four years. So far he was only halfway to achieving his target. He looked at the drawing of his mother on the wall, and wrote on a piece of paper "I LOVE MY MARVELLOUS MOTHER!" and pinned it to his noticeboard. Then he looked at the drawing of Oya and thought about her. If his mother hadn't had a dream about Oya, she wouldn't have asked his father to send him to London. Oya was the main reason for his coming to London. He wrote on another piece of paper "I LOVE MY PRETTY PRINCESS OYA!" and pinned it to the noticeboard.

He remembered what his mother had told him. "You can achieve whatever you want to, if you focus on these three words: Manifestation, Concentration and Determination."

He had had his manifestation, but he wasn't able to concentrate on anything that morning and went to London Fields for a walk. While he was walking under the plane trees, a dog barked at him. He recognised the owner and talked to him.

"Good morning, sir."

"Good morning, young man."

"It was nineteen months ago when I saw you here. Your dog has grown a lot. Is she still a vegetarian?"

He laughed. "Yes, she is. Let me introduce you to her."

Goldash stroked her head and massaged her head and then her back. The dog liked it very much, and he continued it for a while. When he stopped, the dog leaned against his leg.

"She is beautiful. I haven't seen a dog like her before. What breed is she?"

"This lovely dog is a Kerry Blue Terrier. She certainly enjoyed the massage you gave her. It isn't very often she stands so still and quiet. Are you a massage therapist?"

"Yes, I am. This is the first time I've given a massage to a dog, though."

"I usually have a synchronised massage every two weeks. I had no idea my dog would like to have a massage too. Would you be happy to give her a massage every week?"

"Yes, I would. I live on the ground floor of 147 Mentmore Terrace. I can say I have a dog client now."

When he came back from his walk, he sat down and made a study plan for his three exams in December. Three hours' study every morning and two weeks' intensive study before his exams would be good enough to pass at the first attempt. After that he felt confident to impress his examiners, and he suddenly recalled his English teacher. It had been a Friday evening in April 1987 when she had taken him to a restaurant in Greenwich. While they had been enjoying dinner, she had told him some variants of the KISS principle and some cynical quotations.

"Thank you for telling me new things. I've been learning a lot from you since I met you. I want to learn more about English literature."

She had smiled at him and said, "My dear Goldash, I like you very much. You are a nice and naive boy. I think you have many things to learn, not only about English literature."

She squeezed the top of the rose on the table and looked at him. "What do you think about this?"

With a shy smile he said, "I don't understand why you have squeezed it."

"This rose is delicate and smells lovely. If I didn't handle it properly, its thorns would prick my fingers, and I would feel pain. When the top of a rose is squeezed gently, it looks like a love box. It's very nice, isn't it? As a gentleman, first you must learn how to treat ladies, as they are delicate like roses, and then you can enjoy them without having pain and problems."

On Saturday the twenty-eighth of July 1990, Oya came to his flat in the afternoon.

"Samuel and Sylvia are coming to dinner this evening. They want to celebrate my hat-trick of one-four-sevens anniversary. I want to surprise them and cook something special for them."

"I'm sure our friends will enjoy it. As you know, I've been enjoying my sabbatical leave as much as I can. For the last few weeks, I've been busy going to Wimbledon to watch some tennis matches and visiting some of my friends. So I haven't had my treatment and missed your healing hands."

He looked her in the eye and said, "I understand you want me to be in action this afternoon."

She smiled. "I always want my GG Boy to be in action."

The Jamiesons were at his flat at about seven, and dinner was served.

"This meal smells and tastes nice. I haven't had it before. What is it?" asked Sylvia.

"It's called *karnıyarık*, a traditional Turkish meal. As you see, it's stuffed aubergine. It's my sister's favourite meal. I learned how to cook it from her."

"This is delicious. You have been spoiling us, Goldash," said Samuel.

"It's my pleasure to serve my friends."

"He has been spoiling me too. He is a terrific therapist, a good cook, and above all he is a true friend. I am so lucky to have him," said Oya.

"Once, he was a sensational snooker showman. I will never forget the way he had his hat-trick of one-four-sevens last July," said Samuel.

"It was very impressive the way he did his disappearing shots for us. After watching his video many times, I decided to have my own twenty-eight trick shots show on the twenty-eighth of every month. So far I've learned many trick shots, including Goldash's disappearing shot. My first show will be on the twenty-eighth of next month. I will dedicate it to Goldash, as his birthday is on the same day."

"Thank you very much, Sylvia. I am honoured," said Goldash.

"It would be very nice if Goldash were my show partner," said Sylvia.

Oya shook her head and held his hand.

"He is my healer and promised me not to play snooker or hold a cue in his hands again. I wouldn't be happy if he broke his promise. Of course, both of us would love to come to your show. We wish you the best of luck for it."

Sylvia was disappointed and said, "I understand. It was just a thought."

"I am still angry with Henry. He shouldn't have lied to us," said Samuel.

"I still don't understand why he did something like that. I met his wife Hazel a few months ago. She says her husband is still angry with himself for lying to Goldash," said Sylvia.

Oya and Samuel played acey-deucey for the best of three after dinner, and they talked about the world tour.

After the Jamiesons left, there was a gentle silence in the flat. Goldash noticed Oya wanted to say something.

"What is it, my darling? Do you want to say something?"

"Yes, I do. We're going to Istanbul for five weeks next Wednesday and will come back on the fifth of September. I won't be here on your birthday, as I must be there with my parents. My cousin is getting married, and there are also some other things I need to do. I'll start working on the tenth of September."

"I understand you very well. That's fine with me. I will imagine you're with me on my birthday."

It was the twenty-eighth of August 1990. He tried to picture Oya, but no matter how hard he tried, her image didn't come to him; it was all a blank. The Jamiesons came to his flat in the evening; they had dinner and went to a snooker club in East London.

He cleaned the pool table and the balls for Sylvia. Standing next to Samuel, he enjoyed watching her twenty-eight trick shots.

"Well done, Sylvia. That was very impressive. I am proud of you and pleased you are having your show on my monthiversary. I haven't seen some of your trick shots before. I wish Oya would allow me to be your show partner."

"I wish the same thing, Goldash. It would be nice if you joined me and did your disappearing shot with your right hand and left hand. When I tell some people about you, they don't believe you could do something like that."

"We don't need to bother about what other people say. I'm sure you can do it too, if you practise with your left hand."

Samuel smiled at him and said, "If I were you, I wouldn't even think about becoming Sylvia's show partner. Just be happy and obey your pretty princess Oya."

There was still no news from Oya. He was thinking about her and trying to visualise her every day, but he still couldn't get an image of her.

Samuel came to his door on the fourteenth of September. He could barely look Goldash in the eye.

"Good afternoon, Samuel. It looks like you have been crying. What's happened?"

"I was at the hospital for a routine check-up and asked a doctor if Oya had returned. I was told she and her parents had been killed in a traffic accident."

Goldash stared at him and there was a long silence.

"Samuel, are you sure about this?"

"Yes, I'm sure. The doctor cried when she told me about the accident."

Goldash hugged him and then stood there, frozen. Samuel pushed him to the sofa, and he stayed like that for more than half an hour.

He murmured at last, "I'm sorry. Suddenly, I don't know what to say. I always felt it was like a dream. It was my sweetest dream. Now my dream is over. I want to be alone for a while. Thank you for letting me know, my good friend."

Samuel nodded and stood. "Please let me know if there is anything I can do for you."

Goldash phoned the Nesbitts in the evening.

"Hello, Nigel. Can I visit you this evening please?"

"Yes, you can. I was going to call you. I guess you've heard about Oya. You can stay with us for a while."

He looked at the mirror and remembered what Oya had said to him:

"Under all circumstances, we must be strong and steady, my love."

He wore a suit and asked his landlady to take him to the Nesbitts' house in Buckhurst Hill.

When he arrived, Nigel clasped him by the shoulder and led him to the sofa. "I'm so sorry, Goldash. We visited Oya's uncle in Istanbul and came back yesterday. He told us Oya, her parents and her cousin were going to Gulistan to see her therapist's parents on the twenty-seventh of August. There was an accident, and all of them were killed at the scene," said Nigel.

"We told her uncle about you," said Narine.

"Now I understand it. They were going to surprise my parents and celebrate my birthday."

For a while, no one said anything.

"This kind of tragedy can happen to anybody. I'm going to visit her uncle again next month. If you like, we can visit him together," said Nigel.

"I'm going to have my finger operation on the fourth of October. I want to wear the engagement ring Oya bought for me. Why do you want to visit her uncle next month?"

"When Oya, her parents and her uncle visited SP Village last time, Oya thought it would be good to have a retreat centre in the village. Her uncle is a businessman and is thinking of building the Oya Retreat Centre there. He wants to have my advice on the project."

"She told me about the village and her grandmother. Did her uncle tell you the story about why her grandmother lived in SP Village?"

"Yes, he did. Her maternal grandfather was a secret agent

and worked for the Allies during the Second World War. Her grandmother was good at languages and joined him. They worked together from the beginning of the war. They were attacked in Istanbul in September 1943. Her grandfather was killed at the scene. A local hero, Molla Mehmet from Bursa, was passing by. He saved her grandmother and took her to his village. A nanny in Istanbul was looking after Oya's mother. Molla Mehmet and his wife went to Istanbul to take her to SP Village as well in October that year. The password was 'Babies cry, and babies laugh'. After the war, she worked as a conference interpreter in London. She was an admirer of Umm Kulthum, who was a famous singer and one of Egypt's national treasures. She also had a keen interest in Middle East history. Every September, she and Oya's mother used to go to Istanbul, Bursa, SP Village, Beirut, Jerusalem, Alexandria and Cairo."

On Wednesday the third of October 1990, Goldash went to St Bartholomew's Hospital and had his finger operation the following morning. After recovering from the operation, he was happy and thinking of Nurse Oya and Doctor Oya. While his mind was miles away, he fell asleep. He woke up when a nurse brought him a cup of tea.

"Thank you, Oya," he said.

"My name is not Oya."

"I'm sorry, nurse. I must have been dreaming about Nurse Oya and Doctor Oya."

"Enjoy your tea, sir."

He remembered his dream and grinned. In his dream, both Nurse Oya and Doctor Oya had visited him in the hospital. Nurse Oya was on the left side of the bed, checking his blood pressure. Doctor Oya was on the right side of the bed, holding his hand.

"I met Goldash when he came to the hospital for his

stomach operation. I think he was sixteen at that time. He was a nice, naughty and naive boy who wanted to be breastfed by a nurse," said Nurse Oya.

"I met him in a bookshop about two years ago. He is twenty-seven now and still naughty. I think he wants breastfeeding by a doctor this time," said Doctor Oya.

"I had better leave this hungry boy and happy doctor alone, then," said Nurse Oya.

"Thank you, nurse," he said.

The Nesbitts visited him on the ward in the evening.

"How have you been doing, my dear boy?" asked Narine.

"I'm so happy that I'll be able to wear my engagement ring after a few weeks."

Nigel looked around, smiling and said, "I enjoyed working here for many years before my retirement."

"This is a very good hospital. I admire the doctors and nurses here. They are all friendly and hard-working people. Of course, I appreciate the free and first-class service of the National Health Service," said Goldash.

"Yes, we are all lucky to have such a good health service," said Narine.

"I'm going to attend a conference in Bristol tomorrow. Narine will pick you up tomorrow afternoon."

"That's fine with me."

On Friday afternoon, Narine arrived to take him home and helped him to get dressed. His right arm in a sling, he followed her to the car. On the way to the Nesbitts' house, he wanted to collect his textbooks from his flat on Mentmore Terrace. After driving through the City of London, she stopped in front of the flat and waited for him in the car. He came back to the car without his textbooks after twenty minutes.

"Goldash, my dear, you were supposed to collect your textbooks. What is the matter with you?"

"My flat was burgled, and my briefcase was among the things stolen. There were photos and diaries of my world tour with Oya and my short story *The Boy With A Broken Briefcase* in it."

"I'm so sorry to hear it."

"They were very important things to me. First Oya and later her photos have been taken away from me. I don't want to study any more. My life has become meaningless," he said with frustration.

"I see a boy with a broken briefcase has become a man with a broken heart. Sometimes our life is so unpredictable, and I expect anything and everything. Your heart has been broken once, my heart has been broken three times."

Suddenly, she became very emotional, took a tranquilliser tablet and then gave one to him. They were quiet for a while before she started to talk again.

"Oya was an extraordinary doctor. Both Nigel and I loved her unconditionally, as we loved our daughter and son. The three of them are no longer with us. They've all gone, one by one, within a few years."

"I am so sorry, Narine. I never knew you had lost your children."

"Now you begin to understand me, my dear boy. As you see, we are in the same boat. Oya told me about you and your mother. I know how much your mother wants you to be an educated man. For the sake of your mother, Oya, Nigel and me, you must finish your studies. You're very dear to us. We treat you as our son and don't want to lose you too. Please go to your flat and get your textbooks."

"Yes, Narine."

The following morning after breakfast, he read a few pages of his textbook, but he didn't understand anything of what he read because he was unable to concentrate. He took the long walk from Buckhurst Hill to Loughton and did some window shopping. When he came back, he wanted to phone his mother. He was standing next to the telephone in the sitting room but unable to dial her number, as he wasn't sure what to say.

"Goldash, my dear, do you fancy a cup of tea?" asked Narine.

"Yes please."

She made their tea and asked him to sit next to her.

"I understand you want to phone your mother. It's not the right time to call her now. When the right time comes, you can phone her. You're not able to concentrate on your studies either. I've been thinking about you since yesterday. If we find the right female company for you, she may help you to overcome what has happened in the past. We have a doctor friend who lives alone in Blackheath. Kenneth is a surgeon, pianist and playboy. Whenever he visits us, he comes with a different girlfriend. He knows many ladies and can introduce some of them to you. Let me phone him and find out what he thinks."

"You are a doctor and know what is best for me. I would be happy to meet him."

She phoned Kenneth and talked with him for a while.

"Good news, he is happy to meet you and has invited us for lunch tomorrow. Now, let's play acey-deucey," she smiled.

"Yes, that's a good idea."

In the late afternoon, Narine wanted to cook something special for dinner and asked Goldash to go to the shop to buy a few items. On his way, a bicycle hit him from behind. He was knocked over and left unconscious on the ground. Somebody called an ambulance, and he was taken to Whipps Cross Hospital.

"What is your name?" a nurse asked.

"Oya," he answered.

"What is your surname?

"Oya."

"When is your birthday?"

"Oya."

PARTNERS IN PEACE & PLEASURE

IF I SAY

If I say I was thrilled,
I met you in the air.
If I say I was in seventh heaven,
I made love to you.
You came into my life
And gave me the pleasure of being a woman.
From now on,
I always want to be with you.
That is my only desire.
But wherever you go
And whatever you do,
God bless you, Mr Conqueror.

My dearest soulmate Goldash,

Yesterday, my father and I visited your mother and celebrated your sister's birthday. The nurse who visits your mother on your birthdays is the psychic Mrs Gulizar Gulbar. She told your mother that you and Oya had had a traffic accident. Oya died at the scene, and you died in hospital. We couldn't say anything to your mother about you. I am sure there must be a good reason why she told your mother something like that.

I bought a laptop for your sister as a birthday present. When we watched the video of your hat-trick of one-four-sevens, we laughed and cried together. I saw my father cry for the first time. He didn't cry when my grandparents passed away. It was very emotional, and I will never forget it. Your sister got married. She has one son and two daughters, whose names are Goldash, Oya and Ayla. They are all cute kids. Your father passed away on the seventeenth of November 1996, and your favourite goat,

197

Meltem, died on the thirtieth of June 1993. Your sister showed me a photo of Oya milking her.

This afternoon we came to Bursa and will stay here for four days. We met the youngest son of Molla Mehmet. He is taking us to SP Village tomorrow. This evening, the daughter of Molla Mehmet is taking me to a famous Turkish baths. We will go back to Gulistan and stay there for a few days. Your mother will show me how to make kefir. I understand your family is famous for making it. We will also visit Oya's uncle in Istanbul. He will take us to the cemetery to visit the graves of Oya and her parents.

I've added your name to my car insurance, so you can collect the key from my mother. When we return to London, you can meet us at Heathrow Airport.

Hugs and kisses!
Your loving angel
LL

It was the third of May 2001. Goldash woke up early and read Leyla's email. He visualised his mother, Oya, Leyla and Meltem. His life would be so different if Oya were alive. He wished he could tell his mother that he was alive.

He took a walk along the high street, looked at people and wondered what was going on in their minds. Everybody was trying to do the best they could.

After a while, he came back to his flat, had breakfast, and decided to tidy the garden and plant some flowers. It might help refresh his mind. When he had finished tidying the garden, he was thinking about which flowers he should plant that year when Bernie came into the garden.

"Good morning, Goldash. Well done, son. You did a good job. Here you are, have a cup of tea. While you were tidying the garden, Leyla phoned me. She must be a daisy-crazy lady and lectured me about daisies. Apparently, there are approximately thirty-three thousand species of daisy. She talked to me about families, subfamilies and tribes of daisies. I can't remember all the names she told me. I remembered some of them, though, and put them in alphabetical order. Here are those daisies' names: African daisy, all that jazz, annual daisy, blue-eyed daisy, dark-eyed daisy, English daisy, fatal attraction, harvest moon, lemon symphony, lollipop, oxeye daisy, painted daisy, passion mix, pink double delight, Rob Roy daisy, tiger tail, vanilla spoon and women daisy."

"That's surprising. When I was at her parents' house, I didn't see any daisies in their garden. She must have been bored and wanted a new challenge," said Goldash.

"Do you think she wants to be a doctor of daisies?"

"It would be great if she became a triple doctor so we could get more free advice from her."

"You're right, Goldash. She is an incredible investor and has been advising me on what to buy and when to sell for the last few months. I've made good money. It's good enough to sponsor you for at least four years."

"How much have you made?"

"More than fifty thousand pounds."

"Well done, sir."

Bernie laughed. "Well, she helps me to make money. If I get my maximum break on the twenty-eighth of June, she will give me five thousand pounds."

"You support me, and she supports you. I can help you get your maximum break after my exams next month. I'll be your snooker coach, and we will practise every day until your snooker show."

"Leyla told me you did reflexology. You give reflexology to

your lady friends, but not to your sponsor. When would you like to give me reflexology?"

"I can give you reflexology, hand reflexology and ear reflexology on a regular basis so you can become a better snooker player."

"We have to do a few things together today. These are Leyla's requests: first, we have to go to Crews Hill and visit some of the garden centres there. We are to buy two of each of these plants: red English climbing rose, passion fruit, London pride, English daisy, oxeye daisy, French lavender, African marigold, French marigold, dark blue delphinium, light blue delphinium, rosemary and chocolate fruit."

Goldash nodded. "That's good, because I've found it impossible to concentrate on my studies today. Let's go now and spend some time there."

"Let me call Richard's brother. He is a very good gardener and can rearrange our garden."

"That's a good idea, always best to leave it to a professional."

Goldash and Bernie went to Crews Hill and visited a few garden centres there. Both of them enjoyed looking at different flowers and plants for a few hours.

"Shall we have some tea?" said Goldash.

"Good idea. I saw a café over there."

They found a table and sat down.

"Can you remember the names of the flowers and plants we have seen?" asked Goldash.

"No, I can't. There are so many of them, and it's difficult to remember their names. When I was in Paris, I had private French lessons from a friendly teacher. She wanted to teach me flower and bird names in French. I told her there was no point learning them in French as I didn't know them in English."

"I didn't know you spoke French."

"It's beneficial to know more than one language. I worked in France and Germany for a good few years and am fluent in both languages."

"When Oya and I were doing our world tour, we used to say to each other 'I love you' in the language of the country we were in at the time. We enjoyed saying it in different languages. When we were in Germany, she said to me '*Ich liebe dich*' and I said to her '*Ich liebe dich. Ich habe Hunger für dich.*' She smiled at me and said the same thing to me. I liked the way she said it to me."

"You were very lucky. She had desire for you."

"Yes, indeed."

Once they had finished their tea, they found the last few plants on the list and headed back home.

"Our garden will be beautiful this summer," said Goldash.

"Yes, it will be. When Leyla visits us, we can have a barbecue party."

"It'll be nice to invite our neighbours to it, and Leyla can play the violin for all of us."

"Would you like to give me reflexology today?"

"Yes, I will. We'll go to La Lune this evening. Barbara is taking her sons to the restaurant, and she wants us to join them there."

After giving reflexology to Bernie, Goldash left him sleeping on the chair and went into the garden. He looked around and pictured how the garden would look in summer. While he was imagining what it would be like with Leyla there, he wrote a poem.

ASTRAL TRAVEL

My dearest Leyla,
I am your pilot.
You are my navigator.
Let's do our astral travels together.
Let's go to my dream place
Where we can find peace and happiness.
It is not very far from the sea and the mountain.
My dream house and my dream garden are there.
They are designed and decorated by Mimar Sinan.[8]
I call the garden Leyla Garden.
That is my dream place
Where nature can serve us
And we can serve nature.
We don't need to do anything else there.
We can have only pleasure and more pleasure.

On Thursday morning, the tenth of May, he met Mili and her father at the airport.

"I was surprised you didn't tell me you were visiting my mother," said Goldash.

Osman shrugged apologetically. "You don't need to blame me for that. It was all Mili's idea. I always take her request as an order. Whatever she says, I have to listen to her."

"I understand, Mr Tokkan. I do the same thing when she kindly requests me to do something."

"Every language has its own rhythm and rhyme. Your mother and sister called me Osman Bey,[9] and I liked it very much. You can call me Osman Bey."

---

[8] Mimar Sinan (1490–1588), the great Turkish architect.
[9] A formal and social title of respect for men in Turkish.

"Very well, I'll call you that from now on."

Osman nodded. "When we visited your mother, I couldn't tell her we had met you, and felt guilty about it. Next time, we must visit your mother together."

"I hope to visit her in the near future."

"Goldash, I have good news for you," said Mili.

"What is it, our double delight?"

"Oya's uncle and auntie inherited her parents' house, and they have been letting it since then. Her uncle and my uncle are going to set up a manufacturing business in Istanbul. My uncle borrowed money from us, and Oya's uncle needed money, so he and his sister decided to sell the house. I'm buying the house and the original drawings of Oya and her parents from them."

"I'm delighted to hear it. Congratulations!"

"When I buy the house, I will set up Oya's room as she used to keep it. You will have a spare key both for the house and for her room. It will be your room."

"You have surprised me again. That's very sweet of you."

"Samuel has been keeping the original drawings of your mother and *Pigeon Pelin & Company*. I think it will be better if we visit him and take them from him tomorrow. Oya and her parents were killed on their way to meet your mother. They couldn't meet each other on that day, so their drawings must be displayed in the same room together."

"That's a wonderful idea."

"When Samuel retired from the textile trade, he became a reflexologist. These days, he is charging a nominal fee. He is fully booked for the next six months."

"He must be very popular. I haven't seen him for more than ten years."

"I'm sure he would like to give you reflexology tomorrow."

"That would be nice. I haven't had reflexology for a long time."

"You give reflexology to others, not to yourself. I have sympathy for you."

"Would you give me reflexology this afternoon and play snooker with me later?" asked Osman.

"Yes, Osman Bey. It would be my pleasure."

The following day, Leyla and Goldash visited the Jamiesons in Brentwood.

"We've missed you so much, Goldash. The last time I saw you, it was on the fourteenth of September 1990. How come you didn't contact us for more than ten years?" asked Samuel.

"I've missed you too. I'm very sorry that I didn't stay in touch with you. There have been so many ups and downs in my life, and I had no clue what to do. I shouldn't have ignored my good friends, though. You've always treated me as a member of your family. I've been doing very well since I met Leyla. Thank you for taking care of my belongings at 147 Mentmore Terrace, and the drawings of my mother and the pigeons."

"We will always take care of you and pray for you. I'm so delighted to see you again. I've missed your healing hands too," said Sylvia.

"Leyla told me Samuel is now a reflexologist. Don't you get treatment from him?" asked Goldash.

"Yes, I do. He is as good as you, but I prefer you to give me reflexology. Next time, you must stay with us for a few days and give reflexology to all of us."

"Yes, that would be fun. I will visit you on a regular basis. How are your sons these days?"

"Both of them are professional footballers and are married now," said Samuel.

"I haven't had reflexology for a long time. I understand you will be busy this afternoon with your clients. Can I have my treatment before lunch please?" asked Goldash.

"When you gave me reflexology for the first time, I was very impressed and wanted to be a reflexologist like you. I enrolled on a part-time course in October 1990 and qualified in July 1992."

"Well done, Samuel!"

On Saturday afternoon, Mili and Goldash visited the Gulbars in Muswell Hill. After having lunch, Mili asked Gulizar to tell them why she had visited Goldash's parents. She sighed and started telling them what had happened on the twenty-seventh of August 1990.

"It was the summer bank holiday. We planned to visit the Reismanns, have lunch and play bridge in the afternoon. I went upstairs to get ready for the visit. When I was coming down, I felt that Oya, her parents and her cousin had had a terrible accident. Suddenly, I lost my balance, tumbled down the stairs and broke my right leg. Memzar called an ambulance, and I was taken to hospital. On the twenty-eighth of November, I thought about Oya and her parents, and Goldash and his parents. His mother hadn't heard from him and Oya for a while, so she didn't know Oya had died in a traffic accident, or that Goldash had had an accident and lost his memory. She became very worried and was having many sleepless nights. I called her and had to pretend I was a nurse and told her that Oya had died at the scene and he had died in hospital. I said to her that before the accident, Goldash had got the qualification she cared so much about, and he had wanted to visit her on her birthday. Well, she wept and accepted it was destiny and couldn't be helped. She and I became good friends after that phone conversation."

Gulizar hugged Goldash and said, "The Reismanns are coming to dinner this evening. They've been our friends for more than twenty years. Roger is a successful accountant. He is a Fellow of the Association of International Accountants, and Rina is a Fellow of the Chartered Institute of Taxation. They go on holiday twice a year. When they are away, we look after their house. I told Roger about you. He said their trainee would leave the firm at the end of August, and you could start working as a trainee on the first Monday of September."

"I would be very happy to work for them," said Goldash.

"Very well, Goldash, good luck in your studies and training. Now, come and help me prepare dinner," said Gulizar.

Memzar, who had been sitting quietly alongside his wife, stood. "I'm going to the garden centre. Mili, would you like to come and help me choose flowers?"

The following Thursday, Leyla came to Goldash's flat for lunch.

"The gardener prepared the garden as you requested. Our garden will be beautiful this summer. Mr Barnaby has been thinking of having some barbecue parties," said Goldash.

She nodded. "It looks much better now. The gardener did an excellent job. I forgot to tell Mr Barnaby about collecting rainwater. He needs to have a water tank to collect the rainwater from the roof."

"Yes, that's a good idea. Mr Barnaby thinks you are a daisy-crazy lady. How long have you been studying daisies?"

"I always liked daisies but didn't have time to study them properly in the past. These days I have enough time to do so and take photos of the different varieties. When I was in Bursa, I bought silk carpets for my parents' house, my grandmother's house, my house and for the Goldash Shelter. If you like, we can go to 147 Mentmore Terrace and stay there tonight. I would like to play the violin on the silk carpet and have fun with you."

"I haven't had fun on a silk carpet before. You keep surprising me, Leyla."

"When I was in Istanbul, I met Mrs Gloria Goodenough and her husband Gareth. They stayed at the hotel of Oya's uncle and were going to the Derinkuyu underground city and Halfeti, the land of black roses. This Saturday we can go to Cardiff. I want you to meet Katelyn there. She is a gynaecologist and was a friend of Oya. After visiting her, we can go to the Manor House Hotel and stay there for a few nights. The Goodenoughs would like to have reflexology from you. Perhaps you can learn a few recipes from Gareth. He is an excellent chef. While you are preparing your luggage, I'll talk to Mr Barnaby about a couple of things. You are taking your course materials and dinner suit, aren't you?"

"Yes, Leyla."

"Great! You should prepare your luggage now."

"All right, see you soon."

It didn't take long for him to pack his things. When he was done, he sat and waited for her to return.

"I'm sorry, Goldash. It took longer than I expected. I had to explain to Mr Barnaby a few things about his investments."

He stood. "I'm glad you've been advising my sponsor on how to invest successfully."

"I've been instructing him on what to buy and when to sell. Naturally, he always asks me questions about my instructions. You should know I wouldn't advise him on investments if he weren't your sponsor."

"Thank you for taking care of me, Leyla."

"I ordered three hundred and thirty-three red roses from Debbie the florist. First we can go to the flower shop in Muswell Hill to collect them and do the shopping there, then go to the Goldash Shelter. I want you to pamper me today and tomorrow."

"As you wish, my lady."

It was Saturday morning.

"Katelyn is expecting us in the late afternoon. I haven't been to the Uffington White Horse and am thinking of going there via Oxford," said Leyla.

"I haven't been there either. Let's go and see it today."

"Do you like horses?"

He nodded. "Yes, I do. Horses are cute creatures. My parents had a horse. He was a very fast runner, and we called him Uchannal, which means 'flying horseshoe'."

"That's very interesting. My sister Lili has a horse, and his name is Uchannal."

"I didn't know you had a sister."

"She is a double doctor and lives with my maternal grandmother. I told them all about you. When the right time comes, I will introduce you to them."

"I look forward to meeting your sister and grandmother."

After a journey of about two and a half hours, they arrived at White Horse Hill.

"At last, we are here! I've been wondering about this historic monument for a while. Once, my parents visited this place, and my father was very inspired by this masterpiece. When we were on holiday in Milan, we met the artist Bruna X, and my father bought a drawing of a horse from her. The title of the drawing was *The Knight*. Lili liked it very much and wanted to have a horse like that for her twenty-first birthday. My parents bought a yearling for her. She named him Knight. He was professionally trained for racing. Unfortunately, he came last in three races. Lili wasn't happy and changed his name to Uchannal. After that, Uchannal won seventeen races in a row and made us multimillionaires," said Leyla.

"What did you get for your twenty-first birthday?"

"I got a car. I must say Lili's choice was better than mine. I wish I'd got a yearling as well."

He sighed. "I wish my parents had trained our horse."

"You think if your parents had trained your horse, they would be multimillionaires. That is wishful thinking, GG Boy. Your parents wouldn't be millionaires. If you want, you can be a millionaire on your birthday this year."

"You're a joker. My birthday is on the twenty-eighth of August, and I'll be starting my accountancy training the first week of September. How can I be a millionaire on my birthday?"

"Have you forgotten that I'm a double doctor and an investor?"

"No, I haven't. How can your qualifications make me a millionaire?"

"You can be if you sell the drawing of *Now You See Me* to me on your birthday."

"I told you I wouldn't sell it to anybody for any price."

"If you were pragmatic, not dogmatic, life would be much easier for you. I really want you to be a millionaire and expect you to accept my offer."

"I appreciate what you have been doing for me. Honestly, though, I'm not comfortable selling that drawing."

She smiled. "I understand how you feel. Think about it and let me know if you want to receive a cheque for one million pounds on your birthday."

"Yes, I'll think about it after my exams. These days I just want to have a good time with you and concentrate on my exams."

"Very well, GG Boy. Can you take my camera and binoculars from the car please? It's a warm and sunny day, and I want to look around over the hill."

"We're lucky today, for once it's not raining."

They climbed the hill. Leyla had been quiet since they had left the car. She was busy taking photos and using her binoculars, and Goldash wanted to talk to her.

"This is a very interesting place. I enjoy being here very much," said Goldash.

"So do I."

"You haven't talked to me for more than an hour. What have you been thinking, Leyla?"

"About artists and art. True artists don't compete with others; they always contribute something to art. An artist or a group of artists contributed this masterpiece, the Uffington White Horse, thousands of years ago, and we still admire it today. I admire artists and appreciate what they do."

"My dearest Leyla, you are an artist too. I always admire the way you play the violin. If you're in a good mood, would you like to play the violin for me after lunch? I prepared some goose egg sandwiches this morning."

"I'm always in a good mood when spending time with you, GG Boy. You're confused about selling the drawing and becoming a millionaire. I'm going to entertain you and motivate you for your exams."

There was a smile on Goldash's face as they headed back to the car.

She grinned puckishly. "Can you open one of the bottles of wine that Samuel gave us? I would like to have a glass of it. You are driving and must only have a glass of carrot juice," said Leyla.

He opened the wine bottle and they sat down in the lush grass.

"Here is your favourite sandwich," he said.

"I've read some of your Turkish poems and composed music for *Gel Bana – Come To Me*. Now, I'm going to play it for you."

"Can I have a cigarette while you are playing the violin?"

"Yes, of course."

"Thank you, my lady."

Leyla began to play, the sound soft and sweet. He closed his eyes, letting the music wash over him, and remembered dancing with Oya in the snow. As he imagined holding her, he stood and began to dance.

"Are you all right, GG Boy?"

"Yes," he murmured.

"That lady over there called you. Do you know her?"

He opened his eyes. "No, I've never seen her before."

"Why don't you go over and ask her why she called you?"

He went to the woman.

"Excuse me, madam. My friend said you called me. Who are you?"

"My name is Emily, and this is my fiancé Eddie. I live in your neighbourhood. You're a tenant of Mr Barnaby, aren't you?"

"Yes, I am. I must have been blind not to see such a beautiful lady in my neighbourhood."

"Mr Barnaby goes out with my mother. He told us all about you."

Goldash smiled and said, "He is the most interesting man I have ever met."

"You are right. He is a very nice man and brings us presents all the time."

"What's your mother's name?" asked Goldash.

"Her name is Femke."

"Mr Barnaby and I go to a restaurant. The manageress of the restaurant is Felicity. Sometimes he calls her Femke. Now I know why he mixes their names up."

"I think Mr Barnaby loves my mother."

He laughed. "I think Mr Barnaby is crazy for your mother."

"Your girlfriend is rich, beautiful and talented. Are you crazy for her?" asked Emily.

"I can't afford to be. My friend Leyla likes clever people, not crazy people. She wants to know why you called me."

"We like the way she plays the violin and wonder if she would play for us. Eddie and I want to dance."

"She plays the violin when she is in a good mood. I'm sure she will play for you. Let me ask her and get back to you."

He hurried back to Leyla and explained the situation. She smiled broadly. "Of course I'll play for them."

"Great!"

He went back to Emily.

"Leyla said she would play *Romance* for you. Congratulations, Emily, you are eight weeks pregnant."

"How do you know that?"

"Leyla told me. Please don't ask how she knows. I only know that she does. If you dance slowly with Eddie, I'll film you. Can you show me how to use your camera?"

Leyla began to play and swayed in time to the music. Emily and Eddie held each other close and danced slowly for a while. Finally, Leyla whipped the bow from the strings. Emily, Eddie and Goldash cheered and clapped.

"Thank you so much. I'm sure we'll see you soon," said Emily.

"Of course. Perhaps we'll have dinner all together," said Goldash.

"Goodbye for now," said Leyla.

After waving them off, Leyla and Goldash picked up the remains of their picnic and went to the car.

"They are a lovely couple. I think they will remember us and dancing at White Horse Hill," said Leyla.

"I'm sure they will remember you for the rest of their lives. Now, it takes two hours to get to Cardiff from here. We have plenty of time to pass. Do you want to explore the countryside on our way?"

"No, let's go to Cardiff."

"Where in Cardiff does Katelyn live?"

"She bought a new detached house near to the university hospital."

Goldash took his time and drove carefully to Cardiff. They arrived at Katelyn's house at about five o'clock. While he was parking the car, she came out and welcomed them.

"Hello, Leyla! It's so nice to see you. And you must be Goldash. I'm delighted to meet you. Kenneth told me all about you," said Katelyn.

"I haven't seen him for four years. How is he these days?" asked Goldash.

"He is very well and waiting for you in the house."

Leyla giggled, and he glanced at Katelyn. "Leyla knew Dr Kavanagh was here and didn't tell me. She simply doesn't stop surprising me."

They all went inside the house.

"Hello, Goldash. I've missed you, my good friend."

"Hello, Dr Kavanagh. I'm surprised to see you here."

"You don't work for me these days. Please call me Kenneth. I've also missed your healing hands. When you gave me reflexology, I felt you were my doctor and I was your patient. Can you give me reflexology after tea please?"

"Yes, of course."

When they were alone in the therapy room, Kenneth turned to stare into Goldash's face. "You are a heartbreaker, my friend."

"I wasn't expecting you to say something like that out of the blue. What's the problem?"

"Last December, I went to New York for the New Year celebrations. My uncle has a recruitment agency there, and I met his beautiful manageress, Rachel, who is engaged to my cousin. Rachel and I were talking about alternative therapy, and she told me about an interesting therapist and martial arts expert who could challenge four men in combat. I knew that therapist was you. I didn't tell her you were not a martial arts expert. She then told me how you broke her heart by failing to go to New York three times. Last March, I met Georgina in London. She has gained weight. You played games with her and didn't sell your number plate to her. If I were you, I would sell it to her immediately. You left her and broke her heart too."

"I accept I made some mistakes. I've been trying to forget my mistakes of the past. You don't need to remind me of them. Now, I want to concentrate on reflexology. Just close your eyes and enjoy it."

After Goldash had finished the reflexology, Kenneth was asleep, and Goldash went to the kitchen.

"Hello, ladies, can I be of assistance?"

"We're doing all right here. You can lay the table if you like," said Katelyn.

"How does Kenneth feel after the reflexology?" asked Leyla.

"He needed it badly and is snoring on the chair. We can wake him when dinner is ready."

After enjoying their dinner in a happy atmosphere, they went to the sitting room.

"My cousin and Rachel are getting married in September. Katelyn and I are getting married in October. I wonder if the four of us could go to Toronto for my cousin's wedding, and visit Niagara Falls as well. We will go to the Seychelles for our honeymoon. If you like, both of you can join us there," said Kenneth.

"I'm going to start my accountancy training the first week of September, so won't be able to join you. Perhaps you can bring me a coco de mer[10] from the Seychelles. I had one when I was there a long time ago," said Goldash.

"My parents have a hotel in the Seychelles. You can stay there and have a ninety-nine per cent discount. I'll tell my parents it's your honeymoon. They will make the necessary arrangements for you," said Leyla.

"Would you like to be my best man at our wedding?" asked Kenneth.

"No, I am not the right person. One of your doctor friends can be your best man. I can borrow my friend Susanna's royal red Rolls-Royce and be your chauffeur, though," said Goldash.

"I can play *The Wedding March* for you," said Leyla.

"It's all settled, then," said Katelyn.

"I would like to have a glass of vintage wine and enjoy this evening. Perhaps Kenneth can play the piano and Leyla can play the violin for us," said Goldash.

"I'm sure these two talented musicians can improvise music to entertain us," said Katelyn.

"My parents are expecting some guests in July and August, and they are looking for somebody to help them during their

---

[10] The world's largest nut, endemic to the Seychelles.

busy period. I thought you would be the best person to do so. You can cook for them and be a chauffeur for their guests. Would you like to help them, Goldash?" asked Kenneth.

"Yes, I would. I'll be available after my exams in June until September, if Leyla has no other plans."

Leyla nodded. "I'll be away from early June to late August. I will go to Holland and visit some flower producers in Aalsmeer, and then go to Germany to visit a rose producer in Thedinghausen and the Europa-Rosarium in Sangerhausen. After that, I'll go to Texas to meet friends in El Paso. My friends and I will go to Costa Rica for scuba-diving. Thanks to modern technology, I can control my office while I'm away from it."

"Great! I look forward to working with the Kavanaghs," said Goldash.

They all had a peaceful and pleasurable night, and the next day enjoyed a barbecue in the sunny afternoon. On Monday, when Kenneth and Katelyn were back at work, Leyla and Goldash went into Cardiff town centre.

"I have an appointment with one of my father's business associates at eleven o'clock. If you like, you can visit Cardiff Castle. I'll be free at around one," said Leyla.

"I like visiting historic places."

He enjoyed visiting the castle, went to the gift shop there and bought a Welsh recipe book. While he was waiting for Leyla, he perused the book until he received a text message from her. She was at the castle gate.

"How was the meeting, my double delight?"

"It went very well. He is a very nice man. His daughter wants to be an investor, and he wants me to train her. Did you enjoy visiting the castle?"

"Yes, I did. I've bought a Welsh recipe book and want to read a few recipes before we go to the Manor House Hotel. Perhaps Gareth can show me how to prepare these recipes properly. Would you drive today please?"

They arrived at the Manor House Hotel at about five o'clock, after an enjoyable journey.

"Good afternoon. I'm so happy to see both of you again," said Gloria.

"Hello, Gloria. I've missed you and this place. I'm happy to be here again after ten years," said Goldash.

"Hello, Leyla. I hope you had a nice journey. As you requested, I reserved a classic room for both of you."

Gloria showed them to the room.

"We'll check out on Friday morning. I want you to take six mock exams in three days. There are some walks near the hotel. I'll enjoy exploring the surroundings during the day and can review your mock exam papers before dinner. I promised Gloria I would play the violin for the guests in the evenings. I want to rest before dinner. If you like, you can go to the kitchen and watch Gareth."

"Yes, Leyla, rest now and have fun later."

The three days of their stay passed just like that in the pleasant environment. Leyla and Goldash were happy they had made the most of their time.

After having breakfast on Friday, Goldash said, "It takes about three hours to get to Susanna's B&B in the Cotswolds from here."

"I like the couple who run her B&B. They are an honest, hard-working couple, and I would like to visit them this weekend. They have one daughter and two sons. Their daughter is a gifted girl and needs special education. I'm going to ask Susanna to sponsor her. At present, though, I have a problem with you, GG Boy."

"A problem with me, what do you mean?"

"Frankly, I wasn't impressed by your essays. If you want to please the examiner, you must write convincing essays. I think we should go back to London today instead of Susanna's B&B, and you should concentrate on your studies. I'm going to review your essays every day before I go to Europe. When are your exams?"

"They're on the first Monday, Tuesday and Wednesday in June."

"I'm going to Europe on the first Monday in June, so that fits perfectly."

Goldash concentrated on improving his essays, and Leyla reviewed them in the evenings. On Saturday evening, the second of June, they went to La Lune and then to the Goldash Shelter.

"You've improved your essay-writing skills. I'm convinced you'll pass your exams at the first attempt," said Leyla.

"My loving angel helped me again."

"I'm going to Europe by car for a change. Do you want anything bringing back?"

"Yes, I want you to come back safely."

"Good luck in your exams."

"Have a safe and enjoyable trip."

After his exams, he visited the Kavanaghs' art gallery in Mayfair.

"Good afternoon, Mrs Kavanagh."

"Good afternoon, Goldash. I'm so delighted to see you after four years. Come on, my boy, give me a big hug."

"Yes, Mrs Kavanagh. I need a big hug too."

They hugged each other.

"I know why you left Kenneth's house suddenly. Do you remember your old neighbour, the retired history lecturer, Mrs Mathilda Hopper?"

"Yes, I do. I'll always remember her. She was a kind of living history encyclopaedia. I used to ask her many questions about everything from Aztec women to Zulu warriors."

"She told me you and Kenneth had an argument over Ms Georgina Green. After that argument, Kenneth asked you to leave the house immediately. I still haven't told Kenneth that I know. This is between you and me."

"It was entirely my fault. I shouldn't have done something like that and apologise for my actions."

"You don't need to apologise, my dear boy. I was very pleased that you did it. After you left Kenneth's house, he stopped going out with different ladies and settled down with Katelyn."

"I met Kenneth and Katelyn last month. They make a lovely couple."

"They are getting married in October. I look forward to becoming a grandmother."

"I'm puzzled, Mrs Kavanagh. How did Mrs Hopper know about the argument I had with Kenneth?"

Camilla winked. "Well, she is a highly respected historian. I think she used to work as a secret agent when she was young. She is in her late eighties now but looks in her early sixties. She told me that you and Kenneth had all kinds of ladies, from a barmaid to a barrister, when you were staying at his house in Hampstead."

"Bless Mrs Hopper! I would like to give her reflexology on her ninety-ninth birthday. We had lunch together many times. A few times, after lunch, she wanted to have a piece of rhubarb cake. She was alone in the house when I was buying it. Do you think she bugged the house when I was at the shop?"

She laughed. "I wouldn't be surprised."

"Either way, she certainly knew what was going on there. She introduced her granddaughter Helena to me. If she knew Kenneth and I were playboys, why on earth did she introduce her to me?"

"It was obvious she wanted Helena to have a good time with you. It was all right with you, wasn't it? Helena was here a few months ago. She told me she had been working as a journalist. The way she asked me about you, I felt she missed you a lot."

"Helena was a nice but naive girl when I met her for the first time. Once she was writing an essay about the art of criticism and asked me to write a poem about critics."

He recited the poem to her.

CRITICS

I like critics.
They are wicked and wise.
They advise me about anything and everything.
Critics never send me an invoice.

She laughed. "That's true! I don't receive any invoice from my critics."

"Jolly good journalists are the best gossipers of our time. I would like to meet Helena this weekend. Do you know her mobile number?"

"Yes, I do. She lives in Holland Park. Let me send her a text message and give her the good news. I'm sure she will call you in the evening."

"How is Mr Kavanagh doing these days?"

"He is on another business trip in Europe and coming back next week. Let's go to the office. I want to show you Callum's obsession."

He followed her into the gallery office. There was a big noticeboard on the wall. One half of the board was covered by a map of the world, and the other half was covered with pinned paper notes bearing names of different cities.

"Callum has been obsessed by the names of these cities for the last ten years. He thinks these cities' names bring him good luck. What do you think about them?"

"Let me look at them carefully."

EUROPE: Brussels, Bern, Berlin, Bratislava, Budapest, Belgrade, Bucharest.
AFRICA: Banjul, Bissau, Bamako, Bangui, Brazzaville, Bujumbura.
ASIA: Bursa, Baku, Baghdad, Beirut, Bengaluru, Bhopal, Bhubaneswar, Bangkok, Bandar Seri Begawan, Beijing, Bishkek.
NORTH AMERICA: Boise, Baton Rouge, Boston, Bismarck, Basseterre, Belmopan.
SOUTH AMERICA: Bogotá, Brasilia, Buenos Aires.

"There are thirty-three names of cities here. Some of them are the capitals of different countries, some of them are the capitals of different states, and one of them used to be a capital city. I think Mr Kavanagh meets the right people to do business with in these cities. How is his business?"

"His business has been very good, and he has made a lot of money. He enjoys it more than ever. I thought he was going to retire last year, but he didn't."

"Bless him! I want to learn the unwritten laws of business from a brilliant businessman. I wonder if he would take me on one of his trips next year."

"I think he would enjoy your company. Kenneth told me

that you would help us in July and August. Are you going anywhere this month?"

"No, I'm going to help my landlord get his maximum break on the twenty-eighth of this month."

She smiled and said, "I didn't know you played snooker."

"I used to play it, but not these days."

"Callum and I like watching snooker, and we go to the Masters final every year. You must join us for the next final."

"I would like that very much. You should come to our show on the twenty-eighth of this month. My friend Lorna, also known as Miss One-Four-Seven, is an ambidextrous and exceptional snooker player. You must see a genius at work."

"We've never watched a female snooker player before and wouldn't miss such an opportunity. I'm thinking of going to Istanbul in November. I wonder if you could come with me and be my interpreter."

"I start my new job in September and wouldn't want to take time off during my probationary period. Why do you want to go to Istanbul?"

"I'm interested in the harem and want to write a book about it."

"My friend Leyla is fluent in Turkish and has relatives in Istanbul. She can be your interpreter. If I were you, I wouldn't bother about the harem. The modern version of the harem is the Playboy Mansion."

"I guess you would know that better than me," she said with a wink.

"You've made me curious now. I wonder if you worked with Mrs Hopper as a secret agent."

"No, I didn't. I wish I could have worked with her, though."

"It was so nice to see you again. I want to go to Leicester Square and Covent Garden. I haven't been there for a long time.

Please give my kind regards to Mr Kavanagh. See you at our snooker show."

"See you soon, my boy."

He walked to Regent Street, Piccadilly Circus and Leicester Square. As usual during the tourist season, there were many people of different nationalities all around, all of them speaking different languages. Their conversations were like music to his ears.

"I hear them but don't understand them. It's like birds singing. I wonder if birds are speaking when they sing to each other," he thought.

He wanted to stay away from the crowds, and wandered around the side streets of Leicester Square and Covent Garden for a while before entering a restaurant and settling down at a table in the corner. While waiting to be served, he wrote a poem.

WANDERING AROUND IN A WEST END TOWN

I am wandering around in a West End town,
Where sex is the main temptation for old and young.
Somebody is looking for Ms Right,
And somebody is looking for Mr Right.
Good luck to them.
In a West End town, girls are everywhere
And they are trying to sell themselves.
"Hi, honey!"
"Bye, baby, I have no money."
And some guys are selling drugs for a trip,
If I give them a good tip.
And some corrupt preachers are preaching to people.
They think they are fooling God.

And some artists are drawing pictures.
Unfortunately,
They don't draw pictures of happiness.
Love is the power of happiness.
There is no love in a West End town,
But lust is always around.

He put down his pen and glanced at his phone. There were a few missed calls. He checked his text messages and read the first one:

Hi Goldash, I hope you are well. If you like, we can meet at Holland Park station this Saturday at 12.30 p.m. xxx Helena

He replied:

Great, see you then xxx

The second message was from Bernie:

Hi Goldash, I want to talk with you this evening. Can you call me when you are available please?

He replied:

I will be with you within an hour.

Once he had finished his dinner, he hurried out and hailed a black cab and headed home. Bernie was waiting for him.

"Good evening, Mr Barnaby."

"Good evening, Goldash. I haven't talked to you for a few weeks, as you were busy studying. How were your exams?"

"I took my auditing exam on Monday, company law exam on Tuesday and management information exam on Wednesday. I was very happy with them and hope to get pass marks in August."

"Well done, son. I am very proud of you."

"I understand you lost five thousand pounds to Lorna and want to get it back from Leyla. From this evening until the twenty-eighth of June, I'm going to be your humble servant. You should be well prepared and well relaxed for your snooker show. I will give you reflexology tomorrow. You must practise snooker three hours in the morning and four hours in the afternoon each day. I will be your practising partner on weekdays, and Lorna will be your partner on Saturdays. Of course, you can practise with your girlfriend on Sundays."

"My girlfriend has no clue about snooker."

"Come on, Mr Barnaby, I didn't mean you would practise snooker with your girlfriend. You know what to practise with her. I'll be busy with my journalist friend Helena in Holland Park this weekend."

"Journalists can expose anything and everything these days. Be careful with Helena, will you?"

"It has been a long time since I last saw her. She was a lovely lady, but as a journalist she may be different to what she appears to be. I'll listen to you and be very careful with her."

"You're starting to sound like Leyla. I was going to talk to you about my snooker show, but you told me before I could mention it."

"I want to go to bed early tonight. What time would you like to have breakfast tomorrow?"

"At eight please."

"See you tomorrow morning."

Bernie practised snooker for sixteen days and was confident for his show. It was the twenty-eighth of June, at lunchtime.

"I cooked my mother's favourite meal, sultan's delight, for you," said Goldash.

"You've been spoiling me with these delicious meals. Who is going to cook for me after today?"

"Six months ago, you were unable to get a century break. You've had a few maximum breaks on the practice table in the last few days. If you want to, you can go on a cooking course and learn how to cook properly. Perhaps you will start cooking for us after a few months."

"You're right, son. I'm happier than ever and feel I can do whatever I want to."

"Today is your day. Lorna's parents and her brother, my ex-employer and his wife, my doctor friend's parents, my barrister friend and her sons are all coming to watch you. I am sure you will have your maximum break and Leyla will reward you. We'll have fun at the snooker club and then go to La Lune all together."

"Where is Leyla these days?"

Goldash looked away. "She is pursuing her hobby in Europe. I'll give you reflexology and a head massage at four o'clock. You must be well relaxed before the show. We'll go to the snooker club at six."

Goldash and Bernie went to the snooker club and met some guests and members there. While they flocked around Bernie and wished him good luck, Goldash cleaned the table and set the snooker balls carefully. Lorna was ready for another maximum break, Araks had set up her camera, and Richard was ready to do the introduction.

"Good evening, guests and members. We've been talking

about her and watching her maximum break videos for the last few months. We all love her, and she loves us. Here she is again, the magical Miss One-Four-Seven."

Lorna enjoyed taking her time, showing off for the spectators when she changed the cue from her right hand to her left hand and the other way around. Goldash enjoyed re-spotting the black ball and counting how many times he did so. When it had been re-spotted fifteen times, he said to Lorna,

"My job is done. Can I sit down please?"

Lorna turned towards the crowd. "Goldash has worked very hard. Can he sit down or not?"

"Yes!" came a chorus of voices.

She potted the yellow, green, brown, blue and pink balls in style and told the crowd:

"I think my job is done. Can I ask Mr Bernie Barnaby to pot the black ball for me please?"

The crowd cheered, and Bernie took a few shy steps towards the table. He leaned over the table, cue held tight, and potted the black ball.

Everybody applauded Lorna and Bernie. Richard started talking again.

"I thank Lorna, Bernie and Goldash. It was the most entertaining maximum break I have ever seen. Bernie has been a well-respected member of this club for many years. For the last few months, he has been preparing for this event. He is ready to get his maximum break this evening. Let's wish him the best of luck!"

"Good luck, Bernie!" the crowd called.

Goldash whispered to Bernie, "I wish you the best of luck, Mr Barnaby. Take it easy and enjoy your maximum break."

Everybody was quiet and wanted Bernie to get his maximum break. Bernie took his time and started potting the red balls carefully. Lorna re-spotted the black ball. After about twenty minutes it was all over. He shouted, "Yes, I've done it!" First Lorna congratulated him. Goldash whispered to him, "Well done, sir. You've got your five thousand pounds back. Leyla will be very pleased with you."

Goldash eased his way through the cheering crowd and told Richard, "Mr Barnaby is in his early sixties and has just got his first maximum break. You can call him Mr One-Four-Seven now."

"You and Lorna trained Bernie very well. He looks like a brand new man. I want to join the one-four-seven club too. Can you and Lorna train me please?" asked Richard.

"Yes, we can. Now, it is celebration time."

Bernie, Goldash, Lorna, Araks and their guests went to La Lune and enjoyed a lovely dinner. Afterwards, Goldash took Bernie to his house.

"How are you feeling, Mr One-Four-Seven?" asked Goldash.

"I feel great, as if I have conquered the world."

"Come on, Mr Barnaby, nobody can conquer the world. You conquered your stage fright this evening. From now on you can have your own show on the twenty-eighth of each month at the snooker club. Lorna and Araks want me to join them at their house tonight. I know you have two girlfriends, Felicity and Femke. Which one would you like to see tonight?"

"How do you know about Femke?"

"I met her daughter Emily and her fiancé Eddie at White Horse Hill. Emily is expecting a baby, and hopefully Femke is going to be a grandmother in seven months. If I were you, I would visit her tonight."

"Yes, I'll listen to you."

Goldash enjoyed helping the Kavanaghs in July and August. He took one of their guests to Stansted Airport on the twenty-sixth of August and went back to his flat to have a nap in the afternoon. After he had had a nap, his phone rang.

"Hello, GG Boy, how have you been doing?" asked Leyla.

"I've been enjoying myself since my exams."

"Have you received your results yet?"

"I haven't checked my mail yet. Let me check it now."

After opening each envelope, he exclaimed. "Yes! I've passed them all."

"Congratulations. Let's have breakfast at Mr Barnaby's house tomorrow at eight."

"When did you come back, my angel?"

"On the twenty-third of August but didn't bother you as I knew you were busy with the Kavanaghs. See you tomorrow morning."

The next morning, Leyla joined Goldash and Bernie for breakfast.

"What you have done is quite remarkable, Mr Barnaby. Araks sent me your maximum break videos on the twenty-eighth of June and July. My father and I watched them together. You made him envious of you. He is in his early sixties like you and wants to break his maximum break duck. Perhaps he can be your snooker practising partner and will get his maximum break in the future. You can train my father, now you know all the tricks of snooker," said Leyla.

Bernie nodded. "He can practise snooker with me whenever he wants to do so. I couldn't have done it without the help of Lorna and Goldash. Both of them know how to motivate a snooker player."

"Goldash will be busy for the next three years and won't have time for my father."

"Is that so? Well, you and your parents should come to my snooker show tomorrow."

"I can't make it tomorrow. My parents can come to it, though. I've moved to my new place in Hampstead Heath. It's Goldash's birthday tomorrow, and I want to entertain him there."

"Bless Goldash. He has struck lucky again."

After breakfast, Leyla took Goldash to her new place, which she had bought from Oya's uncle and auntie.

"My mother has a keen interest in interior design. She has had the entire house redecorated very well. I told her to keep Oya's room just as it used to be. My mother thinks we must keep the three drawings in there. This is your room now. First, have a look around the room. You can decide later where we should hang the drawings."

"Excuse me, Leyla. Would you mind leaving me alone in here for a while?"

"Yes, of course."

He was very emotional being in Oya's room and wanted to touch everything as if he were touching Oya. First, he opened the window and visualised her smiling face; later, he took his time and touched every item, including the various books and dictionaries in the room. He then sat down and wrote a poem from her point of view.

IN MY ROOM

In my room,
There are all kinds of books,
And two plants;
One of them is winter cherry,
The other one is dragon tree.

And on the wall,
The map of the region
Where I was born and brought up.
And one desktop computer
And two chairs;
One of them is for me,
The other one is for my perfect lover.
In my room,
When I read my books,
I feel hilarious and happy.
When I look at the map of my region,
I feel fresh and free.
And when I think about my perfect lover,
I feel wild and witty.

Leyla knocked on the door.

"Are you all right, Goldash? You've been in there for more than two hours."

He opened the door.

"I'm sorry. I had forgotten all about you."

"Let's go to the park for a walk," said Leyla.

She held his hand and led him downstairs and then to the park. His mind was miles away, and he didn't talk to her for a while.

"Do you have any plans for your birthday tomorrow?" she asked at last.

"No, I haven't celebrated my birthday for the last ten years."

"Lorna wants to take you to her parents' place tomorrow. As you know, they celebrate your birthday every year. You can go to their place another time. I will treat you and make your birthday memorable. Your chef friend Nicole will prepare lunch and dinner for us. Samuel will give you reflexology at eleven o'clock, and the terrific twin therapists will give you a synchronised massage at four o'clock. Debbie and Sylvia will arrange the roses for the Goldash Shelter. We can go there after dinner."

"Splendid! I've never had a synchronised massage. Where did you meet the twin therapists?"

"I met them in Las Vegas. They wanted to visit their distant relatives in Horsham and Glasgow. Their great-grandfather was from Horsham, and their great-grandmother was from Glasgow. They came to London with me and are staying at my parents' place. They gave synchronised massages to my parents, my grandmother and my sister. I'll be their tour guide after tomorrow."

"You are my loving angel indeed. Let's go to a café for lunch. We can do some shopping afterwards. I want to cook a special Welsh meal for you this evening."

The next morning, Goldash woke up early, had cereal and a banana for breakfast, made a cup of coffee and went to Oya's room. He looked at some of Oya's medical, language and travel books.

"This is such an interesting room. I could stay here for days," he thought.

After going through some of the books, he sat down and wrote a poem.

LEYLA LOVEBIRD IN LONDON
On Thursday the twenty-third of August 2001,
Leyla Lovebird flew over to London from southern Texas
And made her love nest somewhere in Hampstead Heath.
On Monday the twenty-seventh of August 2001,
Her poet cooked rabbit with lentils for her.
After dinner they had Turkish coffee.
While he was lying down on a Turkish carpet,
She played her two hundred and

Thirty-one-year-old violin for him.
After playing the violin, she said,
"My beloved poet,
When I play in the key of G
I can see the colour blue.
When I play in the key of C
I can see the colour yellow.
When I play in the key of D
I can see the colour green.
When I play in the key of E
I can see the colour gold."
He said,
"My dearest Leyla, my true friend,
Whenever you play your violin
And whatever you play on your violin
I can see only the colour pink."
She asked,
"Pink, is it your favourite colour?"
He answered,
"Pink, it is every man's favourite colour!"

It was almost noon when Leyla knocked on the door.

"Happy birthday, Goldash. Here you are, I got you these presents: a guitar and a cheque for one million pounds. I want you to be a prosperous poet on your birthday. When you cash it, you can bring me the drawing of *Now You See Me*. I want to have it in my bedroom."

"Thank you so much. These are the best birthday presents I've ever had."

She held his hand and took him to the sitting room.

"When I sing, I play either the piano or the guitar. Today, I'm going to play the piano and sing *Happy Birthday* for you."

Goldash was pampered with special birthday treatments. After dinner, they were in the sitting room.

"I feel young and strong after having reflexology and the synchronised massage. Let's go to the Goldash Shelter."

She grinned. "I see GG Boy is ready for me. Let me be his chauffeur and take him there."

After having a pleasurable night at the Goldash Shelter, they woke up late.

"I received a text message from Mrs Gulbar. She wants me to visit her at lunchtime," said Goldash.

"Very well, you visit her. I'll go to see my parents."

Goldash visited Gulizar at one o'clock.

"I've prepared a nice vegetarian quiche. Let's have lunch together," said Gulizar.

"Isn't Mr Gulbar joining us? How is he?"

"He is well and working in Worcester for a few days."

"What does he do?"

"He is a builder. Sometimes he gets contract jobs outside of London."

"You said you wanted to talk to me. Is it something important?"

"I understand Mili wants to buy the drawing from you, and you don't want to sell it."

"I'm not supposed to sell it, but it is a rare opportunity. I'm not sure whether to sell it or not."

"If I were you, I wouldn't sell it to Mili for one million pounds, but rather borrow one million pounds from her. I've been following Tokkans Investments for a while. Osman is a cautious investor, and invests eighty per cent of his funds in low-risk investments and twenty per cent of them in high-risk investments. Mili is an adventurous investor, and invests forty per cent of her funds in low-risk investments and sixty per cent of them in high-risk investments. She is the author of *The Danger and Delight of Derivatives* and helps her father; at the same time, she runs her own investment company, which is called Uchannal Investments. She makes more money than her father, and does it without him knowing."

"It doesn't make any sense if I borrow a million pounds from her and ask her to invest it for me."

"You're right. It wouldn't make sense. That's why we'll invest it together."

"Are you all right, Mrs Gulbar? Neither of us have any investment experience."

"Yes, I'm perfectly all right. Let me make it very clear to you. I'm in my late fifties and want to have a comfortable retirement. When you borrow the money from Mili, we can invest sixty per cent of it in property and forty per cent of it in the stock exchange. Memzar is a very good builder and knows the right people in that industry. We can buy properties, renovate them and sell them. If necessary, we can remortgage this house, as we have no mortgage. I've been using my psychic skills to access Mili's investments strategy. I followed her and invested ten thousand pounds the way she did last year, and made almost four thousand net profit."

"I see. Are psychics allowed to access that kind of information?"

Gulizar shrugged. "If Mili knew what I had been doing, she wouldn't mind. Remember, she wants you to be a prosperous poet."

"She wants to buy the drawing. If I don't sell it to her, she won't lend me the money."

"Mili can lend you the money for three years and keep the drawing as security. If you are not able to repay her on the due date, she keeps the drawing."

"I understand your business plan. You want to double the money within three years."

"Come on, Goldash. It is our business plan. I wouldn't do it without your help. You must ask her not to interfere in your business, and along the same lines, you shouldn't ask her for business or investment advice during the loan period. She doesn't need to know about our business plan."

"I like the idea. Mili is going to Glasgow tomorrow. When she comes back, I'll talk to her."

He went back to his flat, made himself a cup of tea and settled down on his bed. His head was swimming about Gulizar's idea. He wanted to think about her suggestion properly, and about his business management, financial accounting and management accounting exams in December. A knock at the door shook him from his thoughts.

"You must have had a good time yesterday," said Bernie.

"Yes, I had a jolly good time with Leyla. She treated me very well."

"This parcel came yesterday. I signed the delivery paper for you."

He opened the parcel. It was another drawing, with a letter attached.

My dearest Goldash,

This is another masterpiece by Bruna X for your birthday. The name of the drawing is The Real Twins. *You must not sell this drawing to anybody for any price either, otherwise it may bring you bad luck all the time.*

With all my love

X

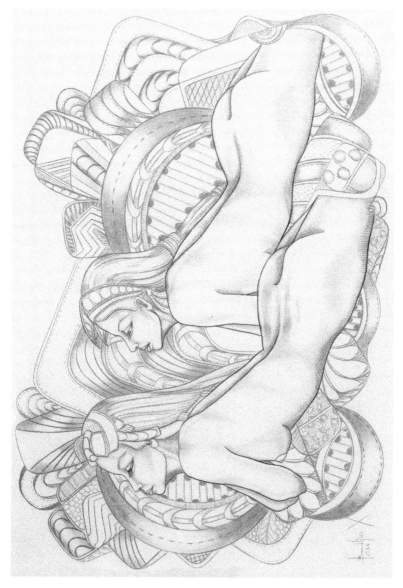

The Real Twins

"I'm puzzled by these drawings. Somebody sent me the small one, *Now You See Me*, last August, and now I've received this larger one, *The Real Twins*. I wonder who it could be."

"You don't need to worry about the person who sent these drawings to you. Some people pay a lot of money for this kind of art. Let's go to the restaurant this evening and have dinner with Fiona and Felicity. Fiona keeps asking me about you."

"Yes, sir, let's go and make them happy tonight."

On Monday the third of September, Goldash arrived at the Reismanns' office in Muswell Hill at nine o'clock. Gulizar beckoned him.

"Good morning, Mrs Gulbar. I'm surprised to see you here."

"Good morning, Goldash. Our secretary isn't well. She is going to have a minor operation, and the Reismanns are on holiday. I'm the secretary here this week. Take a seat please. Our office manageress will be with you shortly."

Gulizar introduced Goldash to the office manageress.

"Let's go to my office. We have to sign a non-disclosure agreement, an employment contract, and a fit and proper declaration," the manageress said.

"I was expecting to meet Mr and Mrs Reismann this morning. Where did they go on holiday?"

"We have clients in Oslo. After visiting them, they want to see the aurora borealis. My husband and I want to go to Norway next summer. Have you been there?"

"Yes, I have. My fiancée and I visited Oslo and Drøbak a long time ago."

"Here are the documents. Please read them carefully before you sign them."

He took his time and read them carefully.

"The hours of work should be nine to five Monday to Friday, not Monday to Wednesday as it states in this contract."

"I'm aware of that. Mrs Gulbar wanted it to be Monday to Wednesday. I understand you have other commitments during the week."

"Bless her. I was so excited about my new job and forgot my other duties."

"All together, we have six full-time staff and three part-time staff. Let me introduce you to the staff who are in the office today."

He was clearing his desk at five o'clock when Gulizar came into his new office.

"Did you enjoy working here today?" she asked.

"Yes, I like this office very much."

"I want to talk to you about something important after dinner. Let's go to the supermarket first and then to my place."

"Sure, let me just finish up here."

"What would you like for dinner?" asked Gulizar.

"I fancy pomfret this evening and can cook it for us."

"That's a good choice. Fish is good for you."

While Goldash was preparing dinner, Gulizar made a phone call.

"Some of my friends like to talk to me for hours and hours. I wish I had the time for all of them," she said when she entered the kitchen.

"Bless our friends. Some of my friends tell me the same thing several times in a short conversation."

"Have you heard about Golden Guide Projection?"

"Yes, I have. I don't really know what it's all about, though."

"The whole purpose of GGP is to be healthy, happy and wealthy. There are usually fifty-two affirmations required for the projection. Thirty-three of them are essential affirmations that are for everybody, and nineteen of them are supplementary ones that depend on what you want. Here, I wrote the essential ones down for you. Would you like to have a look and tell me what you think?"

He read the affirmations a few times.

"I like them very much and understand it would help me to become a better person."

"You're right. You must choose a start date for your GGP. It can be on the first date of a new moon, or the beginning of the spring equinox, summer solstice, autumn equinox or winter solstice. It is an individual choice. You must repeat your affirmations three times every day. It's simple and straightforward. I started my GGP on a spring equinox. I would like you to start yours on the autumn equinox."

"All right, I'll start it as you suggest."

"I wish you the best of luck, my dearest Goldash. You must make the most of yourself and enjoy your life."

On Thursday afternoon, three days before the autumn equinox, Goldash received a text message from Leyla.

Hello, GG Boy, you haven't cashed the cheque yet. Did you lose it?

He thought for a moment before replying.

No, I didn't. I received another drawing for my birthday. Do you want to see it?

Yes, I would love to.

You can come to my place this evening.

See you then xxx

Leyla came to his flat and looked at the new drawing.

"This is so beautiful. I want to buy *The Real Twins* as well."

He showed her the letter that had come with the drawing.

"As you see, I'm not supposed to sell this drawing either. However, I have an offer for you."

"I'm listening," she said curiously.

"You can lend me two million pounds for three years and keep these drawings as security. If I don't repay you the whole loan on the due date, they will be yours."

"You mean you value each drawing at one million pounds?"

"That's correct. Is the price all right with you?"

"Yes, it is. Let me give you another cheque for one million pounds."

"I want to make something very clear to you before you write the cheque. During the loan period, you shouldn't interfere in my business under any circumstances."

"I'm very happy with this arrangement."

She handed the cheque to him.

"Can you take the drawings to my car? I want to celebrate tonight."

"Yes, my lady."

He took the drawings to her car and drove to her house.

"Can you take them to my bedroom please? My mother will hang them in there tomorrow. I'm useless at those sorts of things."

Later, in the sitting room, he opened a bottle of his favourite wine and poured them each a glass.

"I wish you the best of luck in your first business venture. You are excellent at making love and naive at making money, though. You surprised me, GG Boy."

"What do you mean? I raised two million pounds for my business. That's a lot of money."

"I assume you paid me one million pounds for your first business lesson."

"You don't need to confuse me. We are supposed to celebrate tonight, aren't we?"

"Would you be kind enough to keep quiet and listen to me carefully?"

"I'm listening."

"The first rule in every business is to give the right price for the right item, product or service. *The Real Twins* is twice as big as *Now You See Me*. If the value of the smaller drawing is one million pounds, the price of the bigger drawing should be two million pounds. When I saw *The Real Twins*, I was ready and happy to pay you two million pounds. You said one million pounds for the bigger drawing, and I saved one million pounds due to your naivety. You must remember that the price of rare items always goes up, it never goes down."

"Goodness gracious me! I could easily have raised three million pounds for my business."

"It was a million-pound business lesson that only GG Boy could afford."

"I made another mistake. It shouldn't be repeated."

"If you want to be a successful businessman like Mr Kavanagh, you must visit him on a regular basis."

"Yes, he is the right person to cure my weakness."

"Cheers! Come on, GG Boy, show me your lovemaking skills tonight."

On Saturday morning, he woke up early, wrote his fifty-two affirmations in good order and memorised them.

"I'm ready for my GGP and will start it tomorrow," he thought.

He saw a small parcel on the doormat, unwrapped it and found a copy of a book entitled *Astral Projection for Beginners*.

"Somebody sent me another present. It's nice to be loved. I'm going to read this book today," he thought.

He spent the rest of the day reading his new book. After finishing it in the late afternoon, he received a text message.

You can do astral projection too. Can you come to La Lune at seven? Your loving angel wants to surprise you this evening xxx LL

He got ready and went to the restaurant. When he arrived at La Lune, Leyla, Samuel, Sylvia, Georgina, Barbara and her sons were already sitting around a table. They all greeted him warmly. During dinner he was quiet. There were many things on his mind. He thought about how his mother had had a dream about Oya, how Oya had dreamed about his favourite goat Meltem, how Barbara had dreamed about his past. He tuned back into the conversation to hear Samuel explaining how Goldash had got his hat-trick of one-four-sevens on the twenty-eighth of July 1989.

"I didn't know your nickname was Mr One-Four-Seven. Can you come to my place and show your snooker skills to my sons tomorrow afternoon?" asked Barbara.

"Of course I can. I need to play snooker to clear my mind these days. I hope your sons enjoy watching Mr One-Four-Seven in action. Excuse me, I need to go outside."

He went outside the restaurant and had a cigarette. His mind was occupied with GGP and astral projection.

"Hello, Mr One-Four-Seven. Can Georgina and I join you? She fancies a cigarette too," said Leyla.

He handed Georgina a cigarette and started smoking his second one.

"We have a question for our ambidextrous snooker player," said Leyla.

"I'm listening."

"What can a tiger do when he is surrounded by lionesses?"

He took a moment before answering. "I think he should retreat and leave the territory to the lionesses."

"That's a very good answer. A terrific tiger wouldn't waste his energy for nothing," said Leyla.

"Let's get to the point. What can I do for you ladies?"

"My good friend Georgina wants to have a new malachite Mercedes. Of course, for her new car she wants the number plate Y4 TAX."

"She can have my number plate, if she pays me two hundred and forty thousand pounds."

"Georgina doesn't have that amount of money these days."

"That's her problem, not mine."

"No, it's now your problem, not hers. Remember, if a tiger doesn't leave the territory to the lionesses, they will get him quickly. You buy the car that Georgina wants, transfer your number plate to the new car and give it to her. You will be the owner of the car. She will keep the car and maintain it for as long as she wants. Are you happy with this arrangement?"

"Yes, we can complete the formalities after next week."

"Well done, Goldash. I'm going to play the violin for our friends, and you can dance with your lady friends."

When the two cheques from Leyla had cleared in his account, he visited Gulizar.

"I wanted to raise one million pounds for our business, and now we have got two million pounds. It would be better if we incorporated two companies, one for the property business and the other one for the investment business," said Goldash.

"We don't need to remortgage this house at present. If we need extra money in the future, we can do so then. Memzar found an unused factory building close to an underground station. If we buy it and convert it into flats, we can have sixteen flats easily."

"That would be a good investment indeed."

"I must tell you something before we do anything else. We are now business partners and must be frank with each other. I sent those drawings to you."

"Did you pay a lot of money for them?"

"I went to Milan with Oya and her parents. We were very impressed by the artwork of Bruna X. She is a complete artist. Bruna and I have been friends since then. She gave me those drawings as presents."

"I see, so that's why I am not supposed to sell them. Did you also send me the book *Astral Projection for Beginners*?"

"Yes, I did. I want to give you the book *Meditation for Beginners* as well. My husband and I practise meditation on a regular basis. If you like, you can join us at any time."

"That's very kind of you, Mrs Gulbar. I want to do astral projection and meet my parents, Oya and her parents in the astral world."

"You can meet whomever you want in the astral world. We play bridge every Thursday evening. Do you want to be the bridge partner of Ozana?"

He chuckled. "I'm not very good at playing bridge, though."

"She is a good bridge player and can help you to improve your bridge skills. For our business, we need a job-sharing plan.

I look after the legal side, you look after the bookkeeping, accounting and taxation side, and Memzar looks after the construction side of the business."

"That's fine with me, Mrs Gulbar."

"Memzar is coming back from Worcester this Friday. I think your friend Fiona is an excellent architect. You can invite her here for lunch this Saturday. After lunch we can visit the building we want to buy and then go to a classical concert at the Barbican Centre."

"Fantastic! Let me call Fiona now."

Goldash took two weeks' study leave for his December exams and went to the Goldash Shelter to concentrate on his studies. All he wanted was to get pass marks in his exams in the first week of December. He woke up early on the thirtieth of November and wanted to take a walk in London Fields. When he came back from walking, he noticed that somebody had hit his car; the right rear side was damaged. Somebody had also plucked a chrysanthemum from the front of the Goldash Shelter. When he went inside, a poem was forming itself in his mind.

NOVEMBER DAYS

My dearest Leyla,
Today, the end of a nasty November,
Somebody plucked my chrysanthemum,
Somebody damaged my car,
And my business has not been doing well.
Who bothers about them?
I remember those November days
And long for my two ladies.
They are naked and play the music of naked truth.

My two ladies, you and your violin.
Your two audiences, me and my Teddy Tulin.

He emailed the poem to Leyla, had breakfast and read Leyla's email.

My dearest Goldash,
You have had a few cigarettes every day for the last few weeks and have had no sex.
You can come to my place tomorrow. I want to entertain you before your exams.
Always your loving angel
LL

POISONOUS PLEASURE

Smoking is a poisonous pleasure.
We burn it
And it burns us.
We consume it
And it consumes us.
We crave it
And it poisons us.
Smoking is a wicked game.
We play it,
We enjoy it,
But we never win it.
Smoking is a poisonous pleasure.
Our health is our best treasure.
Let's have no more puff-puff!
Let's call this wicked game off!

There had been rhythm and rhyme in his life. It is true that poets need rhythm and rhyme in their lives, as much as they need them in their poetry. Goldash had been lucky enough to have experienced the right balance and the beauty of life. He had been busy and happy working with nice people and appreciating their kindness and generosity. His business partnership with Gulizar had started well. He felt compelled to be useful both to himself and to others.

He went to the Goldash Shelter on the eve of Valentine's Day, cleaned it immaculately, phoned Debbie the florist to order three hundred and thirty-three red roses, and did the shopping. He sent an email and a poem to Leyla.

My dearest Leyla,

I am at the Goldash Shelter. The Jamiesons are so kind. They let me use this place whenever I want. You can come here tomorrow afternoon. It is my turn to entertain you.

Yours passionately

GG Boy

VALENTINE'S GAME

The interesting parts of my body strike lucky
And find other interesting parts of the body.
They are very hilarious and happy.
Their game begins and never ends.
It is always a stalemate!

Leyla came to the Goldash Shelter in the afternoon on Valentine's Day.

"Good afternoon, my gorgeous GG Boy."

"Good afternoon, my lovely Leyla Lovebird."

"I understand you want to surprise me on Valentine's Day."

"Follow me, my lady. We will go to the planet of pleasure together today."

"I am all yours now."

They awoke to bright sunshine.

"That was extraordinary, GG Boy. I slept for more than ten hours and missed my morning meditation for the first time."

"You can blame me for that, my lady. I took you to the planet of pleasure and brought you back."

"I blame nobody, my healer. I want to have coffee and talk to you."

He made two cups of coffee, and she started talking.

"I'm going to Paris this weekend. I want to meet Oya's spiritual parents, Francine and Fernand. Her friends Annabelle and Albert are going to move to Troyes this spring. It would be nice if I bought their flat in Paris. There will be some conferences in Paris and Istanbul that I want to attend. This year I'm going to celebrate my birthday in Gulistan. My cousin is a medical doctor and lives in Bursa. He, his wife and I will go to Gulistan in April. Your mother still celebrates Oya's birthday on the twenty-third of April."

"Excellent! Then there will be a triple celebration this year, Oya's birthday, your birthday and Children's Day."

"My fabulous father is a great admirer of you and Lorna. Sometimes, he watches your maximum break videos and plays snooker afterwards. I suggested he sponsor you and Lorna. He thinks you can do a snooker duet."

"I wouldn't have thought of a snooker duet. What a wonderful idea!"

"You and Lorna are ambidextrous snooker players. There are thirty-six shots in a maximum break. Lorna starts the maximum break, does one shot with her right hand, then another with her left hand, and you continue the break doing the same thing. After potting balls in this order, you pot the pink ball with your right hand and the black ball with your left hand, finishing the break. This kind of maximum break hasn't been done before. My father would be happy to re-spot the black ball and pay you five thousand pounds each on the twenty-eighth of February."

"Lorna and Mr Barnaby have been hosting their own snooker show on the twenty-eighth of each month. There are fourteen days to go before the first maximum break duet in snooker history. I need to polish my snooker skills before the show. Lorna plays better than me these days."

"You know what to do, Mr One-Four-Seven."

"I'm excited about having my snooker show again."

"I wish you the best of luck, GG Boy."

Goldash practised snooker with Bernie in the evenings, and with Lorna on Saturday and Sunday afternoons. He visited the Tokkans on the twenty-eighth of February in the late afternoon.

"I was told you wouldn't be my bridge partner this evening after all," said Ozana.

"I'll be your bridge partner next Thursday. I'm excited about my first snooker show in eleven years. Would you like to come to my show this evening?"

"I'll come to your show when it's not a Thursday evening."

"Mili requested I drive her car today. Can I have the key please?"

"I'm ready. Let's go to the snooker club," said Osman.

Goldash opened the back door of the car for him.

"I want to sit in the front seat and talk to you, Mr One-Four-Seven."

"As you wish, sir."

"Mili said you had been working as a trainee accountant. I wonder if you would like to work for our company."

"I passed my December exams and will take four more exams to complete my studies. When I become a qualified accountant, I can work for your company."

"When I was nineteen, I started working for an investment company as a clerk. I had no idea about investment. They called me the tea boy in those days. I worked hard, read economics, investment and management books, and became a millionaire at the age of twenty-nine."

"Yours is a remarkable success story. I'm thirty-eight years old and still trying to become a qualified accountant. Mili says I am naive when it comes to making money. She calls me GG Boy."

"You don't need to worry about what my daughter says to you or thinks about you. She says I make schoolboy errors in my business sometimes. You are Mr One-Four-Seven and my hero. I reserved all the tables at La Lune. We'll entertain ourselves and our usual guests this evening."

"Yes, sir. I can assure you it will be a memorable evening."

At seven o'clock, Lorna and Bernie started their show. First Lorna started her maximum break and asked Osman to pot the final ball to complete it. Later Bernie did the same thing. Osman enjoyed potting the final black ball for the second time. Richard asked Bernie to do the introduction.

"Good evening, guests and members. Lorna and Goldash are going to get their first maximum break as a snooker duet. Both of them will do a shot with their right hand and another shot with their left hand alternately. This hasn't been done before. We will witness the first maximum break by a snooker duet. Mr Osman Tokkan, the sponsor of this event, will re-spot the black ball. I am as excited as all of you are. Let's wish them the best of luck."

A chorus roared from the assembled crowd, "Good luck!"

There was complete silence in the club. Everybody's eyes were on the snooker table. All of them wanted to make it happen. Lorna was at her best, potted the balls and left the cue ball in inch-perfect positions for Goldash. He was not up to Lorna's playing standards. He took his time potting the balls, and a few times left the cue ball in less than ideal positions. However, she managed to continue the break in style. After fifteen minutes all the balls on the table had been potted. Both of them were delighted to make snooker history.

Osman got excited and shouted, "Yes, they have done it! I knew they would do it." He talked to guests and members and kept saying, "I asked them to do it." Goldash waited for Osman for about fifteen minutes.

"Excuse me, sir. We are supposed to go to the restaurant together with our guests."

"Thank you for reminding me, Goldash. I'd forgotten all about it. I'm so excited that I don't feel hungry at the moment, but we must go there nonetheless."

They went to the restaurant and enjoyed their dinner. Lorna told Osman that Goldash had been a cleaner at her parents' snooker club, how Goldash had become the Mr One-Four-Seven of the club, and why he had chosen his show to be on the twenty-eighth of each month. Osman wrote two cheques for five thousand pounds and gave them to Lorna and Goldash.

"I'm going to give one thousand pounds for the show every month. We must celebrate Goldash's monthiversary."

Goldash took a day off on the twenty-third of April 2002, went to Leyla's house in Hampstead Heath, cleaned the house and cooked his mother's favourite meal. Wearing his dinner suit, he put two empty plates on the table, one for Oya and another one for Leyla. He visualised both of them and said: "Happy birthday, Oya! Happy birthday, Leyla!"

After dinner he wrote a poem and emailed it to Leyla.

FOR YOUR BIRTHDAY
My dearest soulmate,
Let me give you a red rose and a red carnation
For your birthday celebration.
Don't think that you are getting old.
You are always twenty-four carat gold.
I know your heart is kind and sweet.
You know I am an experienced goldsmith.

The following morning, he read Leyla's email and her poem.

My dearest soulmate Goldash,

Thank you for your email and poem. That was so sweet of you.

Yesterday we celebrated Oya's birthday and my birthday. I am so happy to be here. Your mother, sister, brother-in-law, nephew and nieces are all fine. I feel as if I am a member of your family. I bought a goat and a yearling yesterday. Your mother calls my goat Meltem and my yearling Uchannal. Your sister and brother-in-law are going to keep them for me. We are going back to Istanbul after tomorrow. I bought a house there last month, and you can visit me whenever you like.

Hugs and kisses!

Your loving angel

LL

PREACHERS

I listened to preachers of different religions.
They all told me
More or less the same thing about
Happiness,
Honesty,
Equality,
High morality in a society,
Living in peace
And knowing yourself.
The golden rule must be the philosophy of every religion.
So I invited all those preachers to my house for dinner.
Musicians were playing,
Dancing girls were dancing,
And we were having our dinner.
Everything looked so wonderful.
My house turned out to be a little heaven on earth.
Suddenly, the preachers started quarrelling with each other.
Their words became more dangerous than nuclear weapons.
They all made the same bloody mistake
And broke the golden rule.
Great preachers must be great pretenders.
They all speak as it suits them.
They all act as it suits them.

He read Leyla's poem again and thought about her and her house in Istanbul.

"Leyla has been very active these days. Many activities must be going on in that house. Wouldn't it be nice if I visited her at her new house on my astral travels?" he thought.

Goldash was on study leave for his June exams and went to Leyla's house in Hampstead Heath. He wanted to have a daily routine, as she had had for many years, and made a daily plan. Finally, he performed his first astral travel on the night of the twenty-eighth of May. When he awoke, he wrote down what he had seen:

- A big house with a big garden.
- A Kangal dog at the gate of the garden.
- Leyla was walking in the garden.
- She called the dog "Gogua".

He noted in capital letters: NEXT TIME, LOCATE THE HOUSE AND TRY TO GO INSIDE.

He did his morning meditation, had breakfast and checked his emails.

My beloved Goldash,

I had planned to come to London this weekend and entertain you before your exams, but my friend's mother passed away, and I must fly to Texas to attend the funeral.

Good luck in your exams.

Lots of love!

LL

After his exams he decided to stay at Leyla's house for a while to concentrate on his meditations. He had his first out-of-body experience on the twenty-fourth of June and wrote a poem.

OUT-OF-BODY EXPERIENCE

Oh, my dearest!
I am lying on my bed
And the strawberry moon shines through my window.
On my right side is my Teddy Tulin.
On my left side is my Bunny Benny.
I am writing down my daily affirmation.
I am doing my midnight meditation.
It is 23.21 our time.
It must be 16.21 your time.
Oh, my dearest!
You must be having an out-of-body experience!
Suddenly, your image appears on my room's wall.
I can see you are in your golden garden.
I can see your beloved dog Golden Guard.
You are flirting with the sunshine.
I am flirting with the moonshine.
I wonder how you can tell me all the answers
Before I ask you the questions.
You say,
"I want you to play your guitar
As one of the most celebrated guitarists
And write the best love song ever written.
I want you to read the market's mind
And become one of the most incredible investors.
I want you to write a book about checks and balances
And enlighten the public and politicians.
Elected dictators and unelected dictators,
Any kind of dictatorship is a carbuncle on democracy.
Without the control of the Taxpayers Association,
There wouldn't be a proper democracy in any country."
Oh, my dearest!

Even if I were a monumental genius,
I couldn't fulfil your demands and desires.
I had better forget these delightful dreams
And not think about them.
You say,
"I don't want you to be a monumental genius.
I don't want you to be multi-gifted.
I only want you to have the power and
pleasure of an out-of-body experience."

Leyla returned from her long holiday in early August. He met her at the airport, and they shared a long embrace.

"My parents are going to Istanbul for two weeks tomorrow. They'll come back on the twentieth of August. I'll be very busy for the next two weeks. When they come back, we can go to Paris together."

"That sounds lovely. I would love to go to Paris with you."

"Mrs Gulbar told me the Reismanns are very happy with you."

"I enjoy working with them. The last eleven months have passed so quickly. Everybody is friendly in their office. I like their no-nonsense business policy."

"How is your business?"

"It's doing very well, much better than I expected."

"I like your drawings very much. Frankly, I want your business to fail so I can keep them."

He laughed. "Thank you so much for being frank with me."

Leyla and Goldash went to Paris by car on the twenty-third of August. The following day he cleaned the flat and prepared dinner.

"Mrs Tokkan has had this flat decorated very well. I couldn't imagine it any better than this," he said.

"I'm very lucky to have a marvellous mother. She knows what is best for me. I paid twenty-five per cent higher than the market value for this flat."

"That was very thoughtful of you. Oya and I had a jolly good time here."

"Sometimes I am envious of Oya. I want to be loved as much as she is loved."

"Why do you say something like that?" he asked.

"Annabelle showed me the actual-size painting she did of you and Oya."

"I remember she measured our heights and took our photos."

"She wanted to give the painting to you and Oya. Unfortunately, you never visited them again. I offered to buy the painting for the same price as the flat. She said no. I doubled the price. Her answer was still no. I trebled the price. Then Albert intervened with his high-pitched voice and said, 'Listen to me, young lady. This painting is not for sale. We are keeping it for Goldash. When he visits us one day, he can take it. You shouldn't bother us about it again.'"

"Oya dedicated her life to her patients and people in her community. You dedicate your life to your profit and pleasure. That is the difference between you and Oya. How can you be loved as much as she is loved?"

"That's not fair. I make money and help people as much as I can. Do you remember Mélodie, the elder daughter of Francine and Fernand?"

"Yes, I do. What about her?"

"She and her husband had a bakery in Brittany. Sadly, she had breast cancer and passed away last year. I'm going to support her elder daughter Lucie and younger daughter Natalie. I want them to have a good education. They are going to stay in this flat during their studies."

"Thank you for sponsoring my spiritual nieces. Both of them used to call Oya 'auntie'. When I met them, they were little girls. I wouldn't recognise them if I saw them today."

"They didn't know you and Oya were engaged. They thought you were one of her therapist friends. Shall we visit Annabelle and Albert in Troyes tomorrow?"

"No, I'm not comfortable visiting them these days."

"Come on, GG Boy, don't you want to see our friends and get the painting tomorrow?"

"I said no, didn't I?"

"Yes, you did. I know they won't sell the painting to me. You can take it from them, sell it to me and become a multimillionaire on your birthday in Paris."

"Oya and I were in this flat in June 1989. When Annabelle and Albert came back from Troyes, we had dinner. They thought if they spoke French, it would help me to improve my French. I didn't understand what they were saying, but I felt everything they talked about. When Annabelle asked where the two of us had met, Oya told them how we had met in the bookshop. Annabelle became very emotional and started to cry, then we all cried. That was the most enjoyable and emotional dinner I've ever had. If I meet Annabelle and Albert again, they will cry when they see me, but their tears won't be the same tears. I couldn't bear to see their tears of sadness."

"My dear GG Boy, you're still living in the past. I told you to be pragmatic, not dogmatic."

"Damn it, you're a crazy lady. You don't understand me, do you? I'm grateful and appreciate what you've been doing for me. If you talk to me again on this matter though, I won't bother speaking to you ever again."

They slept in separate rooms without saying goodnight to each other. The following morning Leyla knocked on his door.

"Good morning, Goldash. I apologise for upsetting you last night. Shall we go to a café for breakfast? I want to talk to you about something important."

He got ready, and they went out.

"I thought a lot about you and Oya last night. It would be nice if we set up an Oya Oydash Foundation to help people in need. I would be happy to give fifty per cent of my earnings to this charity."

"That's an excellent idea. I can be the treasurer, and Mrs Gulbar can be the chairperson of the foundation, as she was Oya's godmother."

Leyla stood up and kissed him.

"Excuse me, Leyla. Suddenly, something has come to my mind."

"And what is that, GG Boy?"

"If we set up the foundation, Annabelle and Albert would donate the painting to us. You wouldn't try to buy the painting from the foundation, would you?"

"Of course I wouldn't. You shouldn't think something like that, GG Boy."

"I must have your word on it."

"This has been very educational for me. I've learned my lesson and give you my word."

"Well done, my lady. I'm going to pamper you today and tomorrow."

"That's all I need now. I will treat you well on your birthday. The terrific twin therapists are in Paris."

It was mid-September. He prepared their companies' annual accounts and visited Gulizar.

"We have all good news, Mrs Gulbar. I passed my June exams. Our investment business is doing extremely well. If we transfer the profit of the investment company to the property company, we won't have any cash flow problems."

"I'm so happy for both of us. Memzar has been working hard since February. Shall we go to the Manor House Hotel next Thursday and come back on Sunday?"

"Yes, Mrs Gulbar. I will be your chauffeur."

He woke up late on Monday the fourth of November, not in the mood to do anything that day. After having coffee, he wrote a poem.

CHRYSANTHEMUM

My dearest Leyla,
I must have been tired of working and waiting.
Yesterday I slept all day long.
This morning I woke up very late.
I forgot which day it was.
I forgot which month it was.
I opened the curtains of my studio flat.
I saw my chrysanthemums had blossomed.
Chrysanthemums cannot be wrong,
It must be the month of November.
It always makes me happy and wonder
Remembering those days of November.
After all these years,
I still live in the same studio flat.
I still hope to buy a nice house in a nice area
And want to entertain you and your girlfriends.
I still remember what you said to me.
"Don't worry, my precious poet!

You will have it one of these days."
You were very sorry for me, weren't you?
Well, I have been very sorry for myself,
More than anyone else.
I wonder what you have been doing these days.
Perhaps you play your violin in Las Vegas, the city of sin.
Perhaps you receive your holistic massage in a luxury hotel.
Perhaps you flirt with a few men there.
Who knows what my lovebird will do next?
Perhaps I should stop trying to understand women.
Perhaps I should love women
More than ever these days.

He stayed in bed, read the meditation book again, and prepared lunch and dinner while still wearing his pyjamas. After dinner, he wrote another poem.

WHAT HAVE I DONE TODAY?
It was Monday.
I felt very lazy.
I didn't go to the office.
I didn't go out either.
Instead I stayed in all day long.
In the evening, I asked myself,
"What have I done today?"
Oh yes,
I remembered
How many times I met her,
How many times I cooked meals for her,
And how many times I made her scream.
I remembered
How many times I surprised her,

How many times I made her sad,
And how many times I told her silly jokes.
I remembered
How many times we argued over
Politics, religion and sex,
And never had an agreement
After long discussions.
When it was 19.36,
I remembered to call her.
So I called her.
Her mobile phone was switched off!
I asked myself again,
"What have I done today?"
Oh no,
I don't want to remember it.
I forgot to tell her
"I love you."

He watched a comic film on the television and read Leyla's email.

My dearest GG Boy,

Thank you for sending me your poems.

After reading them, I am concerned about you. Whenever I am away, I always miss my GG Boy. I will come to London before your snooker show on the twenty-eighth of November and entertain you before your exams. I really hope these will be your last exams.

Hugs and kisses!
Your loving angel
LL

He took his last exam on taxation and tax planning on the fifth of December. He met Leyla at her place, and they went to La Lune to celebrate. Her face was glowing more than ever.

"I'm glad your exams are over. You did very well, GG Boy."

"When I have pass marks for my exams, then it will all be over."

"I'm confident you will get pass marks. Also, I have good news for you."

"Everybody likes good news. What is it, my double delight?"

"Yesterday, I was in beautiful Barking attending a meeting and met a young medical doctor. She wants to move to Norwich and needs to sell her house at 3 Poet Close. It's a two-bedroom house with a garden. I thought that house could be your first headquarters."

"I don't have enough money to buy a house. All my money is in investments."

"That's not a problem. I'll be the guarantor for your mortgage. You must see the house before you decide. I made an appointment at six o'clock tomorrow. We will go there together. In the meantime, let's enjoy ourselves."

"Yes, my guarantor."

The following day, Leyla took Goldash to the house in Barking.

After they had viewed the house, she asked, "What do you think about this house, GG Boy?"

"I have a good feeling here and want to own it as soon as possible."

"That's good, I feel the same way about it. You could have a nice conservatory built and a shed in the garden. Susanna has been taking my advice on investments and has made good money. She can get the necessary things for this house done. After all, I give her free advice, and she must do us a favour in return. However, we must get the formalities tied up before anything else."

"Yes, my angel."

He received his last exam results, with pass marks, on the twenty-first of February 2003, and remembered receiving his first pass mark, for bookkeeping, in February 1987. It had taken sixteen years to complete his studies. He felt as if he were sweet sixteen, and phoned his sister.

"Hello, this is Goldash. Whom am I talking to?"

"My name is Ayla. You're a joker. My *abi*'s[11] name is Goldash."

"Ayla, my dear niece, I am your uncle Goldash."

"You're not my uncle Goldash. My mum said my uncle had gone to heaven."

"Yes, your mum is right. I'm calling from heaven, everybody has a mobile phone there these days. May I talk to your mum please?"

"My mum is in the garden. She is going to make chestnut kebabs for us."

"I like chestnut kebabs very much. Can you call your mum please?"

"All right, wait, I'm going to call her."

"Thank you, Ayla. You're a very good girl."

He waited for a few minutes.

"Hello, who is this?"

"Hello, my dearest *abla*."

"My dearest brother, have you come back from heaven?"

"No, I haven't been there yet. It's a long story. When I meet you, I will tell you all about it. Can I talk to my mother please?"

---

[11] "Elder brother" in Turkish.

"I'm so sorry, Goldash. She passed away on the sixth of this month."

Suddenly, he dropped the phone from his hand. He remained on the chair, frozen for a while. When his doorbell rang, he jerked as if startled. He managed to compose himself and opened the door. The Gulbars were at the door. Both of them hugged him, offered their condolences and comforted him.

"Goldash, my dear, your sister phoned me and explained what had happened. Let's go to our place. You must stay with us for a few days."

"Yes, Mrs Gulbar."

Leyla took Goldash to Susanna's B&B in the Cotswolds for the Easter break. He enjoyed giving reflexology to the couple who ran it and their children. Each day, she enjoyed walking in the Cotswold Gardens and taking many pretty photos.

"Susanna made the right decision buying this place. We can see everybody is a winner here," said Leyla.

"I'm happy for Susanna and this lovely family."

She looked him in the eye and said, "I'm going to Istanbul next week. Would you like to join me, GG Boy?"

"Not this time."

"Come on, GG Boy. I want to show you my house there and introduce you to my uncle and Oya's uncle and auntie. We can go to Gulistan together and celebrate my birthday and Oya's birthday. Don't you miss your sister and her family?"

"I had intended to go back to Gulistan with a qualification when my mother was alive. It didn't happen during her lifetime. I've now decided to go back there as a prosperous poet."

"Sometimes you're very sensitive on certain matters. I

respect your decision and don't want to interfere with your business."

"Thank you, my angel."

Susanna met Goldash at his new place on the twenty-second of May.

"Everything has been done as Leyla requested: the conservatory, the shed in the garden and the folding ladder to the attic. Mrs Tokkan helped me choose the furniture and decorate. Your gardener friend will sort out the garden for you," said Susanna.

"You've done an excellent job. Thank you so much for everything."

"I wish you the best of luck in becoming a prosperous poet at your new place. Leyla asked me not to interfere with your business."

"Bless her. Sometimes she likes to tease me. We must listen to whatever our investment guru says."

"I adore Leyla. She helped me to make a lot of money over the past two years. I can retire any time I want."

"Excellent! Double-delight Leyla and sexy Susanna strike and make money. The lionesses are in business."

"My sister, her children, my children and I are going to my B&B for the bank holiday break. Here, this is the key to my sister's house. You can clean her house this weekend and my house next week. I want to be pampered next weekend."

"Yes, Susanna. You deserve it."

Goldash had been enjoying his new house and concentrating on his meditation and astral travels. He kept failing to enter Mili's house in Istanbul and was unable to locate it on his astral travels. The dog at the gate of the house barked at him and woke him up before he could open the gate. This happened a few times.

"I must be doing something wrong. There must be a simple solution to this," he thought.

He visited Gulizar and talked to her about his astral travels.

"You concentrate on Mili's house in Istanbul. She may have another house somewhere you don't know of, or it may be one of her relatives' houses. If I were you, I would concentrate on Mili. In astral travel, we can talk to animals as well. When you are at the gate of the house, you must introduce yourself to the dog before touching the gate, so it knows you and your intention. It's as simple as that."

"Thank you for enlightening me, Mrs Gulbar."

"Have you heard from Mili recently?"

"No, I haven't. The last time I talked to her was in April. I refused to go to Istanbul with her. I don't think she is very happy with me."

"She wants me to organise your fortieth birthday party in Gulistan. Here is her email."

Dearest Mrs Gulbar,

I wonder if you would kindly do me a favour and organise Goldash's fortieth birthday party in Gulistan. I believe you are the best person for this. Kindly invite these people:

The Jamiesons,

His snooker partner Lorna, her parents and her brother,

The Nesbitts and their niece Araks,

His doctor friend Kenneth, his wife and his parents,

His ex-neighbour Mathilda Hopper and her granddaughter Helena,

His friends Georgina and Nicole,

His friend Barbara and her assistant Debra,

His friend Susanna,
The Reismanns,
His architect friend Fiona and her mother.
My parents, my uncle and his family, as well as Oya's uncle and auntie and their families, will join you in Istanbul.
I am happy to pay you for all the expenses. Please let me know how much you need and your bank details.
Best wishes
Mili

"I'm very surprised she is doing this for me. Surely she can organise my birthday party if she wants to. You don't need to organise it, Mrs Gulbar."

"Goldash, my dear boy, don't be silly. Everything is going very well. We don't need to wake a sleeping lioness. Remember, a lioness can be more dangerous than a lion. She wants to surprise you and wants you to visit your sister on your birthday. You must be grateful to her. I'm sure we'll have fun all together."

"I told her I would only go back to Gulistan as a prosperous poet."

"When your sister called me, I explained to her why I had lied to your mother about you, as she was in severe emotional trauma. Your sister is a wise lady and understood me. They are all dying to see you. Mili bought a snooker table for your sister's house. She wants you and Lorna to do a maximum break show on your birthday."

"Perhaps we'll go to Gulistan together in the near future, but I am not going there this year."

"Very well, Goldash, you know what is best for you."

Bernie and Goldash went to the snooker club and did their snooker show on the twenty-eighth of August. After the show, both of them went to La Lune.

"I didn't enjoy the show this evening. There was no Lorna, no Araks and not one of our regular guests," said Bernie.

"You are right. It was no fun without our friends and guests."

"Lorna said she and Araks will visit your sister on your birthday. Why haven't you joined them? Is everything all right with you?"

"Everything is fine with me, thank you for asking. Which girlfriend are you visiting tonight?"

"Felicity and her daughter went to Istanbul. I was surprised they didn't ask me to join them."

"I feel a little bit tired. Let me take you to Femke's house."

On his birthday, Goldash did his meditation and wanted to have successful astral travels. When he woke up, he wrote down what he had seen on his astral travels:

- Identical twin sisters Mili and Lili.
- A six-bedroom detached house.
- A Kangal dog.
- An elderly blind lady.
- Epping Forest.
- The CM16 postcode area.

He made a cup of coffee and wrote a poem.

APPRENTICE
My dearest Leyla,
This has been a long year.
My mother passed away

And I could not attend her funeral.
This has been a long summer.
You ignored me.
You sent me neither a postcard nor a letter.
This has been a long month.
I received no cheque and met no client.
This has been a long week.
I went out every night
And met many lovely ladies.
None of them turned me on.
This has been a wonderful weekend.
Yesterday, on my birthday,
Terrific twin sisters tranquillised me.
That was an experience of a lifetime.
Now I am no longer a master of living in pain.
I am lucky enough to be
An apprentice of living in pleasure.

After having his breakfast, he received a text message from Gulizar.

You should visit Mili's sister Lili in Epping Forest this afternoon at two o'clock.

He got ready, drove to Epping Forest and found the house that he had seen on his astral travels, but he didn't enter. Instead, he returned to his house. He did some meditation, had lunch and went back to the house in Epping Forest. There was a Kangal dog at the gate. He talked to the dog as he had done on his astral travels.

"Good afternoon, Gogua. My name is Goldash Goldadash. I know your name Gogua is short for Golden Guard. I have an appointment with her ladyship, Lili Tokkan. May I come in please?"

The dog went to the right side of the gate and turned its snout towards a bell by the gate.

"Thank you, my friend."

He pressed the doorbell,

"Hello, who is this?"

"This is Goldash. Mrs Gulbar asked me to come here."

"I've been waiting for you. Come in please."

He opened the gate, stroked the dog's head and walked to the house. Lili met him at the door.

"Good afternoon, Goldash."

"Good afternoon, Lili. Mili told me about you, but she didn't mention you were her identical twin."

"Thank you for coming. I'm so happy to see you."

"I'm delighted to be here. My dream has come true."

They went inside the house. He noticed an elderly lady sitting there, who was blind.

"Goldash, this is my grandmother."

"My dear boy, give me a big hug."

"My grandmother is a retired concert pianist. She can play the piano for you while I'm making tea."

"I know you are a poet. Before tea I'm going to play *Poet and Peasant*. After tea I will play Lili's masterpiece, *Poet and Princess*, so you can dance with her."

"Thank you, Grandmother, that's so sweet of you," he said.

While he was dancing with Lili, he saw the drawing of Uchannal on the wall.

"That was very beautiful. It's the first time I've listened to *Poet and Princess*."

"I'll play the violin, and you can dance with my grandmother."

After dancing with her grandmother, he looked again at the drawing of Uchannal.

"Do you like this drawing?" asked Lili.

"Yes, I do. I love every artwork by Bruna X. Mili told me about your beloved horse Uchannal. Can you tell me more about him?"

"As you know, his name was originally Knight, and he was a present for my twenty-first birthday. He was trained by a reputable trainer and was ready for racing. He raced half-heartedly and came last in three races. After his third race, I wasn't happy and didn't know what to do with him. Something strange happened that night when I had a dream about Knight. In my dream, he talked to me and requested a new name and a female jockey, and asked me to bet all of my savings on his next race. I told my grandmother and Mili about my dream. My grandmother suggested changing his name to Uchannal, so I changed it. I interviewed a few female jockeys but wasn't sure which one was right for the job. A friend suggested I interview a jockey called Carol. I interviewed her and allowed her to take Uchannal out for a ride. When she returned, I asked her how it had been. She said it was orgasmic. Well, I knew some ladies had orgasms when riding horses and took it as a good sign."

"I never knew horses could be useful for that kind of pleasure."

She smiled at him and said, "Horses can be very useful indeed."

"How did Uchannal make you a multimillionaire?"

"When Carol and Uchannal were ready for their first race, the odds were unbelievably high. Grandmother bet all her savings on Uchannal with different bookies. After the race, Grandmother was a bookies buster. It was her first and last gamble, and she gave all her winnings to me, Mili and Carol. The three of us became instant multimillionaires."

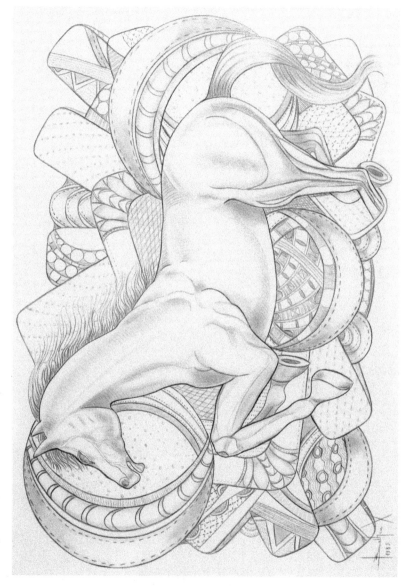

Uchannal

"Wow! That's the most remarkable success story I've ever heard."

"After winning seventeen races in a row, Uchannal became a reputable stud. Half of his earnings go to his charity, the Uchannal Foundation. I am the chairperson of the foundation, and he is the shadow chairperson. We have board meetings during my astral travels, and he instructs me on the activities of the foundation."

"You have an astral office for your board meetings? How interesting."

She smiled. "I'm glad you know about the astral world, not many people do."

"I didn't know anything about it until Mrs Gulbar told me all its beauties."

"Shall we go to the music room? I want to show you my musical skills."

He followed her to the music room. It was full of instruments. He stood by the piano, tickled the keys and looked at different brass and string instruments, some of which he hadn't seen before.

"How long have you been living here with your grandmother?"

"When my grandfather passed away, I was fourteen. My grandmother asked me to stay here and be her companion."

"This is a very pleasant place. I wish I could stay here and be your companion."

"I'm a doctor of music and can play every musical instrument."

She played Mozart's *Turkish March* on the piano and Vivaldi's *Four Seasons – Spring* on the violin. He applauded her and said, "I admire the way you play the piano and the violin. I could listen to you for hours and hours."

She smiled. "I'm a doctor of transference as well. I can transfer one person's skill to another person."

"You mean you transferred Mozart's piano skills and Vivaldi's violin skills to yourself?"

"I could have done so if they were alive or if their live performances were recorded."

"Wow! That's extraordinary. I've learned new things here today."

"What's your favourite musical instrument, Goldash?"

"It's the guitar."

"I'm a right-handed violinist and a left-handed guitarist. What can I play for you on the guitar?"

"*All Along the Watchtower*," he said.

She picked up an electric guitar and demonstrated her playing skills and fascinated him.

"You are a genius, Lili. I haven't heard this version of *All Along the Watchtower* before. I'm convinced Bob Dylan and Jimi Hendrix would like your version of the song too."

"Now it's your turn, my dear Goldash. What can you play for me on the guitar?"

"I can play *Happy Birthday* for you on your birthday, that's all I can manage."

"That would be great. No man has ever played *Happy Birthday* for me."

He smiled. "In that case, I must practise my guitar every day for my big gig."

"If you practise your guitar for an hour every day for a year, you can join me onstage."

"You must be joking, Lili."

"No, I'm not joking. It's true. I will be your guitar teacher if you show me your snooker skills. Let's go to the snooker room."

The room was bigger than his old studio flat.

"This is my snooker table, and this is my cue. I named it GG the Third. I've been trying to transfer your snooker skills to one of our neighbours. She is ambidextrous and has managed to get a century break a few times. Of course, her target is to get a maximum break. She doesn't really need to get one, but it's a kind of personal challenge for her."

"I like this room and could play snooker here every day. I think you should transfer my snooker skills to your father. He is dying to break his maximum break duck."

"My father doesn't think it can be done. Now, I want you to show me a maximum break. You must complete it the way I want, two shots with your right hand and then two shots with your left hand. Then continue the break in that order. If you show me a maximum break today, I'll be your guitar teacher until you play as well as me."

"I accept your offer. May I have an hour to prepare myself for my snooker show?"

"Yes, of course you can."

"It's my snooker show, and this is my room now. Can you leave me alone for a while please?"

"Yes, sir."

As usual, he cleaned the snooker table and balls, and decided to do the Alexander technique on the table before practising snooker. Lili knocked on the door after an hour and entered. He asked her to re-spot the black ball for him and started playing. Lili enjoyed re-spotting the black ball and was excited about being a part of the show. He took more time than he had intended and completed the maximum break in the requested order. She congratulated him and started kissing him.

"Excuse me, Lili. Kissing wasn't in our agreement."

"Your show is over. Now, I run the show. Would you keep quiet and follow my instructions please?"

They spread twelve blankets on the snooker table, then a silk carpet over the top. Then they scattered the petals of three hundred and thirty-three red roses onto the carpet.

"I've been waiting for this moment for a long time. Now, show me your lovemaking skills on the snooker table, GG Boy."

"Yes, my lady."

After completing their two shows in the snooker room, Goldash and Lili returned to the sitting room.

"Grandmother, we are going to the supermarket. What can we get for you today?" asked Lili.

"I fancy tuna steak this evening. You can go to the supermarket. Goldash can stay with me. I want him to give me reflexology."

"All right, I'll bring my reflexology chair from my car," said Goldash.

He brought the chair in and set it up.

"Grandmother, the chair is ready for you."

"Goldash, my dear, when Lili was fulfilling her fantasy with you on the snooker table, Mili phoned me. She was very upset you didn't let her know before you came here. She said you should have given me reflexology before anything else and you must stay here until she comes back from Istanbul. If I were you, I would take her request as an order."

"I'm very sorry, Grandmother. I didn't know you wanted to have reflexology today."

"You don't need to be sorry, my boy. If I were you, I would have done the same thing with a beautiful young lady. Cheer up, GG Boy, and give me relaxing reflexology."

"Yes, Grandmother."

He prepared dinner, and Lili laid the table.

"That was the best tuna steak I've ever had. We always need a man like you in this house. Mili told me you are a very good handyman. You can clean the whole house tomorrow and tidy the garden the day after."

"I'm always at your service, Grandmother."

"Every year we visit different parts of beautiful Britain. Next week, we are going to Brimham Rocks, which are unusual balancing rock formations in North Yorkshire and then to the Lake District. Would you like to join us, Goldash?" asked Lili.

"I'm staying with you until Mili comes back from her long holiday. I saw the Balancing Rock when Oya and I were in Nova Scotia. I haven't heard about Brimham Rocks, though."

"One of our neighbours has been there. She says we must see the Balancing Idol Rock," said Lili.

"If I'm going to clean this house tomorrow, I must get an early night. Which room will be mine?" asked Goldash.

Lili showed him to his room and wished him goodnight. After he'd had a shower in the en-suite, he lay down on the bed and wrote a poem for Mili.

CHECKMATE

My dear lady,
I don't know your next move.
You are as unpredictable
As a chess player.
You always take me.
I cannot move anywhere.

Grandmother, Lili, Goldash and Gogua went to Brimham Rocks on the first of September. They stayed in a farmhouse overnight before heading to wonderful Windermere.

"I like this place very much. We were here a long time ago. You haven't given me reflexology yet. If we hire a boat, could I have it on there?" asked Lili.

"I'm here to serve you, my lady."

They hired a boat, and he gave her reflexology.

"Lili must be so relaxed. She is sleeping on the seat," Grandmother said.

"She can relax for a while, and we can enjoy the wonder of Lake Windermere," Goldash said.

After having a short sleep, Lili woke up and said, "You're amazing, Goldash. I had a delightful dream. The three of us and Gogua were in a glass submarine. Grandmother and I played *Sensation of the Ocean*. I've never played such sweet music before."

"Marvellous! You can play the violin now. I want to hear *Sensation of the Ocean*."

"Yes, my beloved Goldash."

The Gulbars visited Lili and her grandmother on the thirteenth of September, in the afternoon.

"Thank you for looking after our naughty boy. We celebrated his fortieth birthday in Gulistan, and he didn't even attend. When Mili and his employer Rodger were talking, she told him that Goldash had visited her grandmother without telling her, and that he would stay with Grandmother until she comes back to London. Rodger asked her to forgive Goldash, and she accepted it. She is staying in Istanbul and coming back in early October. So he can go to the office on Monday," said Gulizar.

"He has been a very helpful boy and has worked for us as a voluntary butler for the last two weeks. We will miss him," Grandmother said.

"Be happy, Grandmother. I can come here some weekends," said Goldash.

"That's great. I hope to see you soon."

After saying farewell to Grandmother and Lili, the Gulbars and Goldash went to his house and reviewed their companies' accounts.

"Our newly built flats will be ready for sale by next April," said Memzar.

"I've prepared management accounts for both companies. If we sell ten flats next summer, we will recover all our expenses and become millionaires before tax this time next year," said Goldash.

"Fantastic! Let's go to Snowdonia this Thursday and come back on Sunday," said Gulizar.

In early October, Leyla came to his place in the afternoon.

"Have you been enjoying yourself at your new place, GG Boy?"

"Yes, I have. This is an ideal and inspirational place for me and my business. I love living here."

"Excellent! When you become a millionaire, I want a millionaire's treat."

"I want to entertain you as a poet. You may forget having a millionaire's treat or a billionaire's treat, assume you are having a trillionaire's treat today."

"That's very inspirational indeed. Poets are exceptionally imaginative people; their imagination is as big as the world."

"Perhaps you are right. Let me start by giving you relaxing reflexology."

He gave her an hour of reflexology, and she fell asleep on the chair. He covered her with a blanket and went to the kitchen. When she woke up, she called him.

"That was magical, GG Boy. You touched my feet and sent me to the moon. I was in a big glass house. There were so many daisies that I had never seen before. I had a glass of ninety-nine-year-old wine and watched the world from the moon."

"Very good, my lady. I wish I could be as imaginative as you are."

He prepared the massage couch and started giving her a ninety-minute holistic massage. She fell asleep again towards the end of the massage. After waking up, she said, "I had another dream. I'm so thrilled and feel that I am having a trillionaire's treat."

"Tell me all about it, my lady."

"I was on the moon again. We were in a big glass concert hall. It was full of scientists, engineers, entrepreneurs, academics, architects, artists, authors, poets, composers, and representatives of different countries. I was at the front of a big orchestra and played *Sensation of the Moon*. It was the sweetest music I had ever played."

"We would definitely need a trillion-pound investment to host such an event on the moon. I think there are dedicated and diligent scientists and engineers in the world. Perhaps, if the world's billionaires gave twenty-five per cent of their wealth to fund this project, we could make your dream a reality. Those billionaires wouldn't need to worry about losing twenty-five per cent of their wealth; they would still be richer than billions of people in the world."

"You've become very imaginative, GG Boy."

"I think you are the right person to organise this kind of project. It will be a lifetime's challenge for you. We can think about it later. Now we must go upstairs. One thousand red roses and one blue rose are waiting for us. You will be on the moon for the third time today."

"Let me have a shower and join you, GG Boy."

It was mid-December, he wanted to have a quiet weekend. He switched his mobile phone off, went to the market, bought fresh fish, vegetables, fruit and flowers in the morning, read a book about international taxation, practised his guitar in the afternoon, and checked his emails in the late evening. There was an email from Leyla.

My dearest Goldash,

I have been very busy meeting different people in New York and Toronto for the last few weeks. It would be nice if you became my personal assistant after finishing your accountancy training. Today, I am meeting one of my friends in Halifax, Nova Scotia. I will be flying to Paris on the twenty-third of December, and you can join me there on the twenty-seventh. After spending a week there, we can go back to London together.

Lots of love!

Your loving angel

LL

He wanted to have breakfast with Leyla in Paris and took the first Eurostar train on the twenty-seventh of December. She met him at Gare du Nord.

"I've missed you so much, GG Boy. You are the only person I can tease and argue with about anything and everything for hours and hours. The days on my business trips and holidays get longer and longer without you. I think you should join me on my next business trip."

"You like to tease me and want me to please you. *Merci beaucoup, madame.* I am starving and want to join you for breakfast."

They went to a café near to the station and had breakfast.

"I bought a book entitled *Teach Yourself French*. When you

are learning a new language, first learn the numbers in that language."

"I see you want to be my French interpreter and not my French teacher. *Je t'aime*, Leyla."

"*J'aime beaucoup, mon amour Goldash*. I want to have decent conversations with you in French. I can find you a good French teacher, and we can stay in Paris until you learn."

"*Merci beaucoup, madame*."

"I'm going to buy a few dresses today. Can you choose some for me?"

"*Oui*, Leyla."

They spent a good few hours shopping, then they went to Leyla's flat. They enjoyed each other's company and didn't go out the whole day on the twenty-eighth of December. The following morning, she received a text message from her mother.

"My parents are in New York for the New Year celebrations. My father had an accident last night and broke his left arm. I must fly to New York as soon as possible."

"I'm sorry to hear it."

She got ready quickly, took a taxi and went to the airport. He took a long walk through the streets of Paris, knowing how people could be lonely in a big city. Later he returned to the flat, had a cup of tea and wrote a poem.

LEYLA LOVEBIRD IN PARIS

On Tuesday the twenty-third of December 2003,
Leyla Lovebird flew over to Paris from eastern Canada
And made her love nest somewhere in the 7th arrondissement.
On Saturday the twenty-seventh of December 2003,
She met her poet at Gare du Nord.
And later she played

Her favourite piece of music, Romance, for him.
After playing the violin, she said,
"My beloved poet,
Sometimes I visit Paris, the city of pleasure,
And entertain princes and princesses,
Preachers and presidents, poets and politicians."
He asked,
"Politicians? How about them?"
She said,
"Mountains,
From a distance they look small.
When you approach them,
They look bigger and bigger.
Politicians,
From a distance they sound big.
When you approach them,
They sound smaller and smaller."
He asked again,
"Poets? How about them?"
She said,
"Poets,
Sometimes they are silent like a dormant volcano.
Sometimes they explode like an active volcano.
Silence wouldn't be golden for poets.
They should speak out and enlighten politicians."
He said,
"My dearest Leyla, my true friend,
I am hot!
I am very hot!
I am ready to explode!"

On the thirtieth of December, he woke up late and went to a café. He ordered lunch, remembering his first visit to Paris, and visualised Oya. Her image appeared in front of the café, and she winked at him. He winked at her image with his right eye and then his left eye several times.

"Excuse me, sir," a woman said.

"Yes, madam?"

"My name is Mireille, and this is my daughter Adeline. She is a psychic artist."

"My name is Goldash. I'm about to have my lunch. Please join me. I like art and artists."

"Adeline thinks you were here with a beautiful lady about fourteen years ago. Is that right?"

"Yes, it is. I was here in June 1989. It was my first visit to Paris. I haven't met a psychic artist before. Honestly, I didn't know there were such artists. I am delighted to meet you, Adeline."

"She doesn't speak. You must read her lips and try to understand what she is saying," said Mireille.

"Your daughter is extremely beautiful. I haven't seen such a smiling face and long curly hair before. She is a rare jewel indeed."

They had their lunch, and he told them all about Oya and Leyla. The three of them spent the whole afternoon together and had dinner later. Before bidding them farewell for the night, he invited them to Leyla's flat for the New Year celebrations.

On the thirty-first of December in the afternoon, Mireille and Adeline came to the flat. He gave them reflexology and prepared dinner for his guests. They celebrated the New Year together. He had a quiet New Year's Day, and received a text message from Mireille the following morning.

Hi Goldash, Adeline wants to see you. Can we meet at the same café for lunch at 12.30 p.m. please?

He replied:

Yes, of course we can. See you then.

He met Mireille and Adeline at the café and had lunch with them.

"Adeline likes you and wants to spend the day with you. Is that all right?"

"Yes, definitely. I'm alone in Paris and would welcome her company."

"She knows English. You must read her lips carefully."

"I'm sure I can improve my lip-reading skills."

"Very well, I had better leave you together, then."

"Before you go, let me give you the flat's landline number."

After Mireille had left, he looked at Adeline and said, "You don't wear make-up, just like Oya and Leyla. The way you smile at me reminds me of Oya. I want to hold your hand and take a long walk with you. Of course, I'll prepare a nice dinner for you later. What can I cook for you this evening?"

He carefully read her lips. "Fish"

"I fancy fish too."

After they had gone walking and shopping together, he took her to the flat, gave her a holistic massage, and prepared dinner. They had dinner smiling at one another. Afterwards, she cleaned the table and the kitchen. He turned on the television, and she took the remote control and turned it off.

"What's the problem? I want to watch the television to improve my French."

He read her lips and said, "Yes, you can draw Oya's picture. I'll be very quiet and meditate in the armchair."

While he was meditating, he fell asleep. After drawing Oya's picture, Adeline tapped him on his shoulder. He woke up and looked at the picture.

"Yes, this is my beloved Oya. I am amazed. You are an incredible artist."

He hugged and kissed her.

The following morning, he woke up late and wanted to have a bath. He stayed in the bath for a while and wrote a poem.

ALONE ABROAD

My dearest,
Tonight, I am in a wonderful city.
Pretty girls are everywhere.
I fancy all of them.
Some of them smile at me
And I smile back,
But nothing happens.
Then I meet a deaf and dumb girl.
She is beautiful and friendly.
She understands me just the same as you do.
She makes love to me just as well as you do.
And she is every bit as honest as I am.

He came out from the bathroom and wanted to email the poem to Leyla. When he went into the sitting room, he was surprised to find Lucie and Natalie there.

"Good morning, girls. I thought you weren't due here until Sunday. Leyla went to New York last Monday. I have company here."

"Yes, we've met the cleaner lady," said Lucie.

"She is not a cleaner. She is a psychic artist," he said in an angry voice.

"She spoke to us in English with a London accent, and in French with a Parisian accent. Honestly, I didn't think she could be a cleaner. I thought she was a model," said Lucie.

"I agree with you. She should be a model. When I learn French, I want to be a consultant to model agencies in Paris. So far they have failed to recruit the most exotic and erotic girl in Paris."

"No problem, Uncle Goldash. You can stay here as long as you want, and we can teach you French," said Natalie.

"Did she really speak to you?"

"Yes, she did," said Natalie.

"I am puzzled. She didn't say a single word to me. I thought she was deaf and dumb."

He went into the bedroom and found a note on the bed.

It said: "MERCI INFINIMENT, MON MAGICIEN. JE T'AIME BEAUCOUP."

Goldash got dressed and went out for a walk. He stopped at a small café and bought a sandwich and a cup of coffee before returning to the flat, and wondered why Adeline had acted like that.

"While you were out, a woman named Mireille phoned, and I talked to her. She thinks you are a magician. You slept with Adeline last night. Apparently, she has regained her confidence and started to speak again. Now Mireille is a very happy mother. She is very grateful to you," said Lucie.

"I forgot to take my mobile phone with me. I'm confused about this. Did she tell you what had happened to Adeline?"

"Yes, she did. Two years ago, in December, Adeline was

attacked. The intention of the attackers was obvious. She struggled and didn't surrender to them. Her only option was to jump into the cold water of the River Seine on a late evening, and an elderly couple rescued her. After that terrifying experience, she has been unable to speak until this morning."

"I admire her bravery. She must be a rare breed. I'm so happy her suffering is over now."

"Leyla phoned as well. She said her father was all right. She asked me to give you this list," said Natalie.

- Buy clothes, shoes and pearl sets for both Lucie and Natalie this afternoon. They know what to choose.
- Take them to a restaurant this evening.
- Clean the flat tomorrow morning.
- Give them reflexology in the afternoon.
- Prepare a nice dinner in the evening.
- Go back to London on Monday.

"This is great! Girls, let's go shopping!"

"Yes, Uncle Goldash."

It was early April 2004. Goldash visited the Gulbars.

"The flats are ready to be put on the market. There is a big demand for flats in that area, and we will sell them quickly," said Gulizar.

"That's very good. I can repay the loan to Mili before the end of August," said Goldash.

"If I were you, I wouldn't repay the loan to her. Let her keep the drawings," said Gulizar.

"I'm not supposed to sell those drawings. Have you forgotten?"

"No, I haven't."

"I'm not sure what you're trying to say, Mrs Gulbar."

"Memzar, my love, can you bring the drawings from our bedroom please?"

He nodded, went upstairs, and brought *Now You See Me* and *The Real Twins* to the sitting room.

"These are the originals. Mili has the duplicates," said Gulizar.

"Congratulations, Mrs Gulbar. You have outwitted Mili. You planned it right from the beginning, didn't you? If I don't repay the loan, she will wonder how I could have spent two million pounds in three years. When she finds out she has been outwitted, she will crucify me. I must repay the loan to her as soon as possible. You can tell Mili about the duplicates of the drawings when the right time comes."

"I agree with Goldash," said Memzar.

"Fair enough. In the meantime, we must sell ten flats and let out six flats," said Gulizar.

He stayed inside during the Easter break and focused on preparing his companies' management accounts and his tax return. He spent the evening lying on the sofa and listening to the sound of the rain falling down onto the roof of his conservatory. On Sunday, he met one of his friends at the Toby Carvery in Epping Forest. After lunch he took a walk in the rain, came back to his house, wrote a poem and emailed it Leyla.

RAINY AFTERNOON

My dearest soulmate,
This afternoon
I walked in the rain.
I felt calm and comfortable.

While raindrops were stroking my umbrella,
I felt as if your heart were beating at its peak.
While it was raining,
I slept in my car and had a dream about you.
You were playing your guitar
And singing your favourite Turkish song.
"Come to me,
Come, come, come to me, come to me!
With your sweet words and smiling face, come to me!
On your sunny days and rainy days, come to me,
Come, come, come to me, come to me!"

In the late evening, he read Leyla's email and her poem.

My dearest GG Boy,

Thank you for the poem. In fact, I played the guitar and sang the song for you at my place in Istanbul this afternoon. Next week, Grandmother and Lili are visiting me. We will go to Gulistan and celebrate my birthday. You are most welcome to join us.

Always your loving angel.

LL

RAINY EVENING

My precious poet,
This evening I am in Istanbul.
It is raining gently.
I am having a glass of ninety-nine-year-old wine
And thinking about you.
I am wet and wicked.
I remember that
You love to hear the sound of rain

Falling down onto the roof of your conservatory
And make me scream passionately.
I wish you were here!
We would have some creative ideas
About peace, pleasure and prosperity!

He smiled, picturing her relaxing in her house in Istanbul, and replied to her email.

My dearest Leyla,
Thank you for the poem and your invitation. I wish I could join you on your birthday in Gulistan, play the guitar and sing Happy Birthday *for you, Lili and Oya. My accountancy training will finish at the end of August, and I want to be a personal assistant to you and Lili in September.*
Yours passionately
GG Boy

Over the following few months, the Gulbars and Goldash were very busy selling the flats and completing the necessary formalities. There was only one thing on Goldash's mind: repaying the loan to Leyla as soon as possible. At the end of July, the money was in his company's bank account. He went to Leyla's house in Hampstead Heath.

"Hello, GG Boy, you look very happy. What's going on?"

"I have made a lot of money and want to repay your loan today. Here is a cheque for two million pounds. Thank you for trusting me. I'm very grateful, my lady."

"Can I keep the drawings until the twentieth of September? Remember, I lent you the money for three years."

He gave her a smile. "You can keep the drawings as long as you want to."

"So tell me, have you hit the seven-digit sum in your first business venture?"

"Yes, I've been enjoying making money and making love for the last three years. After I pay the corporation tax, it will go down to a six-digit sum, though."

"Congratulations! You are a prosperous poet now. You must make the taxwoman happy as well. Grandmother, Lili and I are going to Paris for two weeks on Monday. When we come back, Lili and I can enjoy a millionaire's treat at your place."

"Mili and Lili are most welcome at my place any time."

"My father wants to have a word with you. Can you visit my parents tomorrow at lunchtime?"

"Yes, Leyla."

He visited the Tokkans. They had lunch together, and later he gave both of them reflexology.

"I haven't played snooker since I had the accident last December. Shall we go to the snooker room and practise together?" asked Osman.

"Excellent idea."

Goldash followed Osman into the snooker room.

"How is your left arm, Osman Bey? Are you fully recovered?"

"Yes, my arm is all right now. I want to practise snooker every day and get my maximum break."

"I'm sure you can get your maximum break and join our snooker team."

He nodded. "I've worked forty-two years continuously and am ready to consider semi-retirement. You can start to work at our company next month. You'll get a very good salary."

"Thank you for the offer, Osman Bey. I started my own business, and it has been doing very well, but I will consider your offer and let you know next month."

"Very well. Mili suggested to me we celebrate your birthday at our place this year. Perhaps you can show us a maximum break at this snooker table on your birthday."

"That will be my pleasure, sir."

It was the twenty-eighth of August 2004. He went to the Tokkans' house. They enjoyed a wonderful lunch. Mili and Lili played their violins. Grandmother, the Tokkans and Nicole sang *Happy Birthday* for Goldash. Ozana read Gulizar's email.

Dear Ozana and Osman,

You must be celebrating Goldash's birthday and having fun at your place today. I am in beautiful Bursa and have bought a house with a big garden in a village for Goldash as a birthday present. It is not very far from the sea and the mountain. Memzar and I are going to go on a world tour next month. After touring the world, I want to write a book and call it In the Footsteps of Oya and Goldash. *If you like, both of you can join us on the twenty-first of September. I am sure Mili, Lili and Goldash can look after your company better than anyone else. I have the originals of* Now You See Me *and* The Real Twins. *I gave duplicates to Goldash, and Mili took them from him. She can keep them for as long as she wants to. The originals have my fingerprints on the back to confirm their authenticity and will be given to the British Museum in the future. Goldash is my trusted executor and will ensure it happens. They must be exhibited at different museums in different countries. Those beauties belong to the people of the world, not individuals.*

I hope to see you soon.
Best wishes
Gulizar

"If you show me a maximum break today, I'll give you one fifth of my shares as your birthday present. The value of our property company is a seven-digit sum. You can work out the value of your shares," said Osman.

"I want Goldash to show me a maximum break today and will be happy to give him one fifth of my shares too," said Ozana.

"If he shows me a maximum break and another one for Lili today, he will get one fifth of both mine and Lili's shares. The five of us will have equal shares in the company," said Mili.

"I am flabbergasted. I wasn't expecting anything like this on my birthday. It is a once-in-a-lifetime opportunity, and I must get four maximum breaks today. The four of you are putting me under a lot of pressure. If Mili and Lili play *The Four Seasons*, I can relax and concentrate on my snooker show."

Mili and Lili played their violins, and Goldash danced with Grandmother, Ozana and Nicole. He requested an hour of preparation time for his biggest snooker show yet and went to the snooker room. As per his normal routine, he prepared himself and the snooker table. The time had come to display his skills and showmanship once and for all.

"I will re-spot the black ball for the first and second break. Ozana will re-spot it for the third and fourth break. We all wish you the best of luck," said Osman.

"Thank you so much, sir."

He started potting balls slowly and brought rhythm and rhyme onto the snooker table. His onlookers' faces were etched with pleasure, and each one was delighted to be witnessing his sensational snooker-playing skills. He completed four maximum breaks within ninety minutes.

Osman came forward, cheering and clapping. "Excellent, just excellent! A genius must be at his best under pressure. I haven't seen anything like that before, and I am so delighted we have been celebrating your birthday here. I have just one question for you."

"Yes, sir."

"Will you be my snooker practising partner for life please?"

"Yes, I will."

"Will you be my bridge partner for life please?" asked Ozana.

"Yes, I will."

"Can Lili and I be your partners for life please?" asked Mili.

"Yes, you can. Now, I have one question for all of you. Will you be my partners in peace and pleasure for life please?"

As one, they said, "Yes, Goldash, we will!"

Dear reader

Thank you for reading my novel.

Once, I read a novel by a Nobel laureate. The protagonist was a poet, and I expected to read poems in the novel. There were titles of poems, but no poems. Poetry is harmonious and meaningful words and sentences which express feelings, thoughts and imaginings. I write poems in English and Turkish. As a bilingual poet, I know it is difficult to translate poems from one language to another. I was disappointed that the quality of his writing was not up to my expectation. It made me think how the Nobel laureate would feel if he went to a restaurant and was given the menu but no meal. Somehow, at the same time, I was inspired by the shortfall, which motivated me to write a novel.

It has become my passion and pleasure to show readers how a novel should be written when the protagonist is a poet. I am happy that I have contributed something to the world of literature. Of course, I am very grateful for the inspiration and motivation of the Swedish Academy and the unconditional support of my family, friends and readers.

I am sure you will remember some characters in the novel and their adventures, affairs, problems and pleasures.

May you be healthy, happy and wealthy!

Yours poetically

G G Gench

THE LIST OF POEMS
AS APPEARING IN THE NOVEL

THE LIST OF POEMS
IN ALPHABETICAL ORDER